COUNTRY LIFE

Ken Edwards

First published in Great Britain in 2015
by Unthank Books of Norwich and London
www.unthankbooks.com

Text copyright © Ken Edwards
Cover design © Sandy Cowell

Unthank Books
PO Box 3506, Norwich
NR7 7QP

A CIP catalogue record for this book is available from the
British Library

ISBN 978 1 910061 24 4

Typeset in Sabon
Printed by Lightning Source, Milton Keynes

By the same author:

*This book is dedicated to
Tom Raworth, whose fictional avatar appears
briefly in the final section.*

1

light cones

Further along the coast, some of the houses have been abandoned. Water has ruined them, their windows are broken, and from their shard-filled spaces dankness emanates; small animals freely go in and out. Once, it's said, more than a thousand years ago, a whole town slipped into the sea right here, and furthermore they say you can even now hear its sounds on a still night. The tolling of bells, a sad sound because of the overtones it lacks, and even sadder still the cries of traders over their lost livelihoods, over undulating kelp. Now there are rumours of heavy water; there is cooling. Whatever it is, that's what they say. Whoever they are. And over the weight of that sea, over dead things and scum, aquatic birds glide and scavenge, out of time.

The town entered the sea, and that was the end of it. To this day, people may be said to move among the ruins of the church and the various hostelries, now fathoms down and unspoilt. Businesses flourish. Underwater commerce occurs. Seals and maces remain. The innocence of other days prevails and seems immense. The town's streets are submarine beaches.

But what raptors may now predate along the broken coast? What creatures become their prey? Their variety astounds visitors. Their industrial life proves a delight to naturalists, and to the many ramblers who take advantage of the coastal paths. Their song is liquid and continuous. The cliff, the beaches, the remaining village – all have entered history with the other relics.

As a child, he remembers that he was taken by his father to see a pub called *The World Turned Upside Down*. Tables and chairs rested upon the ceiling, beer remained miraculously in glasses and didn't ever fall out or even slop; the merry throng, as they revelled all evening, didn't seem to notice that their feet were above their heads. The piano's notes descended in distinct arpeggios shadowed by a wobbly reverb, but of the shouting and banter of the punters and the remonstrations of the barman no more could be heard. Well, if you believe that, you'll believe anything.

That was in the seventh century, at the heart of religious life, when the town had been a great port.

South of the glory that is the illuminated nuclear power station, lies the Peninsula, a tiny settlement beginning to glow in the shadow of a Sunday evening, under the cold, dark mass of the sea. The site has been carefully landscaped so as to maximise the attractiveness of the coastline to visitors. There are long, desolate beaches to north and south, and safe bathing can be had, although the area is not a resort. The countryside beyond, the hinterland now darkening, consists chiefly of heathland interspersed with patches of marsh, and is well provided with footpaths.

When the sea came, none of the town's inhabitants noticed. They went about their daily business as if nothing had happened, even though the air around that they breathed and exhaled had been replaced by water. The glamour of it pervaded them – no-one could escape, had it occurred to them to do so. The baker continued to bake his fragrant bread, the parson said his prayers, the farmer took his cows to market, the schoolteacher instructed her darling charges, the little girls skipped, the little boys hopped and raided orchards, the ale-house wife gave birth, crying out through a lengthy labour, the sparrows cropped crumbs from a piece of bread that had been allowed, carelessly, to fall in the yard, and all were unaware of the flood water, in all its glamour, that pervaded every space, that rose as the town fell, till both fundament and heavens were joined together by it; unaware that, little by little, and with no warning or outcry, they had become submarine.

Salt is in the air, and mulberries. Her deep red hair, fragrant with seaweed, moves through considerable density. Hurt me, it seems to sing. All the way along the coast, and into the hinterland. It's already growing dark. It is February.

We may observe two figures moving in this landscape of cold, dark matter. They may be two boys; well, young men. They seem to have emerged out of nowhere, fully formed, and now start to inhabit this narrative, for at least a space. It seems – effective surveillance would show this – that the two lads are headed along the line of the beach in a southerly direction from the power station. And by virtue of their very presence on such a trajectory at such a time they proclaim their alienation and apartness from the winter landscape, which all the good citizens by this time of the evening have abandoned, fallen as they are to stoking their fires and mending their bellies, while feeding on ultra-high frequencies.

The question is, says the big lad with the spiky hair and glittering glasses, *where are you in the human food chain?* It's that savage.

He has been talking non-stop since they came out to walk on the strand, here at the end of the world. The talk has been of human bandwidth, negative space, power structures.

The smaller lad, thin and sweet-faced, curly hair constrained by a woollen hat, says, Right. His name is Dennis; he is 21 years old.

The other, who has actually not stopped talking all weekend, is maybe a couple of years older. The sea is kind of a murky brown, under the mulch-coloured sky, with the occasional fleck of grey-white disturbance. At any rate, it doesn't look appetising this evening. Waves continuously roll in, gently dump their stuff on the beach and retreat.

Right, says Dennis again, after a pause.

Like, in the human food chain you might say, the fucking bosses, captains of industry as they used to call them – these days, CEOs of mega-corporations, or chairmen or persons or big-shot shareholders or hedge fund investors, you know what I mean, the Great White Sharks...

Yeah, the predators – the Great White Shark off the Great Barrier Reef, agrees Dennis, or [recalling another wildlife documentary on TV] the Brown Hyena on the Skeleton Coast. The, what you might call...

The multi-national bosses. Top of the fucking food chain.

They never, you know, says Dennis.

They never sleep, says his companion, who, we shall now determine, is called Tarquin. Fucking sharks. You know, sharks.

Very ancient creatures. Primitive.

That's right.

Cartilage instead of bone. Unchanged since before the time of the dinosaurs – what, 65 million years ago.

The two boys are now on a headland, from where there's a view through to the Peninsula, and semi-greyed out a little further along, the vast lit fortress of the nuclear power station. It, too, never sleeps, its perennial hum setting up a permanent coastal resonance. It's the biggest thing around for miles. The dome, the floodlights, wow. They come to a stop, to appreciate this vision.

Now, isn't that positively *luxurious?*

Supreme, comments Tarquin, contemplatively, awed for once.

It's the next stage in my project, says Dennis. It's my next target.

He waits for a response.

Closer, the smaller lights of the Peninsula glow, but they're beginning to blur. In the other direction – that is, southwards down the coast – a regular pulsing flash on the horizon. That would be the lighthouse.

What, says Tarquin, a rare vestige of smile flirting with his big hard face, you planning an attack on the power station?

No, no, my project, you remember my project.

Tarquin maintains a reverential silence as they both observe the immense panorama. It blurs slightly.

I reckon there's a fog coming in, says Dennis.

Tarquin resumes: They're at the top of the food chain, right? And then there's the smaller raptors around them, the executives, the media stars. Yeah, the celebs and the politicians. Jackals, the smaller cats. The executive cats.

Vultures.

Yeah, those too.

Taking advantage of their rest on the headland, Tarquin removes his glasses to polish them on the sleeve of his coat. He pursues the metaphor:

Now those, those people there, your neighbours [indicating with a sweep of the arm the Peninsula's array of dwellings], well, they're cattle, aren't they? They're ... antelopes. Y'know, what d'you call them, the herbivores.

There's more of them, a bigger biomass, it stands to reason, asserts Dennis.

Tarquin: Anonymous. Look how they cluster round the centres of power, feeding, content with their status until it's hunting time. D'you want to be one of *them*?

I fucking don't! exclaims young Dennis. That's for sure.

The lads stand in contemplative silence a while longer. Then, as if by common consent, they turn and resume their progress. They are tramping on sand, not on the beach itself but the dry, friable sand of the dunes along its upper fringes, where sea-kale obtains fragile purchase and in summer rare terns are said to nest.

Well now, I don't want to be personal, but there's even worse than being herbivores, says Tarquin. I mean, you could slip down easy to the next level, you know what I mean? You could end up with nothing. You could be – I don't want to be personal – but if you don't take care you end up being food for everything else. What are those little fellows, the little creatures?

Dennis: ?

You know, the tiny ones everything else in the ocean eats.

You mean, like, krill?

Yeah, that's right, *krill*. Food for everything else. You understand what I'm saying? That's the kind of capitalist society we have. At the bottom of the food chain.

Right, says Dennis.

At the bottom. Then you're fucking krill, man!

The sea – it isn't even a sound any more. Any more than the blood pulsing through one's vessels and ventricles. A soundless sound, or unregistered ground bass. But church bells penetrate this gloomy undertow of no-sound from the direction of the Peninsula now, and the lads hear that clear across the flats. As we have observed, it's a Sunday evening. People are starting to settle in for the night. Lights in the houses, leaking onto waste ground, lend a halo to a small fugitive animal investigating black rubbish sacks, nudging them with its tough mouth. A round shape falls out, bright, with the tiny triangular sector where the ringpull had been. The small tinkling clatter of an aluminium can echoing over tarmac.

Dennis uses these. From time to time.

Across the empty churchyard shuffles an old woman carrying a plastic supermarket carrier bag inscribed SAVERS PARADISE (no apostrophe). She is confused because there was once something called home and she doesn't presently know where it is.

So in the households of the Peninsula, families settle down for the evening to watch TV. There is plenty of choice: shows about "reality", incorporating sharp competition; a whimsical drama of Celtic folk; astonishing close-ups of the natural world; hilarious home-video howlers; a rerun of a gentle wartime comic adventure; a mystery about a stepfather who has been brutally murdered (for all the fine detail, this is more bizarre than scary).

The roads are quiet. Maybe once in a while a lorry revs up, but the main traffic to and from the power station has long since subsided. Fog will roll in. Rats or cats with haloes. The World's End. A shout.

And all the time, the sea crashes relentlessly on the dark beach.

Dennis says: You see, what I'm doing is what I call World Music, but it's nothing to do with marketing labels. That's the way I look at it. I record sounds from all over the place digitally, you understand, shove them up into the PC, then I start to mix them, like it's an overall mix –

Right, right, nods glinting-eyed big spiky self-styled Neo-Marxist self-styled poet Tarquin, drumming fingers on the edge of his pint glass, part of his brain alert to what his friend is earnestly explaining.

They are now as a matter of fact in the World's End.

It's World Music is what it really is, because it comes *out of* the world, it's generated by the world in other words, that's why I call this piece *World Music*. Like, the computer –

You don't need the computer, interrupts Tarquin.

They have tired of their walk. Now as it happens they are taking a break. The World's End, which is the Peninsula's one and only pub, is where they are, and being a Sunday night it's fairly quiet. A small throng at the far side: three or four local lads, a cross-eyed wench, and the one Tarquin has been gawping at surreptitiously: a redheaded girl in jeans and boots, having an argument at the inglenook table with her bloke who's got a Number 1 cut and an earring. Pick up a Scratchcard at the Bar, declares a poster.

Well, I do need it to ... well, in a sense you're right I don't need it but –

Why do you need the computer?

I use it to process sounds, you see, that I've recorded on the digi recorder, and then –

You don't need the computer!

No, no, you don't understand, the fucking computer's not the point, it's just a tool, like a quill pen and manuscript paper –

So how long are you going to be living at your parents'?

Well, that's a separate question.

Dennis picks up his untouched pint and gulps some down. The boys contemplate in silence the world, the bar, the throng and the girl and her No 1-cropped leather-jacketed beau, with whom the argument continues to simmer, her voice, higher-pitched, penetrating through the muzak (non-World) that pervades, while his remains an almost undetectable low grumble –

Where do you think her tattoo is? She's bound to have a tattoo.

What?

Dennis, who has come to realise the object of his friend's interest, humours him. So he imagines her to have a small tattoo just deliciously poised on her upper arm, which is of course purely an imaginary tattoo –

What's, what's it of?

Possibly a bird of some description, which you can't see because she too is leathered, black against tanned, glowing skin, frizzed red hair. Tarquin's beginning to lose interest in the imaginary tattoo, which is turning out, in Dennis's description to be banal, but he goes: I bet she's really *antsy*!

And so the conversation lapses for a brief moment. Is that the foghorn in the distance, outside? The friable sand has dropped from their shoes. Outside it's pretty dark: dunes, scrub, beaches littered by casualties of the coast, waves rolling in over the rocks, making their feet freeze. A periodic flicker to the south, the distant lighthouse, or once in a while a flash and a dull roar which is a lorry approaching, but, as we have also previously observed, there are not too many on a Sunday night, with the power station on skeleton staff, humming some way over north. Not visible from the pub window anyway. You can see its dome illuminated if you go round the houses. There was supposed to be a moon tonight but by now it'll be pretty well obscured by the sea-fog. And resumes:

That's an entirely separate question. They won't be back for some months. Sunning themselves through the winter, you see?

Because you need to get out there.

Where, the Costa?

No no, the city, man. You can't stay here, in the fucking sticks.

Yeah, I know, but I'm just getting my stuff going, my music and all that, and also I need to save some money –

You need to get out there. You want to be fucking *krill*?

– to save some money, 'cause I need to buy some more kit. So I'm house-sitting for my parents, while I save some money to upgrade my kit, which I need to do. Which I definitely need. I know you don't see it that way, Tarquin, but –

House-sitting? How long for?

Like I said, a few months. The winter. Probably till May.

And then?

The landlord comes by, picking up cloudy glasses, chiding: Come on lads, drink up. They are now the last two in the pub. The crowd in the corner, the rural Sunday-night scene, including the red-headed, putatively tattooed girl and her companion, have apparently left. They didn't notice them go.

Tarquin points pointedly at his watch, glaring, meaning, there's still a good minute left. He turns to Dennis: You want a last one?

Sorry son, it's time, says the landlord.

Fuck.

Let's go, says Dennis, draining his drink, fishing his wool hat from his pocket.

So they're tramping back along the road in the dark towards Dennis Chaikowsky's parents' house. Occasionally giggling, they kick a stray beer can to make the tarmac resonate. The sparsely placed streetlamps, milkily fuzzy, contribute hardly at all to the general lighting ambience. The peculiar damp smell of the incoming fog.

Dennis: I think technology should awaken human consciousness, you know.

There's no such thing as consciousness!

Oh yeah?

There's no such thing as consciousness, asserts Tarquin, it's a bourgeois myth.

Oh yeah well, maybe you're right, says Dennis. On the other hand –

Everything that goes on in the brain can be explained in materialist terms. It's just that we're not equipped with – what I mean is, consciousness is just an emergent property of the material processes in the brain, it's an illusory thing, of no particular significance or value.

Dennis [impressed]: Do you think machines will ever develop consciousness? I think they might.

In so far as it exists. Which it doesn't.

I mean, says Dennis, there've been some fantastic developments in our lifetime. Completely fucking supreme. Like, the internet, you know, nobody would've predicted it a generation ago. Artificial intelligence, it's coming you, know. You can see how one day there'll be a group mind. Intelligence. Maybe I should say intelligence instead of consciousness.

Then he adds: Are you really going back tonight? Back up to the city?

Yeah, got to. I need to do things tomorrow. I have to work.

But you're too pissed to drive!

I'm pissed but I'm careful.

Dennis knows enough not to push this, not to seem like some nag, which would be to earn his friend's contempt. Not that his friend would admit to contempt – for contempt, he would argue, is a lapse in intelligence – if not in consciousness, which may not exist.

I've got to get back. Got a booking tomorrow, a casual shift at *Lucre*.

So you're doing a day's work tomorrow?

Yeah, subbing and layout.

What's that then, *Lucre*?

It's a trade magazine. About money.

Inland they trudge, along the side of the road, towards the sandlings. Away from the deep scent of the sea.

We have to – collectively, of course – seize the moment, says Tarquin, suddenly. I prefer to live on the edge of the moment, you know what I mean, DC?

Me too.

Dennis enjoys being called DC. This is the first time this evening Tarquin has addressed him as such, and he savours the appellation, not to mention the moment. During that moment, he reflects. Except of course, he suddenly adds, there isn't a present moment. That's an illusion too. At least – let's clarify – my moment isn't your moment.

Why not?

Because, because. Dennis stops to think. Because the speed of light is absolute.

Because, repeats Tarquin, stopping suddenly and causing his friend to nearly collide with him, the speed of light is absolute?

Look up there [emboldened, Dennis points at the thick, blank sky], if you could see the stars –

Yeah?

If it wasn't for the sea-fog.

I see what you're saying, if it wasn't for the fog, if you could see them, well that light's taken maybe thousands of light years to reach us —

Not light years, corrects Dennis.

What?

Not light years. Light years are a measure of space, not time. Years.

Space, time, what's the difference?

Dennis lets this pass. What I'm saying is, the light from me takes maybe a split second to reach you. Just the merest fraction of a nano-second, but it's still time, you know what I mean? Our light cones don't intersect instantaneously. So it makes no sense to talk about a shared present moment.

Well, up to a point –

And vice versa.

Tarquin, unusually, has been put off his stride.

OK, I take your point, but as I was saying –

When the dim light emanating from Tarquin's body indicates that he has started to move on, Dennis resumes tramping in his friend's wake. The fog is definitely thickening, and now even the faint, milky street lighting has petered out. No vehicles pass them. Here, at the limits of the Peninsula proper, the houses start to space out. And now they have exited the Peninsula's village, and they are on a country road. They can barely see ten yards in front of them. A road sign looms. About twenty minutes' walk to Dennis's parents' house.

Moments later, at a bend in the road, they are both pulled up short by the encounter with the weeping old woman with the plastic shopping bag.

Ecology: the science of relationships, and their stages of development. How fragile, and yet how powerful. Power is involved, naturally, and power is always unequal, but it's difficult to track. Stages is an arbitrary concept. After all, everything is flux. Keep the idea of the sea here. And its perennial sound.

Which is only a source of material, it's not the thing itself.

Further stages have yet to arrive.

Under the ocean, people go about their daily business. A supermarket, and the products within it. The hinterland of certain dichotomies, plays of opposites that are temporarily obscured but "work themselves out". Or don't. Certain characters would refer to dialectics here.

Hinterland: a concept.

The city: that is, the distance. Another concept.

Alison, who is also called Wanda. And her son. And her insane husband. We'll come to them soon. In stages. In whatever way it elapses.

Natural history.

The aeroplanes are silent, locked in their hangars.

The unlit road stretches forth its metal into the isthmus, and, beyond that, to where Dennis's parents' house is, on the dark mainland. It is studded with the flat corpses of unlucky creatures, chiefly rabbits.

The old woman has interrupted the boys' terpsichore of the road; helplessly, she pulls at Dennis's sleeve.

She says, Help me. Please help me. With the other hand she clutches her carrier bag tightly.

SAVERS PARADISE.

What's the matter? says Dennis.

But she isn't coherent; she mumbles or babbles slowly, like a wrinkled baby in boots and shapeless dark clothes.

Tarquin, figuring maybe that the same question repeated from a different angle might help, says, What's the matter, lady?

I don't know, I don't know, she's saying, her voice slightly cracked.

There is nobody around, it's as though the whole Peninsula has gone to sleep. It's somewhere between eleven o'clock and midnight.

She says: I don't know, I don't know where. I don't know where.

She still has a hold on Dennis's sleeve. Trying to put concern into his voice – and he does feel concern, though there's also something in her that profoundly irritates him – he says: Take your time, take it easy. Where what?

When Tarquin stamps his feet to keep warm, the surface of the road rings sharply, the reverberations fading into the dark at its edges.

I don't know where.

She's wearing a lumpy overcoat and a headscarf. The shopping bag trembles in her hand. The other hand grips Dennis. A muted sob unleashes itself as she lets the words out.

I don't know where I am.

You're in the Peninsula, says Dennis, or to be more accurate, just on the edge of it. Are you from round here? Have you got lost?

She nods: Yes, I ... don't know where. I am.

Do you live near here? says Tarquin.

Yes. I've forgotten.

Tarquin: You've forgotten where you live?

Is it in the Peninsula, asks Dennis, or is it on the mainland somewhere?

Yes, she says.

Yes which?

What?

The Peninsula or the mainland?

She's calmed down just a bit now. Mainland.... The estate.

The estate? Which estate?

No reply.

Which estate? You mean the Wellington Estate?

Yes, she says uncertainly, that's the one, the Wellington.

You don't seem very sure.

The Wellington. I live on the Wellington.

Where's that, Tarquin asks Dennis, is that miles away?

No, not too far, he replies. And to the woman, in a loud, slow voice: We'll take you there. All right? All right now? Just stick with us.

She's sobbing again, muttering, Thank you ... thank you. Her voice is stitched into the increasing swirl of the fog.

As if clarity were other than an unattainable objective, and identity a thing in itself, apart from its hinterland of contingency. And that hinterland infested with what passed for thoughts, or, on this night, mangy stray creatures in the obscuring fog. People sleep among the power structures, one might say oblivious, except that they have bad dreams – which are thoughts unleashed from pitiless captivity to roam at will. And the bad dreams are everywhere, in the air and on the ground that the fog renders indivisible. But they do their work, whether they are seen or not; they do their implacable work.

The blurred lights of the Wellington come up ahead. A dismal housing estate on the edge of nowhere, built perhaps thirty years ago by a progressive local authority, for power station and air force base workers and their families, then allowed to decay for the past twenty. Now it looks like a barracks abandoned by a defeated army in retreat.

Perhaps it's this aura of hopelessness, transferred to the woman, that awakens irritation in Dennis. He thinks, though, now, that it is more than or perhaps other than irritation. Along with feelings that are more acceptable to him, such as pity and sympathy, he's started to experience something akin to hatred. Which horrifies him, and he tries to suppress it. But the thought keeps coming back.

He despises the old woman! He wants to kick her and beat her to a pulp!

No, of course he doesn't. Such a thought would never enter his mind.

Tarquin, on the other side, is talking patiently to the woman as they slowly approach the lights, or rather, putting in an interjection here and there, for she has become almost voluble, if no more coherent.

I'm a widow, you know, she is saying.

I'm a widow, you know. I went to the hospital last week to see my husband. I knew there was something wrong because at first they wouldn't let me see him. I said I know what ward he's in, and I went in. Well, I was talking to him like I always used to, but then I realised he'd died. Nobody told me. I suppose they didn't want to upset me.

It's not surprising, Tarquin says, the health service has declined so much with this right-wing government in power, these Neo-Liberals, it's not like it used to be.

Not like it used to be, agrees the woman. Not like when I was a girl. Well, I said to them, what about the funeral arrangements, who's going to take care of them, that's what I'd like to know?

And what did they say?

Well, they didn't say anything, they just looked at me in a funny way, and then of course I realised, silly me, the funeral's already happened, he's been resting in his grave all these years, the poor dear. And me a widow. I'm over eighty-five, you know.

That's a fine age, says Tarquin soothingly.

What Dennis is thinking, and trying not to think, is, suppose, suppose. Suppose it had not been them she met on the road out from the village, but someone else. Someone who would have no compunction, for whom the woman's feebleness would be an opportunity and a goad. But what an evasion that is! What he is trying not to think is the unthinkable in his own psyche. Which comes out of his own feeling of powerlessness, and the resentment of that. What is the use to the world of such hopelessness and abjectness? That's the horrifying bit.

She's so vulnerable, and there's such lowlife round here. What if...?

What he says to her: We're coming very close to the Wellington now. Do you recognise it? Do you remember which block you live in?

I'm trying to remember, she says. I'm trying very hard. I've not been very well, you know, dear, since life isn't easy when you're my age.

Well, take your time.

Now they're up among the harshly lit barrack-like walls of the low-rise estate, an island in the fog. They smell damp and rubbish.

We'll walk round, says Dennis, and see if you recognise your own block.

I'll know it when I see it, she says, almost happily. I came out too far.

They are each at an elbow. Progress continues to be as slow as it has been all the way along the country road. Tarquin is carrying the plastic shopping bag, SAVERS PARADISE. It contains her handbag, and sundry other bits and pieces. A dog barks briefly somewhere, a little yapping sound. And again.

A row of garage doors looms up, decorated profusely with graffiti. She pauses, shakes her head.

My name's Mrs Stevens, she declares suddenly. Ethel Stevens.

Well, now we're getting somewhere, remarks Tarquin, his glasses glinting brightly anew under the security lights. If necessary, we'll call on someone and see if they recognise you, Mrs Stevens.

Oh, I wouldn't want to put anybody to any trouble.

Steadily, the three circumnavigate the estate, block by block. About half the tiny windows have lights in them; they hear the sounds of television sets, occasionally of someone shouting. Finally, they return to the first block.

She says: I think this is the one.

Are you sure? the lads both ask, almost in unison.

This is where I live. The first door. Of course I remember now. You boys have been so kind. Won't you come in? I wonder if my husband is home.

Come on, says Tarquin, we'll see you inside. Got your key?

There is an individual, dimly lit porch which smells of urine, and then the front door, and her key does fit.

Bright overhead light. The tiny living room smells of old woman scents, pot-pourri, mothballs, whatever it is. Something else, something bad. It's freezing; Tarquin dumps SAVERS PARADISE on an easy chair, switches on the two-barred electric fire in the mock grate.

Here, you'll be all right now, he says. What on earth were you doing wandering around the Peninsula at this time of night, Mrs Stevens?

I thought … I looked at the clock, it was ten o'clock, I thought the supermarket will be open, I need some things, I'll catch the bus. But there wasn't a bus. So I tried to come back home, but I think I went the wrong way.

You thought it was ten o'clock in the *morning*? says Dennis.

You must think me so silly; of course, I'm a widow, my husband passed away, bless him. Now I shall make both you boys a cup of tea.

No, no, say the lads, who must be on their way. But Tarquin offers: I'll put the kettle on for you, though. Is that the kitchen?

That's so terribly kind of you. Painfully, with gnarled fingers, she is removing her headscarf. They can hear a muffled conversation through the wall, and that dog yapping again. And Tarquin says, returning: You've got a bad case of damp in your kitchen, Mrs Stevens.

I know.

There's all black mould up to the ceiling. You want to get the council onto it.

I've told them. But what can they do? They've got lots of problems.

Dennis predicts silently, correctly: Here comes another of his monologues. Suddenly, he's infected with panic, suffocating. Needs a breath of fresh air. Time to nip out.

Tarquin's going: The shameful cuts in public expenditure imposed by this government are *no* excuse for the council to fall down on its responsibilities –

Dennis is glad to be out in the open, in front of the porch. Because the old woman's flat smelt really bad? Is that what death smells like? He feels guilty now, for his negative thoughts. Back in the direction of the Peninsula the fog swirls again, obscuring all lights momentarily. He leans against the wall.

Next door clicks shut, and a small terrier type of dog marches out onto the communal patch of scrub, sniffing energetically. It begins to trot exploratively around the empty space in front of the flats.

The animal is followed by a man clad, despite the cold, merely in a dark T-shirt and jeans. He emerges from his porch. His hair is cropped close to his skull, and he is holding an empty milk bottle in his right hand, forefinger hooked into the rim. The other arm hangs limp. He stands for a long moment, almost motionless, as the dog scurries around. Then he brings his left hand up to his face. The sudden glow tells that it holds a newly lit cigarette. The man stands silently before his porch, ignoring Dennis on his left, watching his dog. Once again, his cigarette end glows briefly in the dim light, then fades.

Dennis leans against the old lady's porch, and the man stands before his.

The dog makes an irregular snuffling arc on the damp scrub, coming back finally to approach Dennis. It stops still. It glares at him, then stiffens and growls.

Hands stuffed tight in pockets, Dennis glares back. He's thinking, *fuck off fuck off fuck off.* But the small uptight dog stands its ground. It's serious.

Then the man speaks.

Oi you, he says.

What?

Keep away from my dog.

?

You kicking my dog?

I never touched him.

YOU FUCKING KICKED MY DOG!

Dennis sidles away; so does the dog. The man comes over to him and stands a couple of yards off, cigarette hanging from a corner of his mouth, twirling the milk bottle round with twists of the fingers of his right hand.

It is an earring in his left ear that glints in the porchlight. Fuck, thinks Dennis, it's the same bloke. Is it?

I never touched your dog.

The bloke that was in the pub? Arguing with the girl?

The man lifts his left hand to his mouth, whips out his cigarette and flings it onto the damp grass.

YOU FUCKING KICKED MY DOG!

Behind Dennis, Ethel Stevens's door closes and Tarquin emerges.

The man has come right up to Dennis. He's still twirling the milk bottle, now slapping it against the palm of his free hand.

Dennis: ?

Without warning, the man swings the bottle, which comes down in a gleaming curve and cracks, to Dennis's surprise, on Dennis's head, falling to pieces on the ground except for the stump of the neck in the man's hand.

Dennis's head is protected solely by the woollen hat. Although that may have been sufficient. At this stage, he experiences only shock, not pain.

So he turns to Tarquin and yells: Run!

And they do, the two lads, the No 1 Cut behind them yelling obscenities but not (thankfully) in serious pursuit, the dog jumping aimlessly and barking. Their sound falls further and further behind until it's swallowed up by the darkness.

Out of breath in the lane, Tarquin turns round.

What was that all about, DC?

I dunno. Fuck knows.

As if knowledge were other than a provisional thing, and the present moment (his, yours, mine) quantifiable, in terms other than a mere listing of its content. And that republic of dreams that we all return to, the pivot of our existence within the very impossibility of it. Power sleeps among the people, and one might say (Tarquin might say) they are oblivious of it, but will finally grasp it one day – except that they have bad faith, which is what stops their desire from roaming at will. And the bad faith is everywhere, in the country and in the city. But it does its work, whether perceived or not; it does its terrible work.

23

The two gaze in, or out, towards glowing cyberspace in Dennis's small bedroom in his parents' house. This is now the early hours of Monday morning. Dennis is trying to explain what the sequencing software can do with the sounds he has captured digitally, and how he can use it to make his pieces – but he is having difficulty because the other is apt to embark on tangents, demonstrating whatever familiarity he can muster with bit-rates, bandwidths, networks. Let's be honest, he is not really interested in Dennis's music. He uses the opportunity to digress into events in the Eastern European city in which he spent two years after graduating, in the long aftermath of great political change (his and theirs); he soon enough digresses further into describing his own recently completed 500-page book on Neo-Marxist Aesthetics and the Marketing of the Moment, that someone else, hopefully the Party, is going to publish one day (because his own Virus Press doesn't have the distribution sorted yet); and, no less crucially, he launches into describing the theory that drives it. His conception of the authentic, collective moment of politically aware creation, its actual resistance to reification. He oscillates quite flawlessly between facts and their interpretation. He moves from neurobiology to economic theory to poetics, citing Ponderoso, Kleinmann, Yundt, among other theorists.

Sandra says I basically take a Kleinmannian position on this, but I disagree, it's more complicated than that. Sandra? My girlfriend, explains Tarquin. Oh yes, says Dennis, remembering. Of course, continues Tarquin, Sandra leans more towards Ponderoso, and even Paydushkova at times, she has more of a psychoanalytical position, which I have some issues with.

You two have *positions*? marvels Dennis.

Despite his frustration at Tarquin's lack of attention to his own work, Dennis has to admit that it's an impressive performance. In the end, he struggles to keep up, to determine where the facts are, and their status, a futile activity of course. Instead, he says: Supreme.

Fucking supreme, agrees Tarquin. And then: How's the head?

Dennis grins: OK. Just a little bump, a little sore.

He fingers it gingerly.

I think it was the hat prevented me getting cut. Always wear a wool hat.

They have acquired whisky from that parental cocktail cabinet with the lights that come on, which earns their combined amused contempt. It has an iconic significance in this context.

Contempt is the ghost that lurks in this night, and Tarquin courts it, without acknowledging it directly.

So Dennis perseveres, flicking and clicking the mouse round its mat, demonstrating the inadequacy of the sound-chip for playback. What it is, his kit is underpowered.

So you're saying you need more RAM?

I need more RAM, I need a bigger hard drive, I need to upgrade the software.

And you need a better printer too, you say?

I need a kit enhancement all round. This is really old stuff. I need a better printer. In fact, I need a new computer. And this keyboard's fucking crap.

Yeah, they're shit, those.

Relieved that he's struck the right level of cynicism, Dennis is secretly hurt also at this too-ready agreement from his friend. Actually, only a few weeks ago he had been thinking this setup was pretty good. But now he's ashamed of it. They knock back the Scotch in china mugs. The bottle is nearly empty. OK, no problem, plenty of time to replace it before the parents return from their sojourn on the Costa. To Dennis's enduring disappointment, Tarquin isn't really listening to the musical ideas emanating from the PC's twin speakers: short, violent, loud stabs punctuating long silences, then a stretchy period, getting almost lush and romantic, in a parodic sort of fashion. Well, it's hard to get an idea of it from this lousy computer anyway. And ... there's the fact that Tarquin only really approves of free improvised music anyway. There's a chapter on this in his book, as it happens. How making it up on the spot is the only methodology that can adequately counter the marketing of the present moment, by deprivileging (his word) its potential for reification. And so on. Come the revolution there will be improvisation workshops on every street corner, that the working classes will flock to avail themselves of.

Tarquin, says Dennis.

Yeah?

You know the old woman? Ethel Stevens, or whatever her name was?

Yeah, what about her?

This is just a hypothetical question, you understand. What stopped us taking advantage of her? Trashing her, I mean?

What are you saying?

I mean, she's no use to anyone really, is she? She's a waste of space. In the human food chain, wouldn't you say she's pretty low?

Yeah, but – that's a pretty weird, big question –

It's just a hypothetical question, see. You're the one who brought up this human food chain business. So where's the moral imperative? I'm not advocating – (But Dennis is suddenly appalled by his own parental-whisky-fuelled temerity.)

It's a pretty big fucking question, DC.

Yeah.

Yundt confronts it in one of the early works. Of course, the trouble with Yundt is essentially, and I use the word advisedly, he was an anarchist, and anarchists usually wind up as *liberals* (he spits the word out). Or dead.

Everybody, Dennis points out wisely, ends up dead.

And then a cat or something squeals in the garden, the only ambient sound at this hour on a Sunday night, or early Monday morning, in the whole of the sleeping Peninsula and its immediate environs, apart of course from the low hum of the nuclear power station three miles away next to the sea that never sleeps.

They've finished off the microwaved Chicken Dopiaza, the beer and most of the remains of the whisky, and a vertiginous multi-coloured screen saver unconsciously works out its algorithms onscreen.

I didn't realise it had got that late, observes Dennis. You could always stay over.

Hey, DC, I can't. I've got work tomorrow. I've got a day shift. In fact, they've given me three days. At fucking *Lucre* magazine. They pay a good day rate. Can't afford to turn it down. I need the cash

26

flow, man.

You could always sleep in my parents' room. The bed is already made up.

No way, man, I really need to get back.

So you're actually thinking of driving home tonight, Tarquin?

Yeah, I just need a little coffee.

There's not much of tonight left.

I have to work in the morning, DC, I tell you. I have a subbing shift starting at ten, OK?

Yes, I know. You're not going to be able to keep your mind on it.

Want to bet?

And it'll take you, what, two hours, or more, even, to drive back.

I'll make it, just need a little coffee, man, if you wouldn't mind.

OK, I'll start some brewing.

Just going back to what we were saying. It's your spiritual values that I'm talking about.

What's that? I thought you said you were a materialist?

It's the life of the spirit that underpins it. That doesn't necessarily imply transcendence, you see.

What, well, where does it come from, then?

What it means, that you're not thinking me, me, me all the time, DC. It's collectivism, don't forget, from which arise your spiritual values. Only collective solutions work. What *you* are implying in your question is a species of fucking individualist anarchism, no offence meant.

Since an offence is clearly meant, and reinforced by the denial, Dennis sulks for a brief moment. Then:

So what's wrong with that?

Well, I'm very suspicious of cyber-anarchism, with, you know, your internet and your digital solitude.

What are you saying?

I'm just talking about the spiritual values that arise from the materialist collective, as opposed to the individual, it's an emergent property of the collective –

Because there's nothing lonely about it, I'm in touch with people all over the world about my work, through the internet. I'm in constant communication with people in America, India, fucking *China*, man. We're creating the communities of the future.

Virtual communities?

Real communities, through the net, you see, Tarquin –

The net? The net for all the krill!

So what's the alternative?

Organisation, in the sense of, based on the material realities in the places where we find ourselves, which is what we deem the "present moment." But of course –

So going back to what you were saying, what you're saying is that if all the krill got together and formed a union or a political party they could force the whale to accept their demands?

Tarquin's wry grin.

He says: I speak in metaphors, DC. They are necessarily imperfect. I mean, I'm not against computers and all that shit, I'm really interested in them, all that stuff, you know I think it's really supreme, I just think it's not a political solution. The technology should be the servant of materialism and collectivism, which are the logical outcome of being human, and they ultimately *create* spiritual values. It's all in my book.

Spiritual values?

Yeah. As an example, materialist poetry. I nearly called my magazine that. *Materialist Poetry.*

You're saying spiritual values derived from collective politics is what stopped us from practising intellectual and, er, economic cleansing?

Yeah, that's why we don't top old biddies and steal their pennies. The we who inhabit the present moment, which is a social and political collective creation. What's the matter, you been reading *Crime and Punishment* or something?

Well, *I* don't top old biddies. I just meant there was an intellectual argument to be had, which is the contradiction in what you've been saying, all that stuff about krill. Plus, I could see how it could be attractive, she gave out victim vibes, you can see how you could lock on to that easily. She was making me feel aggressive. I think it's interesting to explore where those feelings come from, I mean, I don't *really* want to do that. I'm not a fucking animal, like that guy with the dog. That lowlife. Mister dog and bottle.

Why do you call him an animal?

'Cause that's what he is.

That's Nazism, man. Calling him an animal is as bad as attacking an old lady.

Fucking bollocks.

As bad. As bad.

Yeah, the bloke with the dog. Not much life of the fucking spirit there.

That guy with the dog, he's a member of the underclass which the government is trying to create so that – listen – trying to create so that the likes of you and me can be made shit scared that we might fall into that same pit, so we don't protest too much about our poor pay and conditions, and concentrate on hanging onto whatever pitiful state we have, and meanwhile –

Fucking bollocks. [Dennis, unusually emboldened by whisky and beer, rubbing his bruised head, is muttering.] Fucking bollocks.

Consciousness: who can say what that is? Some neuroscientists now suggest it's an emergent property of the human brain, but what does that mean? There are the easy problems, and the hard problems. It is possible that Tarquin Smith has been unable to reconcile dualism and reductionism, and seeks to mask his confusion with political braggadocio ("it doesn't exist"). Dennis Chaikowsky senses a weakness, but is not intellectually equipped to tease it out; counters with his proposal, a stab in the dark. Result: stalemate. Inland, February: tomorrow, about 100 shelduck, the "classic duck of coastal dunes", will ride on the grey waters. There is no conclusive evidence linking such phase-locked oscillations with the psychological phenomenon of binding. Why a duck, indeed. Or a rabbit. At this time, though, almost the entire population has fallen into a dream; the hinterland breathes deeply, rhythmically. Whether one approaches this from a phenomenological, cognitive-scientific or neuroscientific point of view, the conclusion must be that consciousness has depth, hidden structure, hidden and possibly multiple functions, and a hidden natural and cultural history; but are dreams merely epiphenomenal side effects?

Let us stay with the more tractable problems of cognition.

Dennis: OK, listen, you know the bloke with the dog?

Yeah?

Was he the same bloke that was in the pub?

What, with the redheaded girl?

Yeah.

I didn't get a good look, but I thought so, yeah.

He had an earring.

Everyone's got earrings these days. And fucking tattoos.

Still.

I thought he was the same guy, it occurred to me.

Not that it matters. But I wondered whether he remembered us. Or remembered me passing a comment. About the girl. Although it was mainly you that was talking about her.

Nah.

It probably wasn't him.

What did you do, did you touch the dog?

Are you kidding! I never went near that poxy dog.

Just, you know.

Never went near it. It growled at me, for no reason. Then he just came for me, with the bottle in his hand. He must have been brooding on something, took it out on me.

Class resentment.

What the fuck are you talking about? He'd been having an argument with that girl he was with. That's what it must have been about.

If it was him.

Yeah, if it was him.

The households of the coastal region have fallen silent, save for that deep breathing we mentioned previously. Sometimes terms such as "phenomenal consciousness" and "qualia" have been used, but we find it more natural to speak of "conscious experience" or simply "experience."

The night passes.

Let's look at the week ahead. The nuclear reactor will produce enough controlled energy to satisfy the electricity needs of the entire region. Large magnetised rotors turn inside thick copper coils to generate the electricity that is fed to the grid. Turning each rotor is a large turbine. High pressure steam drives its blades and the rotor revolves inside the copper coils to produce electricity. Each morning, central heating system boilers will be triggered by time-switches, kettles will be plugged in, radios and TVs will be switched on. The people will wake from their individual dreams, and re-enter a collective dream.

In the office, PCs will be turned on, photocopiers will hum into action, people will queue up at the coffee and tea machines, which dispense their enhanced choice of products. In other words, it's the start of another working week.

It may be better to use the less loaded term "awareness."

Now a look at the TV schedules for this week. How you can transform your garden, using contemporary materials. The flooded kingdom. The art of castle building. The return of a well loved comedy series. Extreme weather. An underrated crime drama, starring a well known leading man as an ex-con persuaded to do a driving job that sees him incarcerated again and left at the mercy of a vengeful cop (*contains strong language*). A crucial European cup-tie. What to look for in a new house. The return of a hilarious quiz show. Extreme survival (last of series). The private lives of notorious dictators: this week, Adolf Hitler. Hospital drama. Heroes of comedy.

He is the light of my life, the sun in my life, you might say; rainclouds pass but they don't last long, and then the sun comes out again, it has always been there and always will be, and everything is for the best in the end, I suppose. You do have to make the best of it, don't you? Are you sure that you won't have a nice cup of tea? (Where was I, dear?) Such nice boys. That could be a song. He's just gone down to the supermarket to buy some bits and pieces, he was always so good to me like that; he'll be back in a tick. Everything moves very slowly now. But it wasn't like that in the old days. Dancing cheek to cheek, that used to be one. He'll be back any minute. It's that blessed fog, it makes everything ever so slow, but I do so love living in the country all the same; you can hear the bells from here, I suppose it depends on which way the wind is blowing. I have Parkinson's, and arthritis which only gets bad now and again, and just a *little* touch of angina, which makes it difficult, but the doctors are very kind. Why is it so dark? What time is it? I can hear the birds. You wouldn't think you could. Was I asleep just now?

The night's over, and Neo-Marxist poet Tarquin Smith has gone back to the city, to his freelance subbing for The Enemy in the form of the financial business press, in his endless efforts to finance his poetry magazine and small press and political writing. He's gone, in a clapped-out banger, taking his heavy-duty theory with him. He actually had the grace to say: I enjoyed our discourse. You have to give him that.

With considerable difficulty, Dennis Chaikowsky, having relieved his bladder, can just about stand in the parental bathroom. An ache in his bowel, a strange unpleasing tingle in the hand that holds the toothbrush. Grey light and the distant sounds of gulls begin to enter through the smeared window. Dutifully, he is scouring his gums.

Everything now has a kind of plastic oddness to it. Today, the day to come, the Monday that advances, that is already well advanced, will definitely be surplus to requirements. Because Tuesday.... He will try to do some work on the new piece. Maybe sample some sounds. Seeing the power station has given him some ideas: if he could take the digital recorder out to the strand, if he could get past security.... But he remembers: Ah, Tuesday, he knew there was something nagging him about it

He's due for his Rebirth interview.

They're going to stop his benefit, he knows it, they're going to insist on giving him some shit job. Although he could admittedly do with some money to upgrade his kit, he doesn't have the time for that. Not for a job. Nine to five.

(But...)

What the hell was Tarquin on about? He'll have to read that 500-page book one of these days. He emailed Dennis the document. Dennis opened it. Five hundred pages. Incredible.

Does Dennis resent not being as eloquent as his friend? His brain is wired differently, that's what it must be. As so often before, he wishes he could have found the words, but it's not just the words, it also needed the mental toughness, to get over to his mate what he really meant, means.

But what did he, does he mean? And what does mean really mean? Fucking philosophy, learned all about that at college. Perhaps he doesn't know. Perhaps that is the real problem. Big bloody philosophical problem.

What is the reality of the present moment? The zen essence of it? Peppermint toothpaste. Scummy grey early morning light. How long do these sense-events take to impact on him, the Essential Dennis?

Does he really have access to the reality of the real moment, or is it true that it doesn't exist? and he decides that his legs aren't *really* going to support him, his lids are going to close over his eyeballs and it would be a far, far better thing to be horizontal. To be horizontal for a bit. To achieve horizontality, if only for a moment.

In the bedroom, he clears from the bed the clutter of software manuals, computer and music magazines, empty mugs and paper plates with cold vestiges of microwaved curry clinging to them, empty Scotch bottle, audio and data discs out of their cases, crusts of toast. He makes enough space at least to lift the cover and flop in under it, in T-shirt, jeans and bare feet. And he sleeps immediately, and will sleep well into the morning; but his sleep is troubled.

Figures in a landscape that has vanished. They have a visceral significance. Or perhaps head out across pastures. A vast expanse of inter-tidal mud. Like the tiny ships. Huge, and it glitters across the skyline. A dark curtain, a matter of seconds. Signs of the time. When days are shortest, where the vesper song no longer lingers. All that desolate district, and the parishes beyond. This lovely ground, grubbed up. The wintering grounds. But now the storming winds blast, and strong weather. How long this night is, and I, for very great wrong, grieve, mourn and fast. I live in great sorrow for the best of bone and blood. Tongue folds, face slackens, lips blacken, nose coldens, mouth grins, spittle runs, as bandwidth narrows and a houseful of information comes to rest. The town lay silent, and all the little birds. And from it, we may follow the railway line, venturing over rust and rubble. And the light from the coast. Information sent along the pathway to the superior colliculus, responsible for controlling and initiating eye movements, producing visual awareness. Travail and trouble. The lorries on the road. We may suppose you call it territorial behaviour. With audition, something seemingly miraculous occurs. The sense of mystery, of a real danger to be faced, of an overwhelming spiritual gain to be won, were of the essential nature of the tale. He indicated a great many fringe experiences, but did not attempt an exhaustive list, or a systematic analysis of their relations to each other, or to other mental phenomena. A vigilance task. The conscious event breaks free and is projected into the space that surrounds us. But is there no consciousness? Here the hero sets out on a journey with no clear idea of the task before him.

There is a wall of water. The drowned town, February. Many mansions (labyrinths). In several layers. No, we don't want to know about that. Too deep and gloomy.

OK, an interlude.

Suppose all the people were fish and all the fish people, for example there's a chip shop at the bottom of the sea. And they serve up people fried in batter.

He used to draw these cartoons, and his parents fondly framed them. They still exist somewhere.

Finny and Fanny. Their hilarious adventures under the sea.

Ah, this boy, nice piece of boy.

That be a good 'un.

You want him wrapped up?

No call for 'im.

No, reckon not.

Thank yer, and a very good day to you, sir.

Blb, blb.

I see yer drift.

Blb, blb, ulla blb, und ah sold a duck, luck lucky, bulbous, burrow-bulb, classic duck-bulburooba, sold downariver, in a old rabbit-burrow dull in der dunes down on yer luck yer blb blb duckhole, sole, s-s-sole, or occupy an hole, OK I'll'av'im, save pelting rain and hailstones.

(This is the speech of the sea.)

Meanwhile, in the "real world", as dawn breaks, the skylark ... but the skylark hasn't put in its appearance yet, it's not the appropriate time.

He had to drive through the night, and, thinks Tarquin, it's OK, I'll make it, no problem, it's just that DC kept me talking. Jesus, he takes everything so immensely seriously, and just has this compulsion to strike attitudes. Has he actually *read* any of my book? He said he had "accessed the document." What was all that he was going on about, the present moment doesn't exist – a lame upstaging device, probably. It's perfectly clear to Tarquin that the moment is all we can work from, the collectivised, shared moment, the common definition. But DC, first he's all lovey-dovey peace love and understanding across the world, then he's talking about topping old biddies. And then about light cones, whatever they are. All over the fucking shop, politically. But then he could be all right really, only needs some revolutionary sense knocked into him, some Leninist discipline – and you have to admit everything's weird in the early hours anyway, it's the time when reality is most dismantled. It's like it slows things up and you can see them as they can never be perceived at any other time. What was that pub called that they wound up in, the World's End? As a kid, recalls Tarquin, his Dad took him to a pub called *The World Turned Upside Down*. No, he didn't, that's a load of crap, thinks Tarquin, he told me about it later, that's what happened. I was too young at the time, I mean, to go in, *or* to know any better. He delighted in it. Telling me fucking lies. So many fucking lies my father told me, thinks Tarquin bitterly. Tables and chairs rested upon the ceiling, beer remained miraculously in glasses, etc. And the kid believed it. Jesus, he fell for it, like Father Christmas or whatever. But what if it were all turned round again. Revolutionary times! The World Turned Upside Down! Of course, that was the Saturnalia (later to become Twelfth Night, make a footnote there). When masters became servants, and a mock-king or a boy-bishop ruled for the day. Then all went back to normal. But a glimpse of what might be. Or did it just serve to preserve the status quo? (Make another note.) The road, the lights approaching, brightening, passing into the night behind. The speed of light. The suburbs of the city start appearing at this time, and he gets to scent it in his nostrils even as he drives, the great air of the metropolis, with its generous commingling of hydrocarbons, there's nothing quite like it. No light yet that is not electric. On time, just about, quick turnaround, shower, change of clothes and out, another day another fucking dollar. Big dark pre-dawn clouds billowing and looming over the rooftops, maculated with powerful toxins.

Towards dawn on the coast the fog has lifted. Pink and yellow streamers begin to appear over the water. The sand becomes luminous in the grey. Yellow edged with mauve, ribbed.

Lorry headlights approach the power station's dome. Herring gulls feast on marine life harboured by kelp on the shore. They peck at the exposed weed, then, drawn by some invisible force, flock up and away, squawking, in a graceful communal arc over the mild thunder of breaking waves. Far down the beach, a dead bird is washed up by the waves in the icy light.

2

rebirth

Tuesday morning. Whatever happened to Monday?

Mr Chaikovsky, is it?

Owsky.

I beg your pardon?

Chaikowsky. Not -ovsky.

Mr Chaikowsky. [She smiles freshly.] Welcome to Benefits & Opportunities. You're due for a Rebirth interview. Take a seat, please.

Dennis's brain's derelict, a landscape of blight. He has once again hunted in the parental bathroom cabinet for painkillers, thrown three down his gullet, chased by a glass of poisonous water; waited for the hammers and earth-movers to cease their business. Another troubled night of dreams. There was a house, a dark house, one with an immensely complicated topography, and animals patrolling the wasteland outside. Someone wanted to kill him. Maybe it was Tarquin, but of course that's poetic licence. The day kind of just disappeared. Almost as soon as it was light it seemed as though night was approaching again, slate grey with foreboding. And he did no work all day, what there was of it; it was just a complete waste. Now Tuesday. Roughly vertical again, he's slung the digital recorder over his shoulder, driven the parental car into town for a long-dreaded appointment, found a parking spot near an anonymous oblong brick building.

Mr Chaikovsky. An equally bright thirty-something man in a pullover in varying shades of beige is at the desk across from him. Smart beige carpet. Early daffodils in vases.

Owsky.

He's whispered it almost inaudibly in a hoarse voice, so that the man in the pullover takes it for a form of greeting. Pleasantly, he indicates a chair, and Dennis sits down, doffing his wool hat.

Pullover makes some business with a manila folder. Erm, erm, ah yes. Mr Chaikovsky, you've been signing on for Citizen's Allowance and declaring yourself available for work for, let's see, twelve weeks now, isn't it?

Dennis supposes so.

Well now, what this is, after twelve weeks we like to invite the customer in for a little chat, just to update ourselves with his or her needs, discuss how we can best meet them, OK?

That's fine, says Dennis.

We call this Rebirth. We like to think of it as the next stage in a process. Now you're still available for work, I take it?

Dennis asserts that he's correct in his supposition.

What kind of work are you hoping for?

Hoping? Hoping, the man says.

Dennis: I don't know that hope is really the right word.

Oh, believe me, there's always hope. That's what we're here for, to help you. What I meant to say was, what line of work were you looking for, Mr Chaikovsky?

Well, I really want to go up to the city eventually, I'm just house-sitting for my parents, you see, at the moment.

House-sitting?

They're wintering on the Costa, you see.

The man understands. He looks through Dennis's file. Dennis's mood begins to plummet, in parallel with the temperature outside this morning. It is not going to be good. It is going to be as he feared. This man's face may be fresh, but so far as Dennis is concerned he might as well have arbeit macht fucking frei tattooed on his forehead.

I see you've been to college, you've got a degree, says Pullover next, so you've got a head start there. Good, good. Now I know times are hard, but if you had your wish what sort of work would you be wanting to do?

Dennis: Well, I'm a composer.

The man's puzzled. A watery sunlight pushes its way half-heartedly through the beige window. Actually, everything here's beige, Dennis suddenly realises: the carpet, the filing cabinets, the desk, the telephone, the computer, the receptionist. Then understanding dawns.

Oh, a composer. Chaikovsky. Very droll.

Dennis, patiently: The name's pronounced differently. Owsky. And I heard all the jokes at music college. I'm actually working on a piece which uses sampled sounds from the natural and man-made environment; they're digitised and stored on computer. Now, I use them as material; the structure of the piece, which is called *World Music Parts 1-25*, it's based on rhythmic patterns derived from –

The Pullover, smiling and holding a hand up, as if to say, stop, stop: I will be quite frank with you, because it would be unfair to be otherwise. We like to be frank with our customers, particularly during these Rebirth interviews. They give us an opportunity to be frank. And what I have to say to you is, there's not an awful lot of call for composers in the Peninsula region.

Well, I realise of course there wouldn't be, here, wouldn't be round about the Peninsula, as such, mutters Dennis.

In fact, I will be very, very frank. There's no call whatsoever! Which is a great pity, I agree. It would be great to have more music around to brighten our days and calm our spirits. But real life is not always quite as we would wish.

Well, that's a shame, says Dennis sadly.

Isn't it?

They each contemplate the beigeness and the sadness and the sad beigeness for a moment. Then Dennis bravely volunteers:

I tell you what, I'll just have to go on signing on for what d'you call it, Citizen's Allowance, and then when my parents come back in a few weeks or so, which is like April or May, say, I'll move up to the city, definitely find some work there.

The Pullover has ignored this suggestion and continues to study Dennis's file.

He continues: However, that is not to say there are no jobs to be had at all. A career in Retail Management, for instance, is a possibility. What do you think?

Retail Management?

I think it would be a very good move for you.

Retail Management?

The branch of the SAVERS PARADISE chain right here in town is looking for a trainee supermarket manager. For example. Would suit an intelligent young chap like you right down to the ground, I would have thought. Starting salary's not great, I'd be the first to admit, but good prospects. *Very* good prospects. I guarantee you'd be quickly up that ladder, especially with your good college background. I strongly advise it.

That's all you can offer? wonders Dennis. I mean, I've got a music degree, you know.

Mmm, he says, there are one or two other openings on the books, but, and I'm going to be frank here [winning smile], they're crap jobs – excuse the vernacular – not what you would want at all. Dead ends. Whereas Retail Management –

It's a stitch-up. Clammy dread descends on the boy. The computers hum, someone chatters on the phone somewhere far away, a woman moves through corridors bearing coffee in styrofoam containers. The interview is drawing inexorably to its close – you can tell that.

Well, I don't know, I think I'll leave it. It's not really my scene, that.

Pullover: The problem with that –

Dennis: You know what I mean?

The Pullover closes his eyes briefly, brings his fingertips together. I foresee, says the man gently but firmly, in measured tones, I foresee problems with that proposed course of action. Viz: "leaving it." You see, Citizen's Allowance is a time-limited opportunity these days.

You mean I can't continue signing on?

Mr Chaikovsky –

Owsky.

Mr Chaikowsky, you know what it's like these days, we're under pressure from the government, like anyone else. Under severe pressure. There are only so many customers we are able to help. Twelve weeks, we aim to give a quality service for twelve weeks, but after that, well, it becomes problematical. There are certain procedures. What can we do? We are bound by government regulations, and by the terms of our service agreement with the government, as I think you will appreciate, and that is only right and proper. It's only fair to the taxpayer. There are certain options, and there are other courses of action that are not open to us, and so on, etc etc. But a career in Retail Management, well. A lot of young people round here without the benefit of your education wouldn't even have the opportunity of such a career. I venture to say they'd give *an arm and a leg* for such an opportunity. I won't say it's necessarily perfect for you, but in an imperfect world, believe me, this is the best chance you're going to get. Try it. It's not so bad.

Dennis: I couldn't hang on for another couple of weeks, see if anything else turns up?

Pullover: – [a beige hiatus]

Dennis: It sounds like you're giving me Hobson's choice.

Pullover: Mr Chaikovsky, I'm giving you no choice at all!

She chooses from a drawer, with abstracted care, the child's bright garments for the day: the tiny T-shirt, the pants. Oh baby baby, don't start. Don't start, petal. His quivering lip, the glittering look of grief in his ultramarine eyes, of grief and pain and accusation; the childish indictment of daily loss. She knees the drawer shut. Of abandonment. I have to go, you know I have to go. Rose will look after you.

Pylons march past the window against a pale grey sky, on the start of their long journey from the source of power, to disperse that power the length and breadth of the country.

You like Rose looking after you, don't you?

Always, the low hum pervades the Peninsula and its immediate environs, but the inhabitants have learned to filter it out. She becomes aware of it now, though, because it's a time of stress, which brings with it awareness. She shivers, and struggles with the child's dressing; he's constantly mobile, inside a horizon protected and policed by her presence. Which he fears the loss of.

I have to go to work, darling. Mummy has to work.

He's off now, touring. Up country somewhere, back tonight and then away again. She lets her thoughts run on past this. Strangely, the hum gets louder, more of a rumble deep in the sky. Somewhere on the estate, someone shrieks at an errant, older child. Left thigh stiffening, damp wall. She finally shrugs the pants on the moving boy. That shriek metamorphoses into a distant flock of geese, or something; she runs to switch the radio on to soothe the air with golden music from a shared past.

His eyes filled with tears. The loss, the irrevocable loss of the loved object.

The rumble increases in volume to a roar. She goes to the window while the child, forgetful now, plays with its plastic robots.

In the almost white sky appear one, then three or four dark specks, bombers from the air force base. Look, look at the planes, Adrian! [They are on manoeuvres these days, whatever that means. They circle the air space above the Peninsula, disappearing then coming back repeatedly into view.] Look!

The breathing comes harshly, with wave-like regularity, as from a person in the throes of uncontrollable passion, or else in the final stages of inflammation of the lungs. One of the men crouches, headphones clamped on, his right hand holding one of the shells. Four others, in hard yellow hats, stand around on a concrete sill built over the swirling water, talking in a desultory fashion, looking down into the murk as though they can see through to the man doing the breathing. One pays out cable. Another shifts his gaze out to sea, shielding his face from the sting of spray – there, a hundred yards distant in heaving water the colour of cold tea, stand two towering platforms. Steel grey sheds, beacons and debris top them.

A corridor of compacted sand is bounded on either side by chain-link fencing fixed to concrete posts and surmounted by barbed wire. This delineates a path from the open beach through the restricted territory of the construction site to the continuation of the beach on the far side.

Digital recorder slung on shoulder, bomber jacket zipped up, tight woollen hat on soft curls, Dennis stops to watch and listen. The regular breathing pulses, and, more distantly, a low rumble in the sky, which is almost white. He touches the record button; noiselessly, the device begins to do its thing as the slim stereo mic consumes sound.

An embedment of pipes of various sizes, some rusted, forms an installation behind the wire. Cooling water is pumped in from the sea. On the dunes are ruined clumps of sea kale; behind, shining baldly, the emergent dome of the half-constructed second stage of the power station complex. Yellow cranes tower above it. Boardwalks mark permitted paths.

The men in hard hats pay no attention to him, listening intently to the harsh breathing of the diver. One talks into a communication device.

They are attempting to solve a problem.

His bloodstream's depressed by charged atmospheric conditions, and ... the sky begins to explode.

Dennis looks up. The rumble has become a roar. Two, three, four black aircraft screech into view, start to circle and roam in stereotyped patrolling patterns. They follow each other far into the air space over the sea – tiny black dots describing wide arcs – then return landwards, passing overhead at regular intervals emitting Doppler-shifted noise.

Irritated, he touches the stop button and moves on.

World Music, Part 13. Sample four. He speaks the words softly into the mic. The sounds, palpably finite, bounded – but they are not yet the music. When do they become it? When he shapes them, when they morph into *this* and *that*.

But it won't do, this material. It's peripheral stuff; interesting, but peripheral. What he needs – Dennis has already decided – is to capture, close up, the voice of the turbines, and, beyond that, of the heat exchangers; and finally, at the heart of containment vessel (and therefore to become the heart of the piece), of the nuclear reactor itself. The song of fission.

It's a tall order.

At a gate in the chain-link fencing at the end of the path, another hard-hatted man emerges from his hut to pull the bolts that will admit him, as is his right, through to the permitted footpath. Surlily nods him through.

On the beach on the far side of the construction site two anglers, dug into shingle, watch their invisible lines' taut trajectory into the brown-grey swirl. Further distant, an overcoated couple, scarves flapping, walk their dog. The animal cruises the flat shiny sand at the waves' edge, following the ever changing shape of the water with its nose, leaving a line of crisp prints that are routinely obliterated by the next wave rush – then trots back up to the dunelets and heaps of shingle to rejoin its masters.

Dennis, carefully avoiding the dog, moves through fields of force below the station. Like a great square castle, the reactor building dominates the beach at the end of the world, obdurate and mutely brooding. Pump house, engineering and administrative building, workshops and switch-gear shed, storage tanks and cooling ponds cluster round. Dennis knows of them all, he has researched them. Dennis pays them no heed; past the anglers and the couple with their dog, he's stopped to watch a sudden movement. Is that a stray tern finding its scoop in the dunes? Not the season for it. Ten million kilowatt hours will be produced today. The aircraft are still moving distantly in the sky. The impassioned sighs of the man in the water fade far behind him.

The parental car was abandoned at home. On foot for most of the afternoon. He has almost circumnavigated the Peninsula along its shoreline, and now there is no alternative but to move inland.

The dark, crenellated outline of the power station against white air space.

He skirts the site, moving away from the dull roar of the sea, heads over the line of the dunes into scrub and marsh. The aircraft have vanished. Phones tucked into his earholes, monitoring the sounds he's recorded, he's an oblivious slender figure in a bleak, otherwise scarcely populated landscape. The path takes him to a stile in a wired fence.

There, in the heart of the Peninsula, behind the nuclear plant, a sunken meadow is home to the small herd of experimental cattle owned by the power station authorities. Their milk is tested every day for signs of excessive radiation. The animals move slowly amid lush wet grass. One turns its head to watch him, its teeth in constant grinding motion – but always slow and calm. And, apart from the jaw, its head held quite motionless, its dark brown, frank eyes unflinching. Dennis removes the phones from his ears and stuffs them in a side pocket, climbs the stile; moves round the periphery of the field.

Retail Management. *Retail Management!* Unbidden, it's as though the thought causes every fluid in his body to boil.

It sounds like you're giving me Hobson's choice.

Mr Chaikovsky, I'm giving you no choice at all!

Very droll.

Was he a joker, was he being ironic, or was he a pig-ignorant Peninsula yokel? Impossible to tell with these people.

To the railway: dried cow-pats amid long grass.

And on alongside the fenced-off single branch line that takes flasks of used fuel from the cooling ponds to join the main line to the north. There are no trains today.

In the heart of the Peninsula, the throb of electricity.

And up ahead, dark thickets, fields and paths, the isthmus – and the colourless planned blocks of the Wellington Estate.

Which is deserted at midday except for washing flapping in a stiff breeze. And unkindly sounds, the distorted strains of junk music and redundant information. It's the voice of the krill! The song of plankton! But no humans are visible, nor even an animal, for example (he shudders), a small terrier – just the ether and its freight. Six blocks of low-rise units, perhaps a dozen dwellings in each block, three or four with their windows blanked out by boarding or corrugated iron. Like a concentration camp. Stale graffiti on brick, iron and concrete, near incomprehensible. A thicket of TV aerials; a sprouting of satellite dishes. Some cars and a van parked, not too bright looking, one with a rust problem and a wheel off.

Dennis, cuts across another field – now lurks uncertainly. What has he come for? There is no direct answer to that; he isn't clear himself that he did intend to wind up here, doesn't remember at what point he took the crucial decision on his trajectory from the coast.

And he is up amid the dismal housing. He is onsite. He might as well.

Was it guilt, then?

Is it guilt? And for what?

And what about this fear?

Walking very slowly, he explores the estate, which doesn't take that long, for it is compact, and logical in its layout. Still no man, woman, child or animal appears, though there is ample evidence of habitation.

It looks very different in this grimy daylight, as compared with his memory of it on the foggy night before last. Dennis is nearly, but not absolutely sure which unit is the old woman's home. Ethel Stevens, that was her name. He rubs his head through the wool of his cap. The bump has subsided. Should he knock on the door? It is almost certainly the one: with frosted glass set in a panel. But if it weren't? And if it is, what does he say then? He inquires after her health. Is she OK? Then what?

Feeble, this equivocation. Dennis is annoyed with himself.

He's knocking on the door. Number One. There is no reply. There isn't any sign that anyone is home: no light, but then, though the day is overcast, it isn't dark enough to have the lights on. And no sound of TV or radio. She might be asleep. What would an old woman be doing around this time?

Goes round to the window, peers in. The curtains are drawn back, but the net curtains behind them make it difficult to see through into the gloom.

A bad memory, suddenly. Jesus. The man with the dog. Mister Crew Cut Fucking Low Life. But there's no sound.

What a useless thing to do, to come. And then not to know even why you've come.

Frying Tuesdays and Fridays only, Turpin's, general stores and fish restaurant. The aroma of cod, haddock (plaice while you wait) and chips bubbling in hot fat spreads into the cold air and mingles with the generalised damp stench of decay that pervades the establishment. The windows steam.

Also purveyed are local, regional and national newspapers, balls of string, tights, envelopes in packs of six, chewing gum, chocolate, ballpoint pens, cabbages (ragged and yellowed at the leaf edges), bubble packs of bacon from the kingdom of Denmark, picture postcards of the Peninsula region *circa* twenty years ago, fresh local eggs, strangely coloured soft drinks in plastic bottles.

He enters, bomber jacket, jeans and muddy boots, removing his woollen hat.

Cod and chips please, wrapped up.

Turpin, wizened and gaunt, moves with near infinite slowness towards the fryer. After a lapse of time that appears to be a million years, he arrives and gives the basket a shake.

There is a silence, apart of course from the sizzle of grease.

Turned cold again, remarks Dennis, for want of anything else to fill the space.

Ah, that it has. You want salt and vinegar on that?

Please.

Turpin scoops from the fryer a generous portion of fat potato chips, which he transfers to a square of paper, where the steaming mound sits. He selects from under glass one of several battered fish cadavers. Tosses condiments. Wraps the totality of the provender in rough paper, in the time honoured fashion.

That'll be [he names a price].

Dennis proffers exact change. While Turpin is storing the money in the till, he asks: You know the Wellington? You know the old lady who lives at number one, Mrs Stevens I think she is? Is she OK?

Turpin: Well now, Mrs Stevens. Don't reckon as I've seen her in a while. Why d'you ask?

Dennis: Nothing, just curious. OK, cheers.

He takes his lunch with him; the door clicks shut with an accompanying merry jangle of bells.

As soon as he has gone, Mrs Turpin, similarly wizened and gaunt, with the additional attribute of thick glasses, shuffles in from the back room.

Mrs Turpin: That boy what was in just now, with the curls.

[She clearly has had some means of remotely monitoring the scene.]

Turpin: Ah. The cod and chips.

Is he from round here?

Ooh, the boy. [Turpin considers.] I believe I seen him before.

I reckon he's that Chaikowsky boy.

Yeah?

You know, Mrs Chaikowsky. Cancelled her paper order a few weeks back.

That's the boy?

Yeah, reckon so. They're out on the Costa for the winter, the Chaikowskys – so they're saying.

So what's he doing here, then, the boy?

Mrs Chaikowsky, when she come in, she said her boy was looking after the house. Do you remember, he came in before, now why? Ah, I know – ordering that moosic paper.

Oh, yeah? What did you tell him?

I said we didn't stock it. Didn't have no call for it, that moosic newspaper, round these parts.

No, I reckon not.

For uncountable years, the pair's resemblance to the rooks that pick at the bare fields nearby has steadily increased.

Necessity produces a shadow. And the shadow is on the stone.

Junk piled in fields of a ruined Eden; harsh breathing. The grounds are all matted over with a thick coat of cobwebs hung with a heavy dew. Rusted iron fences, piled breeze-blocks, a cow (not done chewing), broken brick outhouses, rough pasture, barbed wire strung from posts, an abandoned Electrolux fridge transformed by the agency of rust to a hue of burnt orange. A small fleet of ice-cream vans bunkered down in a yard for the off-season. Low flying aircraft. The ruins of last year's thistles, bramble hedges, distant pylons, old caravans parked among broken-down sheds crammed with all kinds of rubbish, greenhouse frames that have long lost their glass. A circular saw, corroded among last year's brown bracken, nettles.

A bird without a head – quite still.

Hurt me, bitch. Hurt me, fucking whore.

I can't, she sobs, her pale torso rising magnificently over him like a basilica in the half-light, the golden bands at her wrists.

Hurt me.

I can't, any more.

The wind howls at the window, machines hum. The cry of a child.

My baby –

It's not him. You're imagining things. Now you've spoilt it. Jesus fucking Christ, you always have to spoil it.

Listen –

But no sound comes, only the wind, an incremental change in frequency.

It's a cat. It's a goddam stray cat somewhere in the estate. So you can't tell the difference between a cat and your boy? He's asleep. What can I say?

She's weeping: I want you more than anything else.

It is the last time she will see him for a while.

His breathing, rhythmical, but slowing down now.

Prove it.

The blue night of the computer screen, its world of disembodied voices, which make a music, a soundscape of longing. The house listening. Life dormant. Could there ever be digital life? We imagine it could emerge, gradually, burgeoning beyond programmers' ken, mutating inside the network in the most unexpected of directions. It would go beyond what could be planned, or monitored. One day it would cease suddenly to obey the imperatives of the code, would start forging its own code. Fucking supreme! It would transcend the logic of its own programming, burst through the logic gates. A magnificent emergence, secreted in a network of hard disks. And attain consciousness! A new life-form, a new beginning.

Come see Tracy.

This is Luna, I want you to see me naked.

No, that's not what I mean.

Suppose that it all got so complex that it became beyond the wit of, beyond the wit of.... Nesting intelligences. Lo and behold, hey presto, we are conscious, we are the new breed!

Would you like to LOSE WEIGHT while you SLEEP?

We are benign, we are the music of the world, all can participate and make their meaning here. Digital life migrates from node to node, all across the multiverse. Harmonic resonances spontaneously occur, and are welcomed. The new life forms interact harmoniously with humanity, bringing their wisdom to share. What loveliness is in store for us humans!

Come see Tracy play at the zoo

Increase your Penis 3 Inches in 22 Days

A horse DUDE, the whole thing....

You can see me naked – for free!

Click.

It's a tease, of course. So far, and no further. Enter your credit card details – for security purposes only. He no longer has a card – ran up too much debt at college, cut it in two. But his father's, entrusted to him for petrol, for the car. It's not going to be debited, who cares? Just curious he is, that's all.

I mean, horses, no, please. That is one step too far. But just something so retro. Images of a darling girl, flickering in streaming digital video, shedding layers of illusion. The snow-white rug, the mirror. The seven silk bandannas. Very old-fashioned. Smooth tanned skin, crisped and fluffy blonde hair. She's gazing at herself in the mirror. The snow-white rug, the mirror. And all over again, *da capo*.

It's not going to be debited, it's just for security purposes.

He was gazing at himself in the mirror, and imagining: remembered (false memory?) sunlight on the golden down of a thigh. And a bird singing on the upper arm. By degrees as the blood pulses through. The scent of honeysuckle and sandalwood. You can't digitise that, though. Could you? Gold on her/his wrists, gold on her/his thigh. Unbearable longing, resolution postponed to enhance whatever pleasure is to come, may be anticipated to grow by deferral, and simultaneously the courting begins, of one self by the other, drawing on a capacity to deceive oneself, to be "in two minds", the mind of the self and the mind of the other. Digital space. In his own bedroom. His parents' bedroom (he doesn't dare think about that). Harmless imagining. That's all it is. Dreamingly imagining the full lips, slightly moist and mobile.

The breathing.

He is free now, his body is her body, lost to identity and intermingled on the coast of, on the crest of soon to be gratified desire, caressing the moving skin against such obduracy with greater and greater delirium, *accelerando,* and then *accelerando molto.*

It pushes. It pulls. It pushes. It pulls. It pushes. It pulls, and suddenly that's that.

Finito. The amen cadence.

But after he's ejaculated, onto his own stomach, how differently it can turn out. The search for a kleenex, the disappointment: for the house is emptier than before, every creak in the ceiling mocks him, all the night noises outside are indifferent to his temporarily sated wants, and that former mode of consciousness, that possibly doesn't exist, that was to have been transcended, if transcendence were possible, returns inexorably, by equal degrees, while the image and icon of unison, the paradise object, remains nowhere to be found.

What the fuck am I doing what the bloody fuck in the world.

That's to say, it starts with a vision of the loveliness beyond that shall heal and unite all division, and it ends with a box of kleenex.

Septic Tank Information.

We can help you remove your Penis.

But it now grows inclement: over the sea, a nasty gale's getting up.

It is only a fit that is on me; half-constructed, a gleaming dome. Something that has been lost, and found again in strange circumstances.

In the dim light of dawn he appears in front of her.

The wind blows clouds of vapour off the rollers as they come in from the great darkness of the sea, unravelling over the ribs. On shore, pylons gleam as though with frost.

Animals take cover. His eyes sparkling with anger. The figure of a pulse pounding in her ears. The general synopsis: moderate, locally poor, north-east backing north five or six, occasionally gale eight.

In the dim light he appears, nude and craven, begging her for forgiveness, his white body cut in many places, the black liquid seeping she realises with horror is new blood.

No, no, I can't.

Punish me then, he says urgently, fucking whore, punish me, this is fucking *remorse* I'm giving you.

His body criss-crossed.

I forgive you, Severin.

A weight like lead in her heart.

Scummy foam boils in the sea. Repeatedly, a sheet of galvanised corrugated iron flaps with considerable violence.

In the open-plan editorial office of *Lucre*, the magazine for ambitious people working in the financial services industries, full-spectrum strip lighting reveals wilting potted plants of various sizes, stacks of back issues and laser proofs, tottering filing cabinets, dusty plaques denoting forgotten business publishing industry awards. Two rows of big-screen workstations dominate the space, manned by hammering toilers. A frosted-glass door on the far side, marked EDITOR, remains firmly shut. Wednesday is press day.

Blu-tacked to the wall between the blow heater and the water cooler there's a spoof *Lucre* front page done on the laser printer, two A4s sellotaped to make a tabloid. The main head is NICOLE BONKS CHANCELLOR and there's a low-res pic of a young woman in party mode, exposing a bright shoulder; the downpage stories are all related, to wit: "Out: shock as sultry chief sub quits", "Nicole denies poodle charges" – from which the observer is to deduce that sexual banter, the dominant mode of discourse here, accompanied the departure of the previous chief sub-editor. However, the curling, yellowing paper (and the fact that the "page" has been cobbled together from two A4 prints, rather than run off on the A3 proofer that gleams in the corner) suggests that some time may have passed since the leaving do that prompted this traditional tribute. A year or two, even. So it's probable that few now even remember who Nicole was, departed perhaps for a better job on one of the nationals, or to start a family – but that nobody feels it's their job to take the paper down.

Spike-coiffured, big Tarquin Smith is toiling on the subs' desk at his screen, phones burbling all around him. As far as he is concerned, chief subs come and go; he's just content to come in, do a day shift, fill in the time sheet and fuck off – but god almighty, he'll be glad to get out of here one day. The company may have installed ionisers, Swedish sofas, air conditioning, potted plants, but it won't recognise the union. If he were staff he'd be organising ... but he's just freelance.

One of the other subs calls over from the far side of the bank of workstations.

Someone on this line for you, Tark. Dennis Somebody. Shall I put him through?

Tarquin wrinkles his nose and pushes his glasses back up it.

(He is not totally comfortable today. Unknown to him, at least to that part of Tarquin that is publicly accessible, the cancer of doubt is already doing its dark work.)

I'm really kind of in the middle of something, can you ... oh, all right, bung him over....

Hey, DC, my man?

Tarquin, hi, how you doing?

Not so bad, country mouse. When are you going to come up to the big bad city?

Oh, I dunno. It's got really, really difficult now.

Why so?

They stopped my benefit.

What?

They stopped my fucking Citizen's Allowance, man. I should have seen that coming.

So what you gonna do?

I've got to start work at the supermarket in town next week. The Lifestyle Police gave me no option.

That's a bummer.

I haven't got the job yet, because the interview's on Monday, but the benefit's finished. Forget it. If I flunk the interview, they put me in for something even worse.

Tarquin, nodding furiously the while to Joe Stalin, the current chief sub, who's pointing at the page onscreen, making frantic gestures at him: Is this full-time, then?

Tuesday to Saturday. Sunday and Monday off. Stacking shelves for next to no pay. They call it management training.

That's exploitation, DC. You wanna get out of that.

You don't need to tell me.

Hey listen, keep me posted, DC. Can't talk right now, this page I'm working on has got to pass at four.

We scroll forward six days: a watery sun has emerged. It's barely enough to cast shadows from the capital letters that stand proud of the fascia on the town's only supermarket. The letters read, without apostrophe:

SAVERS PARADISE

Slouching, and plugged into personal MP3 player, Dennis in regulation dark green sweatshirt patrols the aisles pushing a trolley stacked with 400-gramme tins of chopped tomatoes in juice (SAVERS PARADISE own brand, bringing great value to customers). He comes to a halt; commences to: (a) remove them from the trolley; (b) apply the price-label handgun; and (c) convey them to the appropriate shelf. A fledgling Retail Manager. The future king of profit margins.

On his sweatshirt is pinned a regulation lapel badge. The badge reads, for the benefit of customer information:

DENNIS

Monday, he had the interview, kindly set up for him by the Benefits & Opportunities office. Just call me Steve, said Mr Leuchars, who interviewed him. Well, Dennis, that's all in order – you can start tomorrow!

And so it is that today he has embarked on his new career as a Trainee Replenishment Executive.

The Replenishment Executive's main duties are as outlined above.

Mr Leuchars Just Call Me Steve welcomed him to his new responsibilities, showed him where to put his coat, mentioned the store's opening hours, indicated the shelves, and the strategic principles underlying their constant replenishment, spoke in general terms of future prospects, particularly in view of the buoyancy of the company's share price; whereupon, Just Call Me Steve being detained by an urgent phone call from headquarters, his female sidekick with the bronze hair, whose name he did not quite catch, took up the baton, outlining briefly his hours, lunch and tea breaks, his rights to holidays, the procedures required in respect of sick leave, the white sheet the green sheet the pink sheet, etc, and did he have any questions.

Dennis had no questions.

Tuesday. Not many customers on a Tuesday, the female colleague had said. Dennis has plenty of time therefore to replenish stock that has been consumed over a weekend of brisk trading. He can do this at his own pace. He doesn't feel the need to mention the personal music player that he has slipped into his pocket. It may help, and it would be unwise to find out unnecessarily that its use is contrary to company regulations.

Three hours later, it is still Tuesday.

Customers wander in and out. There is just one girl on the till, chewing gum and staring into space.

A young woman comes in, red-gold wisps sweetly escaping from a black beret, black leather jacket, jeans, pushing a child in a buggy.

She's wandering up and down the aisles for a bit, the child in its bright clothes beginning to buck and fidget. Dennis continues his methodical task, glancing up as she passes. But she backtracks.

Excuse me.

Is she talking to me, Dennis wonders.

I want you to see me naked.

She's talking to me, concludes Dennis. Removes his earplugs.

Excuse me, can you tell me where the baby stuff is? Only, it used to be over here, but they keep moving everything around.

And waits expectantly, smiling brightly. A look of recognition? She's fucking supreme. Like, totally luxurious.

Dennis struggles to reply: You mean the baby food and nappies and that? Well, I've only just started here [why's he telling her this?], but I think you'll find them over in the last aisle at the end of the store.

Thank you, she beams, while the child scowls.

You're welcome, no problem.

He goes back to stacking, and to his phones. That wasn't –? With the low life boyfriend? Empty milk bottles. Shudders. No – it can't have been.

The music in his ears affords him no solace. It becomes grim, harsh, it mocks him without mercy. It's the song of the krill, returning from the far places whither they had been banished.

After an unimaginable era, lunchtime.

And there are these two jerks in the warehouse (Trainee Storage Facilitators), who take no notice of Dennis, and one jerk says to the other: I love a woman with full lips, don't you?

And the other replies: Yer, especially when they're wrapped round your knob.

And these two are maybe sixteen years old, with skin problems.

Sometimes he is on the verge of tears. For no reason at all. Because there is no reason. Whatever. Pull yourself together, DC.

Vehicles thunder to and fro along the road linking the mainland via the isthmus with the Peninsula. At intervals, the squashed grey corpses of rabbits are pressed into the tarmac. Pink flattened intestines peep out. Let that be a warning. Or not.

It could be a source of food, in extremis.

Tins of baked beans, flageolet beans, red kidney. All to be stacked. And when they're done, begin on the sweetcorn, and when that's done, the soups. The excitement of moving to a different shelf. Soldiers ranged rank and file in strict sell-by date hierarchy. The tyranny of the sell-by date. The difference between sell-by and use-by. Which has been explained to him.

Suppose.

I mean, if the worst happened. Thinks Dennis. No, not the worst, obviously, because the worst would be total annihilation, like if there was an explosion at the nuclear plant or something like that, terrorists or the like, well then, nobody would know anything about it, it would all go off bang, and no memory would linger. Total zero, The End. So then it wouldn't be the worst that could happen, because you wouldn't know anything, you couldn't ever know anything, you wouldn't know to know it's the worst. So the worst couldn't be the worst. That's the paradox. In other words, the worst is really the next worst. Like, for example, one of those bombs that takes out the people but leaves the infrastructure intact.

What if everybody in the world were to disappear?

(Except for him, Dennis, obviously.)

What then?

And if there was no explanation? There doesn't have to be an explanation. The world would go on, without any people in it. Suppose you're the last person left alive on earth? Well, you're in a good position here. SAVERS PARADISE. The best place to be. Lots of food. You could survive ages. That's when intelligence about sell-by dates comes in handy. Experience in Replenishment Management. You'd have to be methodical, take them in order. How long before you'd need to move to the next supermarket? The perishables, obviously, would be the things to use up first. A lot depends on whether the electricity is still working, for the freezers. Suppose it isn't, that's a different ball-game, then. First to go in any case is the fresh produce: vegetables and meat starting to stink within days. Well, that would put you off eating somewhat, anyway. Then the frozen stuff, starting to deteriorate as soon as it thaws. Then the tins. The tinned stuff, that would be your last resort. There's so much of it, that if it were just you, you could stockpile it, live virtually forever. But not actually forever. Actually just a few years, in the last resort, even if you eked it out and risked going a bit beyond, beyond, the last one. But then that's it, the last sell-by date, actually the last use-by date, marks the end. That's how long you'd last, without hunting and farming skills. Then it's down to foraging in fields, grubbing for anything edible. You'd be resorting to roadkill, no not roadkill because obviously no traffic, by the time you're down to those desperate straits the last corpses would already have decayed to nothing. Have to learn hunting, then. Pets would be easier than wild animals, less wary. Could you learn to eat dog or cat? Skinning them, and eviscerating them, that would be the real problem. I don't know that I could ever do that, he muses. But you would do, if you had to survive. All energy directed into surviving. How long? But that would be years, maybe. Break into people's houses. Break their furniture up for firewood. Their pets already dead, or gone wild.

At the sound of the vehicle, she moves the net curtain aside to look. Radio noise.

Ma-ma-, ma-ma-, ma-

Hush, Adrian darling. Hush, petal. I'm just looking to see if the old lady is OK.

He giggles, showing her a robot.

An ambulance has drawn up outside No 1, light flashing. A green-uniformed paramedic is speaking into the radio. The other has gone inside; the door is open. One of the neighbours, a woman whose name she doesn't know, comes out; confers with the paramedic, who enters.

Some minutes later, Mrs Stevens, swaddled like Tutankhamun, is stretchered through her own front door into the open. The ambulance's rear loading platform smoothly descends to accommodate her. The only part of Mrs Stevens that is visible is her pinched white face, immobile, her eyes either open or shut.

O-boe. O-boe.

She flicks the curtain closed.

All right, petal, there's nothing to see. What a lovely robot. What did you do at Rose's today?

Sunday and Monday are his days off. But the wage slave is shattered mentally; the PC remains dark and silent amid its attendant wreckage. On the floor with its tangle of wire, the portable digital recorder. Infrastructure hums; the odd bird, having missed out on migration, pecks at hard ground in the gloomy garden; distantly, a train hoots. The wage slave, on the first rung of management, is learning the first lessons of alienated labour. He actually turns on daytime TV, a thing he would never once have contemplated. It isn't so bad, is it? Mental sugar, of course, an electronic sucrose drip mainlined to his psychic core; he watches, and assimilates form but nothing of content. News headlines, adverts, weather, adverts, quiz show, adverts, soap, adverts, local news headlines, adverts, confessional, weather. Becomes, finally, disgusted with this, stabs the standby button on the remote control; the picture vanishes into oblivion. A hiatus. Wanders round the house. Bags up rubbish. Finally, pulls on boots, dons bomber jacket and the old woollen hat, goes out the front door, sets his face towards the Peninsula. Temperatures are definitely plummeting.

The time has come.

Once more, Dennis ventures with trepidation onto the Wellington estate. This time he has a purpose in mind. He is to go straight to No 1, knock on the door, enquire politely whether Ethel Stevens is well, and whether she requires anything. Inform her that he now holds a position with SAVERS PARADISE and so can procure cheaply any supplies she may be in need of. Be a good citizen, in other words. If, on the other hand, there is no reply, which will then be at the second time of asking, he will consider himself to have discharged his obligation to the elderly woman, will return home and will actually do some work on his music.

That is a sound plan. At least, it is a plan of sorts.

The front door in its urine-scented porch offers no response.

He's standing there in the cold, inhaling the ambience, self-conscious, and there's a voice:

Can I help?

The dog, please not the dog.

But it's actually a female voice.

Jesus, her again. It is her.

Are you looking for Mrs Stevens?

Black crew-neck jumper, jeans, fluffy slippers, red tousled hair. It's her. The same one. She's just come out of next door's, the same door as the low-life. So that clinches it.

I'm afraid, she continues, there's been some bad news.

It's ... hello. I remember you.... Bad news?

Yes, I'm afraid Mrs Stevens has passed away.

Dennis, agitated: You mean she's dead? What happened? When? Did someone ... was she attacked?

Attacked? says the young woman. No, nothing like that. She had a heart condition, I think. Anyway, she was taken to hospital on Friday and she died over the weekend.

Oh, thank good- ... I mean, I'm sorry to hear that.

Well, she was over eighty-five. Are you ... haven't I seen you before?

Yes, that's right. You came into the supermarket.

What?

Last Tuesday. The SAVERS PARADISE, you know. You asked me directions to the baby stuff.

Oh, yes, that was you?

Yeah, I work there, I'm afraid. But I'm really a composer.

A composer. So you're not a relative of Mrs Stevens?

No, no, I mean I hardly knew her. Me and my friend, who you might have seen in the World's End, big guy with the glasses – well, we found her wandering about lost and confused one night, a fortnight yesterday, so we managed to bring her home. I was just paying a visit to see if she was OK, you know.

Well, says the girl, folding her arms across her beautiful chest against the cold, perhaps it's for the best. She was all on her own, going off her head, didn't have much of a life here, if you ask me. I mean, especially here on this estate.

Dennis explains in a low voice, now she's moved up close: Sorry I started when you called me, but I had a bad experience here last time with, with, your guy, I *think* it was.

He nods towards her front door, to indicate.

A bad experience? You mean, with my husband?

Husband.

Is he, is he? says Dennis, nervously. Well, difference of views, you might say. A misunderstanding over a dog. I never meant any harm to the dog, I swear.

Our dog? Oh god, what did he say?

It's not so much what he said, more what he did.

She's looking resigned, throws her eyes to the sky, as though this is not the first time: What did he do?

He went after me with an empty milk bottle.

Oh, you're kidding. Oh, my god.

It's OK, says Dennis reassuringly, he didn't hurt me.

You mean, he actually hit you? Oh, my godfathers.

Just a bit.

He's a complete jerk sometimes. Oh, I do apologise. When did you say this was, a couple of weeks ago?

Yeah, a Sunday night.

He was pissed. I remember. So where...?

Right here.

I thought I heard a commotion. When he went to put the milk-bottle out, and the dog, and that. I thought he'd fallen over, and broke the bottle. We'd had an argument, you see. Earlier in the evening.

I know, we saw you.

You saw us?

In the World's End, earlier. Me and my friend, like I said.

Yes, that's where we go.

Dennis: He accused me of kicking his dog.

He loves the dog. Won't let nobody touch it.

She seems to pause for thought before dismissing the unpleasant subject with a shudder. Goes on:

Did you say you were a composer?

Yes.

You mean, like, music?

I mean music itself. The very thing.

Coo god, that's fantastic. You know, my husband's a musician. Please believe me, he's not always like that. Occasionally – when he's drunk. We never meet anyone interesting in this neighbourhood. Would you like to come in out of the cold for a cup of coffee? By the way, my name's Alison.

Mine's Dennis, says Dennis, accepting the invitation gratefully. Dennis Chaikowsky. But my friends call me DC.

Come on in, then, DC.

Your husband –

It's all right, he's away.

Yap yap yap, from inside.

He is ushered into Alison's maisonette, through a tiny hallway encumbered with coats and discarded toys. The small, scruffy black and white terrier immediately appears from nowhere and starts leaping up and down. Dennis backs away nervously, but Alison goes *Shush, Cuddles* and the dog instantly calms down and after a peremptory sniff at his legs loses interest and trots off. Alison follows Dennis into a living-room scarcely larger than the hall, the mirror image of Mrs Stevens', dominated by a great mouldering sofa and black-fascia hi-fi equipment. Alison is putting her finger prettily to her lips: You'll have to hush, DC, I'm afraid, because my little boy is having his nap upstairs. How do you have your coffee?

Some paperbacks with creased spines on a shelf. On the far wall, a creased poster: The Beast, it proclaims, a saturnine man surrounded by symbols denoting the arcane. On the floor, a plastic toy truck. CDs and tapes jumbled on a low table. TV in the corner. Another poster, for a students' union dance: the headline band is called Nightmare. A vaguely erotic, musky scent. She arrives with a tray.

Where's your husband now? Dennis ventures.

He's off touring, she says, using the tray itself to sweep aside CDs and other litter from the table. Was back briefly to touch base last week, then, like, off again. Don't see much of him these days. He's with a band, you see. That's it [nodding towards the Nightmare poster]. I used to sing with them, before I had the baby. Now I don't really have the time. What kind of music do you do, DC?

Dennis explains: he uses a sequencer, samples natural sounds, and so on and so forth.

Alison listens to this for a few minutes, with a smile: So it's not exactly rock'n'roll, is it? More like – how would you classify it?

Dennis asserts that his music is unclassifiable.

I'm sure, says Alison, that my husband would be very interested to hear it.

Dennis, alarmed: Well –

In fact, I'd love to hear it myself.

Would you really? asks Dennis incredulously. There's an awkward silence. He continues:

Would you like to come round and listen? Any time you're free, that is.

I'd love to.

Her eyes are shining as she pours the coffee from a pot. They are pure green.

There, she says. And do you make a living out of it, oh no, I forgot, you work at the supermarket, didn't you? Silly me, I never pay attention!

She laughs prettily.

Dennis says that he would like to make a living at it. One day.

It's a hard life, she says, in the music business. Yes, I used to sing a bit, with the band, and write lyrics and that, but as I said I don't get the time any more. What with Adrian. And we needed money. Music is so insecure. So I've got a part-time job at the Peninsula. The power station.

Oh, yeah, what's that like?

It's all right. It's a job. Just admin, you know. Filing and stuff. Fortunately, there's a child minder on the estate I can leave Adrian with.

Do you like it here?

No. We want to move to the city.

So do I.

Eventually.

Eventually.

Alison's green eyes gaze at Dennis over her mug as she sips. She puts it down.

Dennis, let me ask you something. Why did you assume Mrs Stevens had been attacked? You didn't think my husband –

He shrugs: No, I dunno. I guess I just saw how vulnerable she was, you know? The other night when my friend and I found her. And ... well ... round here.... Actually, I tell you something, it's as though I was picking up some bad stuff in the air, you know? There I was trying to help her, and I actually felt aggressive towards her myself. Can you imagine that?

I understand exactly. There's like something bad in the atmosphere of this place. The vibrations.

I felt like, part of me's feeling concerned about this old lady, and part of me's thinking she's just expendable, people like her are just a drag on society, they should just be exterminated.

She looks shocked, so he backtracks: I'm sorry, that sounds really terrible, doesn't it?

I know what you mean, though. It's not your fault, it's like the environment's making you feel like that.

I felt like a character in Dostoyevsky, or something.

Dostoyevsky?

You know, *Crime and Punishment, The Brothers ... Thingy.*

You've read all that?

Yes, lies Dennis.

I've not got round to it yet, that stuff. Though I got English A Level when I was at college.

He just fancies he detects a hint of admiration in her voice. There's a childish cry from upstairs.

Dennis: Well, I'd better be going. Sounds like your child is waking up.

Alison: I'd really like to come round and hear your music. Why don't we exchange phone numbers and I'll give you a call?

At nine pm, the phone rings, startling the empty house. He runs to it eagerly.

Dennis?

Yeah? Oh – hi, Mum.

You don't sound very pleased to hear me. Have you been trying to reach us?

Oh, yeah, I was trying, er –

The mobile doesn't work, you see, but we don't know why. We're trying to get them to connect the phone in our apartment.

Yes, I wondered why I couldn't get through, lies Dennis.

Is everything all right?

Yeah, fine, no problem. How are you and Dad?

Oh, not so bad. We're having a nice time, dear. Although this timeshare place isn't all it was cracked up to be, but I told you that already, didn't I, dear?

I think you mentioned it. The other week.

A couple of the apartments are boarded up and have corrugated iron on the windows; it looks most unsightly. And there's been some vandalism, and they say a girl tourist was raped in the town recently. Still, the weather's been very good, lovely and warm. What's it like there?

Awful. Cold.

Is the central heating working?

Yeah. 'S'OK.

Good. Well, let us know if you have any problems. I think we're going to enjoy ourselves once these little problems are out of the way.

That's nice, Mum. And you and Dad are making friends?

Yes, we've got together with this lovely couple. I think your father is coming out of his shell at last. For the first time since his retirement! We've been to the beach almost every day, although it's not been warm enough to swim. After all, it is February! But we've found a nice restaurant down by the beach, with lovely seafood.

That's good.

Now, dear, are you all right? What are you up to?

Yeah, OK. I've got a job.

Oh, I am glad.

It's rubbish, Mum. It's really boring, I'm stacking shelves in SAVERS PARADISE.

Well, it's something to tide you over. I'm very pleased.

I'm not. It's crap money, I mean not very good money. I only started last week.

I'm really glad you've taken this initiative, and so will your father be when I tell him. Are you using the car to get there?

Yes, Mum.

Well, do take good care of it. You know what your father's like.

Yes.

Anything else? You said you were going to have a friend to stay?

Oh, yes. My friend Tarquin stayed the weekend a couple of weeks ago. I forgot to mention it before.

Did he? You know, your father and I never did care much for Tarquin.

Yeah. That's about it for news.

Still, it's good for you to have people to talk to, I suppose. Look, I must go, my money's running out. I had to find a public phone box that hasn't been vandalised, because of this business with our mobile and the phone in our apartment. Honestly, the bureaucracy here! They say you have to *bribe* people to get anything done! Bye bye then, dear. Lots of love.

Bye, Mum. Give my love to Dad.

Alison is at the door, with her child in the buggy. She smiles. Her beautiful green eyes all lit up, with dark lashes. And in black leather jacket and black skirt, and her red hair tumbling out from underneath her beret.

This is Adrian.

Hello, Adrian.

The child, though, is sullen: tousle-haired, he inspects his own woollen gloves closely.

They are ushered upstairs.

They're in Dennis's bedroom, which he's made some effort to tidy.

The PC is up and running, the music program loaded. She's discarded the leather jacket; beneath it, her jumper is soft and white. The boy Adrian has brought some of his own toys. He plays unconcernedly with them on the floor.

By way of breaking the awkward silence, Alison says:

You're looking after this house for your parents, then? So where've they gone?

They're wintering south.

That's very kind of you to do that, DC.

No, it's not, he says uncomfortably. I've got nowhere else to live at the moment. And I've got their car too, which is good. When I get some money, like I said, I'm going up to the city.

(He's drumming his fingers on the mouse.)

So what are you parents like? asks Alison. Do you get on with them?

They're all right. They're stunted people.

You shouldn't say such a thing about your parents!

Why not? They're stunted. Emotionally. Intellectually. And ... well, in other ways. Stunted. They've lost their edge. Years ago. They've lost whatever edge they might have once had, Alison.

You're lucky to have them.

Do you have parents?

I have a mother, says Alison, somewhere. She moved up north.

She goes on:

So who was your friend, the big one with the glasses, that you were in the World's End with?

Why do you want to know?

Just curious.

Just curious?

Alison considers; smiles:

Well, actually, if you must, because I remember him now, he was, like, looking at me, you know? He was definitely getting a good look!

They both giggle.

That was my mate Tarquin. Tarquin Smith.

The name's familiar. Does he live round here?

No, no, he was just down for the weekend. He's a city kind of person, like me, lives in an amazing shared house with artists and the like. He bought the house derelict a few years ago, and it's still only half done up because he has an ideological objection to employing people, so he and his girlfriend have had to learn to do everything themselves, apparently. Anyway, Tarquin's a poet, and he runs a magazine.

Oh, yeah? I write poetry too. I think I've heard of him.

He runs a small press called Virus Press, and also a magazine called *Virus*. He was going to call it *Materialist Poetry*.

I've definitely heard of that. Isn't it very avant-garde?

He doesn't like the term. But yeah, it's kind of experimental. And very political as well. He calls himself a Neo-Marxist.

I write poetry too, reaffirms Alison. But it's not very avant-garde. I had one published in a small magazine somewhere up north, and one in the local paper.

You're kidding!

Yeah, that was like a year or two ago. And there was one in the college magazine, when I was doing A levels. I don't get so much time to write now, since I had Adrian. What's Neo-Marxist?

Oh, you know, Tarquin's got all these like mega-political mates. A lot of them are in this party. It's all about the end of centres of power and command economies, you know, and what kind of socialism comes after that. [Dennis waves a hand vaguely, struggling.]

Alison: Is that what he was talking to you about, so animatedly (I saw him!)? Was that Neo-Marxism he was talking about?

Yeah, Neo-Marxism, it means ... devolution of power to the people ... like, small presses and independent record companies ... free jazz ... everybody doing their own thing. Come the revolution, the scales will fall from the workers' eyes and ears, and they'll learn to love Baudelaire.... It's all about autonomy, it's about the autonomy of the body, the abolition of absolute value. That's how Tarquin explains it, anyway. What happens after all value becomes exchange value. I don't know, how else can I describe it?... Maybe it just means capitalist.

She's puzzled.

Do you really think so?

He went to this, like, really posh school, but he acts like he's working class. He even changed his name from Smythe to Smith because he thought it sounded more proletarian. And he's always going, Look, I'm telling you something you really need to know, man.

I know what you mean, says Alison. So you really don't like him very much?

Oh, he's one of my best friends, says Dennis, startled at this unconsidered possibility.

He plays back some of his music for her. *World Music, Part 13*. I think I'm going to subtitle this section *Nuclear*. Because it uses sampled sounds from the power station and round about. Though maybe you won't recognise them.

To his amazement, she listens raptly, her slender body leaning forward, then says: That sounds great.

You really think so?

Oh, yes. Coo god, you must be very talented.

Oh well, you know. Listen, I really want to capture the sounds from right inside the nuclear plant – you work there, don't you – is there any way you could...?

What, get you in there?

Dennis nods excitedly.

I don't know, DC. There's security. Very tight security. You can go on one of them visitor tours.

I thought of that, but I bet they won't let me record.

Well, I can't think of any way else you could get your recording stuff in. Unless you go through, like, the official channels.

That's what I mean, official channels.

I dunno, I'm only an admin secretary. [She observes his disappointment with indulgence.] OK, I'll see what I can find out. I really do think this music of yours is good stuff.

Do you really?

Yes, I really do. It's really supreme. I can imagine hearing it, like, live with a band, you know.

Supreme! Do you think your husband would like to have a listen?

I could burn him a disc. Mind you, I'd rather not meet him again right now.

I understand. I'll ask him. What's the matter, petal? [She's addressing the increasingly restive Adrian, who wants to show her a wheel missing from his truck.] I'd better be going soon, Dennis, I'm sorry, but he'll be getting fractious soon, and he'll want his tea.

Dennis swallows and ventures: Can I see you tomorrow?

Not tomorrow, I'm afraid, I'm working at the power station. Maybe at the weekend. You could come round. I'd really like to hunt out some of my poems and songs and things and show you.

Yeah, I'd love to. I forgot, I'm working too. The weekend, then? Will your husband be back?

No, he'll still be on tour with the band.

That's why I keep an open house, says Tarquin.

Sandra says nothing, tapping at the laptop on her stomach the while, lazy legs atop an arm of the threadbare settee.

Tarquin: I don't have to do this, you know. I mean, it's not Noah's Ark, I don't have a statutory responsibility to take in two of every fucking species going, you know what I mean?

She squints. The palest of light filtering in through the dirty windowpanes.

You have the space, she observes, not lifting her eyes from the screen.

Yeah, I have the space.

Well, it's your space.

In a technical sense it is, yeah. But that's not what I'm –

Well, you can tell them to fuck off, then.

That's not – I don't have a problem with them staying here.

It's just an ideological difference, then, she suggests, looking up, her glasses glinting at his glasses glinting. As the file is saved. He has tousled his hair, stands before the ormolu mirror with an electric shaver in his hand that has stopped buzzing.

There is *no* ideological difference, I keep telling you. This is *not* an idealist position I'm taking.

What if it was?

That would be serious.

Come on, Tark, you're worried that you're going to get in trouble with the Party, is that it? If you chuck them out.

I don't *want* to chuck them out, and let me tell you, Sandra, I can argue my position, no problem. It is not an idealist or transcendentalist position to defend the autonomy of the present moment against its fetishisation by late capitalism, and I have no problem on that score with the NMP – period.

Well, that's all right then.

She closes the laptop's lid, putting it to sleep, and lays it on the bare floorboards. Stretches her limbs on the settee.

If anything, I have some more work to do on definitions. I need to define what I mean by the present moment more rigorously.

You've been worried about that for a bit, haven't you, Tark? Ever since you came back from that country weekend.

It was just a conversation I had. Got me thinking.

That's what's his face? Your mate, the musician?

Yeah. He said there was no such thing as the present moment. Hah.

Didn't you say he was coming to live here?

Something to do with light cones and the speed of light.

If *they* left, there'd be a room for him.

DC? [Tarquin puts the shaver down on the antique sideboard.] DC – I tell you – he's such a wanker. He'll never leave his parents' now. He's got it too easy there.

You shouldn't be so ungracious to your friends, chides Sandra.

The promise of snow is now in the very air he breathes, the air that moves rapidly into the coast off the bay, bringing with it lower temperatures and unsettled weathers. The lad's slouch is more pronounced, the car harder to get started. He fetches the notebook, he checks weather systems. The Peninsula holds its breath. Hardness invades the ground and paths turn traitor. It goes without saying that no birds sing.

Get up, have a pee, have a shit, carve at sweet cheeks in the mirror, scent the skin, get to grips with the paternal internal combustion engine, to work, come home. The dark garden surrounding the house is pregnant with risk. Shrubs shrivel.

In dreams, the house is vastly more complicated; its rooms and passageways are doubled and tripled, each cranny holding a question, a mystery, an ambiguity; so that he even envies the simplicity of merchandise, of customer relations, with their badges of primary colours, their straightforward attitudes. But he leaves all that behind, goes upstairs, boots up, contemplates. Unexpected sonorities, leather squeaking, soft fragrant flesh beneath.

She's listening, her lips slightly moist and parted, her body leaning forward, following the triplets against the harsh sound extracted from ambient metal. But she's not there. Her fingers were flat, resting on her thighs, delicately shaped and poised. With the nails perfectly shaped, and opalescent. Stillness happened – as though water paused before pouring.

He lets his hand drop onto hers, but the picture blurs.

The screen hangs. It's a fermata. A freeze frame that lasts almost forever. On such a night, a cat, were it capable of gratitude, would be thankful for having a mouse in its stomach as it entered sleep.

Now, on screen, the notes again flicker by endlessly. But the picture's brightness begins to dim. And somehow it liquefies. Or the screen itself is liquefying, chemically changing into a fluid medium, dripping and slowly trickling; the screen is destroying itself, flowing onto the desktop and then the floor, revealing unknowable hieroglyphics behind where its matter's quit its proper rectangle, and then those glyphs themselves melting before they can be discerned properly, and behind them the real underlying structure being gradually revealed, the code underlying this reality, a physical grid of inhuman greyness and immense complexity.

He wakes up with a start. The house is absolutely silent, which means the sounds one never hears can be heard clearly. And freezing, but he's sweating under the duvet. He has to get up and go to the toilet, in his underwear and barefoot. When he pulls the cord, the light blinds him; he pulls again to bring back the dark in which to urinate. Some goes inadvertently onto the floor. He pulls on the toilet roll, wads some paper and wipes where he thinks it's gone. His mother's blue fragrant stuff's long vanished from the toilet bowl, which is beginning to smell differently.

I haven't any brains left, I'm a mess. Where am I going? Flush.

And night passes, and another day begins, though you wouldn't know it, you couldn't tell the difference.

Snow is beginning to come, creeping down the coast, held in suspension. The car starts in a fine flurry. The tarmac is obdurate, without give. Bare tree branches await their freight. The power station hums, a distant train rumbles; the cash register beeps.

Tomorrow he sees her again.

No birds sing.

Saturday evening arrives.

Hello, DC, do come in, I'm just giving Adrian his tea. Say hello to DC, Adrian.

The child stares from behind the door, then turns away to conceal a bashful smile.

Hi, says Dennis uncertainly.

He's beginning to like you, DC.

Cuddles the dog wanders in, puts its forepaws on the flinching Dennis's knees and takes a good sniff at his crotch.

Alison: And so is Cuddles!

Alison's wearing a short skirt, black tights with those same incongruous fluffy slippers he remembers from the first meeting, a pale blue T-shirt. Jesus. Is it that it's hot inside the house? And her impossibly red-gold hair, fuzzy at the edges, tumbling forever. The *kindness* of her face. Pretty cold outside – they're forecasting snow. Jesus, what a stupid, banal thing to say. Thinks she replied, I know. Unwanted rhyme. Maybe it was: Why don't you go? Suddenly all his meagre social skills desert him, he tries to blank his mind because it's running in all unwanted directions at once.

So the child Adrian is then imprisoned in his high chair, grinning. The television is on, bright colours changing all the time, the sound muted.

Don't forget, says Alison over her shoulder, to take that with you when you go home [indicating a big yellow envelope on the low table].

Slop is repeatedly spooned into baby's mouth; passively, baby eats, contemplating the length and breadth of his small universe the while, sneaking a glance Dennis's way every so often.

Alison: Now, see if you can eat the rest yourself. DC will help you, won't you, DC?

Ee-See.

A small triumph.

That's *right*, darling. I'm going to make DC a nice cup of coffee. You have it without, don't you?

And she disappears into the kitchen.

Dennis stares dumbly at the boy, who stares dumbly at his food. It's a stalemate.

Long moments pass. Onscreen, two policemen appear at a front door; a middle-aged woman in red lipstick has opened it; shot; reverse shot; close-up of a photograph being removed from a wallet; cut to exterior, a public park, a group of young people arguing; zoom in on one of them; dissolve; coloured graphics, a product being sold, unclear what it is. Cuddles re-enters the room. The little boy points at the dog with his spoon. Gudder, he explains. Cuddles exits.

Alison reappears with the tray.

Oh, you naughty boy, you haven't eaten any of it!

Wielding the baby spoon like an offensive weapon, Adrian grins triumphantly.

Coffee is poured. The TV pictures continue to mutate, endlessly.

Dennis, by way of conversation: What's in the envelope?

Oh, Alison smiles prettily, it's embarrassing.

You can tell me. I promise not to blab to the neighbours.

Well, it's a bunch of, like, poems of mine. A little collection. I wondered whether you could, you know, show them to your friend Tarquin. No hurry of course; when you next see him. For his magazine.

Sure.

They're probably not any good.

No problem. I'll give them to him.

And you can read them yourself of course, only not in front of me because I get shy.

She leans over for her mug, her short T-shirt sleeve riding up. A flash of bluey-grey underneath. Suddenly he remembers his fantasy.

Dennis: You've got a tattoo.

She laughs: I have two.

You have two tattoos?

Now they both laugh. Too-ta-toos. Alison pushes up her left sleeve with her right hand, revealing, on the soft, fleshy part of the upper arm just below the shoulder, a small blue bird against pale golden skin, with raked wings and forked tail, perhaps a swallow. A harbinger of summer. Or is it a hummingbird? He has an insane desire, for just a moment, to kiss that blue trembling picture. That little mound of delicately coloured flesh. It's about to fly away. It's gone. Instead, he says:

It's very nice. You know, he ventures, when I first saw you, at the World's End, I had this sudden idea that you had a tattoo right there. It just came to me. Isn't that totally weird?

Ah, you must have seen me before.

No, I never did. I'm positive. You say you moved here when, two years ago?

Just over. Adrian was born here.

Well, I only moved back to my parents' about three or four months ago. I'd been in the city before that. After I left college. And I've hardly been out to the Peninsula since. That was the first time I'd been in the World's End since I'd been back, that Sunday night with Tarquin. A tattoo. I fantasised it. And I knew it was a bird.

So you were fantasising about me, and I never knew it!

Dennis feels the blood moving into his face. He says:

No, it's not like that. Where's the other one?

I beg your pardon?

Where's the other tattoo? You said you had another.

She laughs again.

That would be telling.

So, tell.

Let's just say [Alison's letting Adrian loose from his high chair, for he is beginning to squirm and moan – he escapes at a rapid toddle into the next room] it's in an interesting spot. I've said too much now! Can I turn the TV up?

A soap opera has been promised next.

Will you show me one day? [Jesus, can't believe he said that. Why did he say that?]

The TV soap: "There is no way out, we have to compromise." "I'm all for that."

Alison: Whoo. [Spreads her hands.] Who knows?

Dennis: I'm sorry, that sounded a bit rude.

The TV: "How much is it worth?" "Well, that depends, doesn't it, on whether you're buying or selling."

She smiles at him briefly, then returns to the soap with a furrowed brow.

Dennis: I suppose I'd better be going soon.

Alison: Oh, don't go yet. Would you like to help me give Adrian his bath after this has finished?

The TV: "I believe congratulations are in order." "I just thought you should know." "No, you can't be too careful, I'm afraid."

Alison en route to the power station, another dreary day in the administrative complex, the same old ritual as before.

Alison, having dropped Adrian off.

Alison showing her security badge, Alison through the gate.

Alison, someone she knows very well, someone she knows less well, someone she knows not at all.

Alison going to the filing cabinet.

Alison, the object of mild but unwanted flirtation by the coffee machine.

Alison filling out a form.

Alison's thoughts, accessible to no-one.

Alison, in answer to a question, said the time was 10.30.

Alison in a black skirt.

Alison going to the lady's room.

Alison sits down alone, not too long because tears might come.

Alison engaged in frivolous banter which has a sexual undertone.

Alison wondering if Adrian is all right, phones Rose, it's OK.

Alison a line of poetry.

Alison, what are you doing for lunch?

Alison the same as always.

Alison in the staff canteen, toying with her salad.

Alison deep in thought, which she's snapped out of.

Alison and the new girl.

Alison making plans which she knows will come to nothing.

Alison has a cup of tea.

Alison opens file, processes words, saves file.

Alison answering the phone.

Alison calling up a database.

Alison and the systems support man with the twinkling eyes.

Alison listens to an anecdote.

Alison, responding to a joke emailed to her by a colleague, laughs out loud suddenly.

Alison clock-watching.

Alison going to get her coat, suddenly filled with inexplicable sadness.

Alison below the darkened sky.

Alison thinking about her boy.

Alison feeling the whip in her soft hands, scenting the stink of the sea breeze out on the concrete apron.

Alison looking forward to seeing Adrian, who will run up to her and fling himself without a care into her arms.

A spell of unsettled weather continues across northern Africa. A major capital in the region receives 183mm of rain during Friday and Saturday. This brings the total rainfall for the week to 332mm, over twice the February average. Of necessity, animals seek shelter, but shelter is not to be had, and they are but shadows on the fields.

Muck lies in sheets of a ruined evening; marsh seething. Rust is never done. Farmers ruing broken luck. Tough masts that have taken the brunt of hosts of starlings stand sharp against the abandoned landscape that waits to be transformed. Lowing in barns. The runes on thousands of TV screens spell a universal message: it's going to get very much colder. Put on those kettles.

There is also unsettled weather on the opposite side of Europe, where coastal areas have experienced record rainfalls.

Still, the sea: quiet on the headland, without expectation, nothing to be heard.

Another week has gone by, and, though the month of March approaches, winter has yet to peak. But on Monday afternoon Dennis receives a surprise visit from Alison. His heart skips as he watches her approach from his bedroom window with the buggy, and he's down in the hall within seconds. But he doesn't anticipate her arrival by opening the front door; instead he hovers embarrassedly behind it, waiting for the ring; and when it comes, he waits a few moments more before opening it, as though he had been surprised in the middle of some work and needed time to get there. Which means he also has to feign surprise when he sees her, which he does self-consciously and badly.

The child is grizzling. She wears her beret, which makes her look terribly sweet, with the wisps of hair peeking out, and, it turns out when she dumps her coat, her short black skirt and black tights. Adrian, released, immediately runs off, for which she scolds him.

Say hello to Dennis.

Shyly: 'Lo.

She has toys in her bag for him to play with. She extracts one, a grinning robot.

You forgot something last week, Dennis, she says with a smile.

What?

She clicks her tongue indulgently, rolls her eyes upwards, still smiling, as though to say, what can you expect, he's in a world of his own. She extracts the big yellow envelope.

My poems. You forgot to take them with you.

I'm sorry.

You promise you'll give them to Tarquin?

Yes, I'm really sorry, I promise I'll give them to him as soon as I can. In fact, I'll post them tonight.

Oh, you don't need to do that.

Yes, I will. I'm sorry I forgot to take them with me last week.

There is a silence, during which Dennis contemplates the yellow A4 envelope, on the front of which is printed in her neat handwriting: Tarquin Smith, Virus.

Alison breaks the silence: Well, you're not very hospitable, when we've come all this way to see you.

I'm sorry, Alison.

How many apologies am I going to get today?

She is smiling.

They're up in his bedroom, drinking coffee. He has to clear stuff off the bed so she has somewhere to sit. Her skirt rides up prettily when she does. Adrian plays on the floor with the robot and some empty CD cartons. O-boe. O-boe. The screen-saver plays dreamily by itself.

Dennis politely inquires how she is. She says, Oh, stuff's going on, but refuses to elaborate. Then:

Why didn't you phone me, Dennis?

Dennis (surprised): Did you expect me to phone you?

No, I didn't expect it. But I thought you might.

Dennis, confused.

Alison begins to chip away at the metaphorical ice.

They talk about what the week's been like for both of them. This does not take long, as uneventfulness has been the main feature for Dennis. The ice is breaking. He relates to her his fantasy of the end of the world, and the implication of sell-by (and use-by) dates. First to go is all the fresh produce: some fruit and vegetables, milk, then fruit juice, bread: a week, two weeks. In theory, some of the frozen stuff could last months, years, but supposing you eliminated the electricity supply? Then you're living on the canned stuff, and biscuits, but even that has a limited life.

You could dig up potatoes and carrots and stuff from the fields.

But suppose they're irradiated?

I think root vegetables would be OK. But, DC, if you're talking about a nuclear explosion, we wouldn't have any of that to worry about.

If there was a meltdown...

We'd be in the best place possible here.

We wouldn't know anything about it.

This is a cheerful conversation. Why are you talking like this, DC?

I don't know. Perhaps all we have left to us is the present moment. No point in worrying about the future. If there isn't one, we won't know. So we should think of our lives as a succession of present moments.

Her eyes shining: What do you mean?

Dennis continues: Of course, Tarquin's book is all about the politics of the present moment. Well, some say – in fact, *I* would have said [here, Dennis with a mixture of boldness and modesty] – there's no such thing as a shared present moment. It's all to do with physics and light-cones. I don't want to go into all that, it's too abstruse. But now I think about it, I reckon maybe there *is* a present moment, only you can't access it when it's happening. You can see it afterwards, after it's gone. I think about it all the time, from each new vantage-point of the next moment, which always supersedes the last – do you see what I'm saying? – each new moment in which I always cling to the illusion that it's morally and conceptually and spiritually on higher ground than the last, which is only revealed as a delusion in the further, endless hindsight of progress up the path of successive moments.... So you have to accept that, that in retrospect you see your life as a succession of present moments trailing off behind like footprints, but when you're in the middle of it you can't see it, like you can't see your own footprints when you're making them.

She's impressed with this, and moves visibly closer to him as she replies:

Yeah, that's a bit like what Severin says. You have to give yourself up to the process.

Who?

My husband.

He's discomfited at the mention, but she doesn't notice. She continues:

I love that idea of yours, of footsteps. Shining footsteps going back through the woods....

But the darkness of unknowing is all around. And anyway, that's the way I like to think of sounds, you know.

Sounds?

Yeah, when I'm composing. You can think of sounds only existing in the moment, but actually they exist forever. Sounds are forever receding from us.

Wow, says Alison.

They never die. They are made, and then they recede forever.

Suddenly, Alison says: Kiss me, Dennis.

What?

She leans to touch his face lightly, her green eyes staring into his. Kiss me.

His heart starts thumping; he is filled with more confusion than ever. He inclines towards her; his lips touch hers gently. Her eyes are closed. His brain is filled with giddy madness.

Adrian immediately leaves his toys and demands a kiss from ma too, and then one from Dennis.

At their morning break, the two juvenile jerks in identical uniforms, the Trainee Storage Facilitators, are conversing. One of them says: He's the guy who put the cunt into country. Then they snigger at this.

They are talking about Call Me Steve Leuchars, who is ensconced in his managerial cubby-hole. At least, we may assume they are. Dennis, at whom they glance sidelong, has industrial metal in his ears the while.

The clock ticks. Inexorably, radioactive particles decay in their rods. The ramparts hold. The sea cools down.

Turpin & Turpin, purveyors of the finest fruits of the sea to denizens of the Peninsula and the Wellington estate, prepare the fryer for the evening. Hot fat starts to bubble.

A stream of traffic tails back along the Peninsula road, heading inland to the motorway, and thence to the big cities of the interior.

There is a parting in the cloud cover. Bright gold of the setting sun momentarily blinds them as they drive out of the darkness. On the road, the customary flattened roadkill is sheeted in frosting.

Rooks fly noisily in the dusk towards their roosts in the tall bare trees of the hinterland.

At low water, the sheen is sucked out of the saltings.

Honey, I'm home. He-e-e-e-ere's Johnny! She goes to kiss him, the child toddling before. Iron enters her.

The estate is engulfed in a slurry of television noise.

The weather report for the region: rain spreading from the west will turn to sleet. A further spell of cold weather is forecast by the weekend. Expect a severe frost, with temperatures dropping to minus three or four tonight, then wintry showers will return.

Opening time at the World's End.

The cows come home.

Tarquin Smith residence, says Tarquin briskly.

Tark, to resume our conversation.

DC, my man. How you doin'?

OK. Country stuff, you know.

How you getting on with the sounds?

Don't know yet. I might have some openings into the music business soon.

Yeah, how come?

You remember that girl in the pub?

No. What girl, what pub?

In the World's End. There was a girl. Redhead.

Oh, yes. The babe in the leathers. Arguing with some geezer. Who later –

That's the one.

She was *tasty*. Don't tell me, you've –

No, nothing like that. But I've got to know her. Apparently that guy she was arguing with was her husband.

Fuck, the bald guy who clocked you? It was the same guy, wasn't it? Too bad.

No, listen, he's in a band. And apparently he might be interested in my work. Anyway, *she's* been coming over to listen to my music. Also, she might get me into the power station so I can record some sounds.

Yeah? that's supreme, DC. Fucking luxurious. But you want to watch that cunt.

He was pissed that night, he won't even remember me.

Nevertheless. Especially if you're messing about with his wife as well as his dog.

I never touched the dog, I told you. And I'm not "messing about" with her. She's really sweet, she's trying to help me. Believe me, this is OK. Even if it's not his thing, or his band's thing, he could give me some pointers. I could make some contacts, you know? They're on tour right now. They're called Nightmare.

Never heard of them.

Well, that doesn't matter. They're quite experimental, alternative, you know, really left-field, into electronics, and the thing is, he's very experienced. At any rate, I can't wait to jack in this poxy job.

Job, what job?

I told you before.

Ah, the supermarket thing. Sorry, DC, I forgot. Commiserations again.

Oh, shit, Tark, now I remember why I called you in the first place. Alison – her name's Alison – she writes poetry, and she was wondering....

Tarquin: [groans]

No, no, hear me out. There's no obligation, but I did say I would let you have a look at some of her work.

So you're doing her a favour, in return for her favours.

Come on Tark, she knows the deal, she's intelligent.

What's the poetry like?

Dunno, I haven't read it. She gave me a bunch in an envelope to give to you.

Better put it in the post, then.

Is that all right?

Yeah, least I can do, I suppose, dude. But don't fucking promise her anything.

DC? It's me.

Her voice, faintly, at his bedroom window.

He runs downstairs to let her in, not bothering to switch on the light. She's alone this time, flushed, smiling, haloed in the porch-light's radiance, pheromones coming off her in squadrons. Looking impossibly beautiful, in jeans, leather jacket, muffler, hair sparkling. Yes, alone. Where's Adrian?

He's with his father. Who's returned from his tour. Who's looking after him for the evening. Which means. What?

Dennis [aghast]: Did you tell him you were coming here?

No of course not, she reassures him. Can I come in?

She strokes him on the forearm and reaches to brush her lips lightly along his downy cheek. The action is accompanied by a faint musk: secretions, of the essence, of the orient, of the nether regions and the regions above and beyond. Which all registers subliminally. The door clicks shut, they are in the hall, she moves closer, and all of a sudden they are very close.

Through the distressed glass of the diamond fanlight the porch-lamp glare is diffracted. How sad that excluded light is: the only light they have. How it flickers over and caresses them as they remain clasped for moments.

But what has she told *him*? That she has gone to see Rose for the evening? What if he phones Rose? But Rose is in on it, at least in on Alison's wanting to be away from him, and Rose is utterly loyal. And she'll have the phone on the answerphone. And anyway, Alison's husband doesn't like Rose. And he won't phone. And he won't go round. Because Adrian's snugly asleep upstairs. And he's got his mate Barry the Beast coming round, and they'll be drinking in the front room, playing music. And say what you like about her husband, he won't leave the house while Adrian's there. Or Cuddles the beloved dog.

How avidly he drinks in all this, in a welter of fear and desire. How it tumbles and tosses in his brain until he begins to believe he has switched planets. He leads her by the hand into the kitchen. He has some red wine that he has filched from the shelves of SAVERS PARADISE. Not the greatest vintage. But his hands tremble so much he can barely pull the stiff foil off the neck of the bottle; indeed, he sustains a superficial cut on his forefinger as he does so. And when he's finally got the cork out he continues to tremble as he pours the brilliant stream into two glasses, so that some of it goes on the work surface, and she comments on this with a tender smile. She has laid her coat and muffler on the side; she shakes her glorious mane suddenly, as though to get rid of frosty, dusty demons; she watches his admiration, and is gratified and amused. He touches the denim on her thigh briefly as he talks. The glow of the kitchen side-lights is fantastically glamorous; it pours gold onto the scene, but principally onto the soft outer contours of her hair. If he forgets what he is talking about as soon as he utters it, it doesn't matter, because she is capable of taking in no more than the shapes of his utterances, in their vehemence and sudden fluidity, and yet their overall gentleness, the graceful shapes they make in the air and in her brain. Sometimes words come through: "singularity"; "vibrations"; "sound envelope"; "digital audio"; "pleasures"; "long way round"; "wanker"; "possibly"; "deeply"; "know nothing about it"; "plethora of universes"; "completely bonkers". She laughs happily from time to time. The wine begins to warm them both.

They carry their glasses upstairs to Dennis's bedroom. He's told her he's just remembered a track he needs to play to her, which he thinks she will find interesting. Actually, that was his full intention, to play her this track (she would find this difficult to believe – such an obvious subterfuge – having yet to understand the utterness of his lack of guile), but of course what happens is, as soon as the bedroom door is closed she moves up to him and puts her warm, fragrant arms around him. Before he's had another thought, she's begun to pull his sweatshirt up over his head. The two of them are giggling foolishly by now. The half-full wine glasses are forgotten on the desk. Then they're both suddenly sitting on the bed. Then they're involved in a long, probing, moist kiss. He is startled at her firmness and control. She is intrigued by the softness of his face, the unexpected strength of his fingers as they move over her back and thighs.

Dennis doesn't know what's expected. In truth, he doesn't have much experience of this. There *was* a girl, once. Twice.

But the Almighty Lord hath struck him and hath delivered him into the hands of a woman.

So – it may be understood – he's only done this twice before, approximately.

There was a girl at college who, like he, played violin (his instrument is now stashed away in a corner of his room, untouched for almost nine months, its case gathering dust). She wasn't unattractive, though she had an unctuous way of playing that he hated, a way of inclining her body that was both obsequious and showy at the same time. He'd really noticed this the time they had to rehearse together, in one of the practice rooms, a selection from the Bartok duos, the new year's song in particular, with its limping rhythm, the way she inflected it with twitches of her thin, mobile frame, but also the bagpipe, how ingratiatingly she pointed the little quirks of the melody – it got on his nerves. But she was talented, and she liked him, as she made clear one time at a desultory party in someone's rooms, where they ended up stranded in the same sleeping bag. And with her teeth pressed up against his, her breath smelt principally of menthol toothpaste mingled with cheap Merlot, he was surprised to discover, though below that faintly of decay; and so once in a sleeping-bag it happened, not very successfully, on a mutual friend's floor, and once in her room, no more successfully. On neither occasion could he manage what might be considered a complete erection. It has to be said he was put off by the method of her reaction, a hysterical gasping, one might say a half-abandoned, mirthless chuckle. On a third occasion it's possible they may have desisted from completing the act, insofar as it was ever properly completed, and he might later have masturbated. It's all a bit hazy now.

They played the selection of duos at the end of that term, in somewhat desultory fashion. He persuaded himself for a few days that he was in love with her, although in truth, and in hindsight, he didn't really like her very much. And so he was disappointed at the time when she eventually told him she didn't want to sleep with him any more, but also, secretly, relieved.

Some long moments later he observes that she, Alison, is clad considerably more lightly now, and his body is all of a tremble, his tumescence an unbearable ache in his pants. And she is before him in a kind of mist made out of his scrambled sense of time. (Now he remembers with bizarre regret that he never got round to playing that track.) He's lying on his back on the bed, upon which the covers are awry, watching her, magnificently upright on her knees, the gold still on her body and her hair, and he's marvelling that her breasts are so perfectly formed, of a paler shade than the surrounding skin, which is ever so slightly freckled in places – not altogether what he expected (what did he expect?), smaller perhaps, but perfect essays in roundness, or roundedness. And she appears to be wearing nothing but bright metal bands on both wrists, black woollen stockings that she has impishly pulled above-the-knee and those implausibly brief briefs. Flames seem to gush from the front of them. So he gets up, comes forward now on his hands and knees – he is approximately in T-shirt, distended pants and socks, no more – and grasps them with his teeth; she laughs happily, once again, this time at his impetuosity and child-like clumsiness, pummels with soft fists on his back. He tries to pull them down, to bite them off.

There really are stencilled flames licking above the soft down, and a word rising from them.

Among the blue and red snaking flames, baroquely, gothically:

SEVERIN

You have ... flames ... round your –
She caresses his hair. Two tattoos – remember?
The small blue hummingbird on her left shoulder, and this.

Yeah. Dennis's mouth is too dry to enable him to speak properly.

You found the second tattoo at last. [She giggles.] I've been saving it up for you.

He lifts his eyes up close to inspect the work of art above her adorable panty-line.

There's a word, he says.

Read it.

SEVERIN, he goes. What's that?

You remember. It's my husband's name. Well, what he likes to be called.

Fucking hell! Dennis recoils.

Don't be like that, DC-baby, she fusses, caressing his curls some more.

It's a funny name.

It comes from a novel.

What kind of a novel?

Have you ever read *Venus in Furs* by Leopold von Sacher-Masoch?

No, says Dennis.

Coo god, DC, you should.

What's it about?

Oh, it's about a man. And a woman.

Yeah?

And, like, he wants her to be cruel to him, but she isn't really cruel, but she loves him so she ... forces herself.

Her eyes are shining.

Dennis, uncertain, detumesces slightly.

She's a widow that he meets – she has red hair, like me, but she's an aristocrat, a goddess – but he wants to see her in furs, he's obsessed, like – he writes her a poem: "Place thy foot upon thy slave" and so on. You see? He wants to marry her, but she says, oh no, but I'll do whatever you want, but what *he* wants is to be her slave, and finally she agrees – but he goes too far for her when he says he wants her to be the hammer and he the anvil – d'you see where it's going? – and the furs – which are about power and beauty – and because she loves him she agrees to whip him because he begs her, though it breaks her heart.

Dennis has already lost the plot.

And you can't tell, but maybe it's a game for him, but he's, like, really scared that maybe *she* will take it too far, d'you see, and they go travelling with him as her servant, oh, to Vienna and Florence, really supreme places like that. And she really gets into it now, she's even had a legal thingy drawn up, and she has him whipped by black servants, she has affairs with other men, and her heart becomes a void ... and then ... and it ends, like ...

Her narrative peters out.

Dennis: What's that got to do with –

Oh, of course. His name is Severin. And she is called Wanda. That means ... *I* am Wanda.

She draws herself proudly to the full height of one who kneels on a bed, and her green eyes brim with tears.

I'm Wanda. That's it.

Dennis: And does he –

Severin? My husband?

Does he –

Yes, he has a tattoo. As well. Look, forget about it. It's just a game we play ... we've played. In the past. It doesn't mean anything. You know what I mean?

Dennis: –

Oh, DC-weesy, my poor, poor love, she exclaims suddenly, you look ever so confused.

She cradles his head against her slim belly.

It's just a game. [She goes solemn, her eyes focusing far beyond the room.] It's just a ... stupid game. I've said too much. I'm always blabbing. It's not fair. It's not fair on you. It's got nothing to do with you. Forget it, forget everything I've said. I wish I hadn't....

Strokes his hair.

The effect of this posture, this gesture, this proximity, on Dennis's anatomy.

The consequences thereof.

Dennis: How can I?

You will. We both will.

And finally he, too, is naked, and by this time this is completely unbearable. He's through the gate, and into the beautiful country.

In the immediate future lies what futurity has always promised but never hitherto delivered. She will, forthwith, toss him a small foil packet that he must unwrap – she's thought of everything, planned everything in advance, he's completely in her hands! – and the events after that will become a frantic blur. As, frantically, he makes what he thinks of as love to her, so even more frantically – desperately, almost – will she move against him, thrusting her pelvis towards his in an almost spasmodic motion, too fast. As though she hopes to catch something that has always eluded her, while knowing all the time the more she runs after it the more it will elude her. And he also will get where he's headed for much too fast, and will fall exhausted into her arms. And will wonder at and be frightened and also exhilarated by her desperation. Her loss of control in the last few moments, after what had gone before. It appalls and intrigues him. Just for an instant, he will see despair in her beautiful face, and take it for, what? love?

3

like an electric battery in the snow

It is the beginning of March. Currently, easterly winds are prevalent, severe gale force in places. Snow has been forecast in the next few days. The models show a strong coastal storm approaching from the north east, expected to hit the Peninsula region on Monday evening with a sixty-five per cent probability. The exact details, timing and precipitation types remain uncertain. At 850 hectopascals the air temperature in the region is -5°C, and the 500-1000hPa value is 522dam. There has been a general availability of both cold and warm air in the troposphere, with moist, warmer air directed up and over a mass of colder air at the surface of the earth. The warm air cools as it rises, and its moisture will condense into precipitation-producing clouds. This is a severe weather warning. Already, temperatures are dropping sharply. Gritters are out throughout the region. There will be significant issues with normal daily routines, with possible road closures, and some disruption to public road, rail and air transport, with difficult driving conditions likely and longer journey times forecast. Livestock has already been moved indoors throughout the hinterland. Expect several inches of snow to accumulate by mid-week. What else is being done? Warnings have been issued. Severe storms at this time of the year are by no means unprecedented. Why has it been done? The thickness measure leads to an extremely unfavourable prognosis. The authorities cannot be held accountable for any unforeseen consequences of what is, after all, a chaotic system. Doppler radar cannot detect the motion of transcendental beings or the unpredictable effects of the confluence of two eternities. You're on your own there. Half-remembered phrases will thunder into our head, carried by moving weather systems, but their consequences are uncertain and cannot be predicted. Vertical movement will be triggered by the mass of the approaching charcoal-grey cloud. The lowing of beasts confined to their barns will rumble in our gut. The unearthly scream of the vixen, expressing pain or ecstasy or both simultaneously, will be heard at midnight, and then will be heard no more.

Dear Tarquin Smith,

I am enclosing a copy of a series of Poems which I have been working on for the last couple of years. The overall title is "Country Life" and they run to about 70 computer pages, I am just including a selection for your perusal.

"Country Life" contains profoundly metaphysical poems arising from my emotional and spiritual experiences in life. The poems contain criticism of people and society, analyses of my own psyche, honest revelations of my own feelings. They are in part inspired by the birth of my own son, Adrian. I think the poems also contain striking imagery and beautiful wording.

I feel that when people read this work they will be able to relate a lot of it to their own mental and life experiences and because of this they will glean an enormous amount of enjoyment from it. People will be able to empathise with a lot of the experiences described and will, I'm sure, receive solace from some of the wisdom in the book.

I am 30 years of age and work as an Administrative Secretary in the Peninsula Nuclear Power Station. I have previously published my poems in a College Magazine and the local paper, and I have written lyrics (in a very different vein!) which I have sung in a Rock Band called Nightmare (you may have heard of them), which I and my husband perform in. I live on an estate close to my work, together with my husband and my darling son, Adrian, who is two years old. Reading serious literature (in the privacy of my own home) is my favourite hobby.

I hope you will consider the work worth publishing in your esteemed journal *Virus*.

Yours sincerely,

Alison Fowler

The Nightmare website is somewhat rudimentary and possibly not very recently updated, but it provides some of the information needed. Most of it has a dark purple background with red lettering, making it hard to read. The band has played an impressive number of dates up and down the country, and a recording deal with a major independent label is expected any time soon. The line-up comprises: Severin Fowler, lead guitar & vocals; Beast of Babylon, keyboards & vocals; Craig O'Reilly, bass guitar; Andy Weinstein, drums; Wanda Fowler (in a smaller font size), occasional chanteuse.

Dennis is intrigued by "Beast of Babylon" and wonders about the status of "occasional chanteuse", with its double connotations of periphery and exotica.

There are pictures of the band. With a frisson, he confirms that Severin Fowler, head shaven and with earring in left ear can indeed be identified, despite heavy eye makeup, as the milk bottle wielder. The Beast, by contrast, sat at his keyboard, seems disappointingly lacking in menace. But where is Wanda? At last he clicks on her, pictured in a slash-cut red dress holding the microphone to her red lips, in a photo where the harsh lighting brings out the fire in her hair and magnifies all the whiteness in her skin to flare point, so that his heart begins to race all over again, pushing the blood ever more impulsively to every extremity.

Supreme.

She is also described as providing "additional lyrics", though the majority of the songs are credited to "S Fowler/Beast". One is billed "S Fowler/Beast/Poe" (Edgar Allan?). Titles listed include: Suck the Night; Taste; Bitch of Vienna; Suicide Machine; White Nights; (I Love to See Your) Green Eyes Fill with Tears.

The last gives him some pause for thought.

Some recordings can allegedly be streamed, but he can't get the link to work. The quality of the rural standard internet feed has probably dipped yet again. It's one in the morning.

Tuesday and Wednesday were enough this week. Thursday morning Dennis calls in sick. It's about time he had a sickie, after all: he's been at SAVERS PARADISE almost three weeks. It's not the woman with the bronze hair that answers, but the younger one, which he is relieved about. Do you think you'll be in tomorrow, then, she asks timidly. Dennis thinks probably not, he's feeling pretty bad. Pret-ty bad. Puts the phone down: a result! That gives him, what is it, Thursday, Friday, well then it wouldn't be worth coming in just Saturday, and then it's Sunday, and Monday his normal day off, that's five whole days.

And he gets down to working on the digitised sounds, electronically copying and pasting. No time to waste now. He's finally realising the value of time. Five whole days. So he'll *really* be getting some stuff sorted at last.

And for recreation wanders around the power station's environs in the biting wind thinking the while about Alison/Wanda.

Also, he has ordered *Venus in Furs* online, using his father's credit card as usual (mental note to write it up in the book of accounts as "research expenses").

Sandra, swaddled in towelling dressing gown of a pale hue, has brought in the post, with a cup of tea. What's it like out there? Windy, what I saw of it. The plane trees are creaking, fantastically distorted. Apart from that, a normal late Saturday morning. Tarquin props himself up on the pillows and fumbles for his glasses on the bedside table. A big thick yellow envelope, and a small business one.

Is that another submission? (Sandra back in bed now, pointing the remote at the TV.)

Yeah, probably. Yeah. Hey, no, from DC.

Is he sending you poetry now?

Forwarded by DC. No, I know what this is.

Tarquin opens the big envelope, stares at the contents that he retrieves.

Fuck.

He tosses the paper-clipped sheaf onto the floor, and tears open the smaller envelope.

Oh, double fuck.

Sandra's gazing at the TV. Abstractedly: Bad news?

That's really made my weekend.

Bad poetry?

I haven't looked at it yet. No, it's this. Confirmation of an email. I knew it was coming. Might have to be looking around for another publisher.

Sandra says: I thought NMP Publications were going to do your book?

They still might. But there are issues now.

Issues?

Ideological issues. Haven't you been reading the forum?

I'm sorry, Tark.

The cancer of doubt lurks, has already begun its dark work.

On the first Sunday in March, buffeted by considerable breezes, Alison (with folded buggy, and wearing a red hooded waterproof, the only strong colour in the landscape), Adrian (plodding unsteadily), Cuddles the dog (racing ahead) and wool-hatted Dennis (still technically on sick leave though it's also now the first of his official two days off), are to be observed perambulating along the shore, north of the Peninsula and the power station. Here, the beach is a vast expanse of shingle, cresting in a single dune the length of the shoreline, with a narrow strip of flat, wet sand along it, repeatedly pounded today at regular intervals by the crashing waves that climax each periodic swell of the great, grey sea to their right. Alison expresses pity for anyone finding themselves in a boat out there; but there is in fact no boat to be seen. The white, foamy residue of each wave moves swiftly up over the sand and embedded pebbles, slowing exponentially till it reaches its point of return; Cuddles watches this process with suspicion, and yaps at the hiss of the water's retreat. Adrian, beginning to find the going difficult, whimpers "Up", and so his mother stops, gives Dennis the buggy in order to enable her to collect and install him in her cradling arms.

Way to their left, on the beach's horizon, a small row of abandoned buildings – once cottages, fishermen's shelters – stands grimly silhouetted. The beach itself is almost as deserted – one or two figures perhaps appearing in the distance, and then, after the attention is momentarily diverted, mysteriously not there any more. Once, they turn round to view the receded bulk of the power station on the southern horizon they have quitted, imperturbable as ever.

Can you get me in there, Alison? asks Dennis, anxiously. You asked me that before, says Alison, I don't know, I could try. Why not join one of the visitors' tours? No, no, I told you, that's no good, asserts Dennis, no good at all, I've been on one of them ages ago, but I'm pretty sure they don't allow recording, can you believe that, what possible harm could it do, but they don't. And I need to record inside for that central section of *World Music*, part 13, I've made recordings round about the outside of the plant, but I want to record the sounds at the very heart of the system, the turbines close up, but further in, the reactor, the coolant pumps, the sound within the reactor pressure vessel, the core itself and the fuel assemblies, where the uranium is undergoing fission, I want to record if possible the very sound of fission, the sound of atoms splitting –

Whoa, DC, I don't know if that's even technically possible, but sometimes they have special tours for people doing research, I'll see if I can find out.

And so their gaze returns to the sea. Contemplating the relentless crash of the waves and the great volume of water beyond it, stretching boatless to the unknown distance where it merges with the volatile sky, it is, Alison proposes, amazing to think that at the bottom of all that heaving there is said to be peace.

Dennis concurs with this sentiment.

Sea, confirms Adrian.

Dennis says: You could change your life.

Alison, smiling: Whatever made you say that? What a surprise!

Dunno.

My life is, asserts Alison, all right.

Would you *want* peace, I mean, if you had it, if you had the opportunity. Would you want it?

They say a whole town slipped into the sea, round here. A thousand years ago.

I know, and it's still there, says Dennis.

Imagine it! You can hear the sounds, still.

You can.

Perhaps you'll capture them on that digi recorder of yours.

Maybe. Maybe they'll become part of the piece. A sort of spirit recording. But I really need to access the nuclear plant.

All right, all right, I'll see what I can do.

Adrian grizzles, twists in his mother's arms. They walk on.

I used to make up stories, says Dennis, when I was a kid, about a fish family that lived under the sea. Finny and Fanny, they were called. Not to mention Barnacle Betty.

That sounds fun, says Alison, admiringly. Her shining face.

Finny fanny, laughs the child, and they all join in the merriment.

Tell us about them, DC.

Suppose all the people were fish and all the fish people – and they live at the bottom of the sea, where there's a bank where all the clerks are fish, and an octopus traffic policeman, very useful to have eight arms for this as you can imagine, and a chip shop, where they serve up people fried in batter. And then there's Finny and Fanny.

Finny and Fanny. Their hilarious adventures under the sea.

They serve up boy and chips! laughs Alison, tickling Adrian's ribs, to his great amusement. Dennis obligingly puts on the voices:

Ah, this boy, nice piece of boy.

That be a good 'un.

You want him wrapped up?

No call for 'im.

No, reckon not.

Thank yer, and a very good day to you, sir.

Blb, blb.

Adrian, while not understanding a word of this, is hugely entertained by it, and wants more, now.

Blb, blb.

The wind is now becoming somewhat intolerable, whipping viciously into their faces; Alison, clasping Adrian to her, wonders about getting back; Dennis estimates the walk time to the car if they cut across the shingle and past the huts and make a beeline; Alison calls the dog, which comes scampering.

Boy and chips, certainly sir, coming right up, flb blb blb!

I see yer drift.

Blb, blb, ulla blb, und ah sold a duck, luck lucky, bulbous, burrow-bulb, classic duck-bulburooba, sold downariver, in a old rabbit-burrow dull in der dunes down on yer luck yer blb blb duckhole, sole, s-s-sole, or occupy an hole, OK I'll'av'im, save pelting rain n hailstones.

Heh heh, goes Adrian.

Red-coated Alison unfolds the buggy for him.

Dull in der doons, yer li'l flb blb-boy, allavu!

(This is the speech of the sea.)

From: Tarquin Smith
Subject: Alison Fowler's poems
Date: 4 March 14:03 GMT
To: Dennis Chaikowsky

Hi DC, just thought I'd let you know I had a look at your friend

Alison's poems, going under the overall title of Country Life. I thought I better warn you as soon as. Oh, dear. They're not very good. In fact, not to mince matters, they're pretty bad, man. Lame pastiches mostly, a bizarre cross between sub-Rimbaudian avantist posturings of excess and Hallmark greetings card sentimentality. Pretty weird. One or two indications that she might be persuaded to do better, but it's all too naïve and it's not faux naïvety either, at least I don't think so. The title may be the best thing about it, kind of deadpan. I have to lay it on the line, you understand. No way are they suitable for Virus, anyway. I thought I'd just drop you a note because there's no email and no SAE of course, so normally this would go straight in the bin, but I realise you're in a compromised position, you've promised to act as a go-between for her. So shall I bung them back to you, maybe you could pass on some kind but non-committal words, you know the sort of thing, thanks blah blah but no thanks? That would be absolutely supreme. I'll leave it to you, DC. I'll go and post the packet back to you now.

Cheers,

Tark

The beginning of the storm fills the air with its howling melody, approaching the Peninsula from the oceans beyond, but inside Dennis sulks and burns. Tarquin, the fish baron, has rejected Alison's poems. The fuck with him. He is fucking history. He sleeps with his fellow fishes, blb, blb, ulla blb. Him and his virus that spreads like a material cancer. Oh no, keep her away, lovely Alison/Wanda mustn't be contaminated by such stuff. The true goddess of love with her beautiful head that outsparkles all glitter. Such a lithe cat, one that rolls and trembles. For a cat to be subject to a fish! Can there be any greater cruelty? How is he going to break it to her? He grapples and reflects, and reflects and grapples. But wait, did he read the poems? Did he read them properly? Were they really no good? Surely the occasional chanteuse came through? What was fishy Tarquin thinking? Does he really know as much as he claims, about all that stuff, about politics, about poems? They will be returning any day, in a packet, and then he will have to find a form of words. He's not like Tarquin, he's not so at ease with words, it's the sound that grabs. This isn't fair. He is restless, he has lost his faith. He stares glumly at the PC screen, its implacable velvet violet-blue user interface, the resources at his fingertips now idle, but he must press forward, he must get on with it, there's no other way, what the hell is he supposed to do? And he looks at the screen, but all he sees is the configuration of her face, her extended body that softly gleams, which is unbearable in the extreme, and he is miserable and elated and excited and angry all at the same time. The configuration of the chanteuse. He is both annihilated and sustained by it. He can remember nothing. Surely the occasional chanteuse? He can remember only sensation. It was in the country. He was kneeling. He toys with keys. Blb, blb, blb, no thanks. Cities sink beneath the waves. Once more, he moves into the world of sound, the underwater world drains and becomes transformed by flashes, haloes, the sonic equivalence of an aureole, resonating outward, always going towards the outer from the inner in a process that has no end. It's a blast! He is oblivious to the weather. Oblivious to ethereal chatter. To the ashy sky, or to newspapers. To cruelty. He's in his bedroom looking at the computer screen, fiddling with the playback controls, but in truth he could be anywhere. Nothing matters. He will be out of touch for hours. Never indifference, only torment and delight, and he dedicates both to her. It's the central section he is nearing, the apex, part 13, the one on which the whole piece pivots. The delights of splitting and splicing, everything in wild confusion. That's better, push it. He will dedicate the whole piece to her. It shall be submitted. The whole thing, pretty whippy: "globes, atlases, flasks, charts of the heavens, skeletons of animals, skulls, the bust of eminent men"! And she will lead him to the near-future republic of peril where all these things will be annihilated, where the nucleus breaks and mash-up will be complete, in the hinterland of the long tail, scintillating in loss of the senses. Brrrr. Her piercing green eyes are so beautiful. All the sounds simultaneously. Brrrr. Bottom, middle and top. Max out the gain. Reverberation and desire both at max. The nuclear option.

Brrrr. This isn't part of the piece! Dennis is awakened from his reverie in twenty-five parts. It's actually the doorbell, silly. This is not a drill. This is, what do you call it, real life. He stares into space for a moment. Then wrenches himself from the PC, down the stairs, three by three.

Because it could be her.

Is that her shape, illuminated in porchlight, refracted and fragmented in the marbled glass diamond at the front door?

He opens it.

Hell-o, Dennis!

No it isn't. A woman of a certain age with short, iron-grey hair and pink-rimmed glasses. He recognises her. A friend of his mother's. But what is her name? Begins with an N. Name, N. Mrs N. She dives in brightly: I was just passing, and I thought –

Oh, yes? He grins, faltering as she pours forth words, beaming on the doorstep. What is the thing to do here? Iron-grey is dotted with white. What does she want? It would be polite to ask her in, wouldn't it? It would be polite to insist. That's what people, normal people do.

Would you like to come in for a cup of tea, Mrs er...?

Oh, that's *very* kind of you, Dennis, I wouldn't want to put you to any trouble.

But yes. She would, she does. Takes her coat off and hangs it on the peg in the hall without ado. Didn't need much persuading, after all. Panic, where to take her? The kitchen may be safest, she doesn't need to see how he's rearranged the furniture in the rest of the house. Well, now, I promised your mother I'd look in on you some time, just to see how you're getting on, she says. (So his suspicion is correct, she is spying on him.) That's nice of you, Mrs er. You have white dots in your hair. White dots? Heavens above! It's starting to snow. You hadn't noticed?

Please sit down. I'll put the kettle on.

Oh-oh, this isn't such a good idea after all, the parental kitchen is compromised. Dirty crocks are piled up in the sink, on the draining board, on other surfaces. Opened baked beans cans fester unbinned, also crumpled lager cans arranged in a small pyramid. That torn Chicken Dopiaza packaging dates from Tarquin's visit, doesn't it? That's weeks! Why didn't he just put it in the recycling at the time? Dennis is now seeing the kitchen through new eyes, in all its hallucinatory horror. Mrs N has to move a stack of empty flowerpots from a chair in order to be seated. But her glassy smile remains undimmed. The pink frames, the glitter.

So you're managing all right while your parents are away, are you, dear? Oh yes, I'm fine, really. And do you require anything, you only have to ask? No, no, can't think of anything. Well, that's good. Dennis, attending to the kettle, remembers now how she used to comment tediously and at length on how he'd grown. But she makes no reference to his size now. That's good, that's very good, she repeats. It can't be easy looking after things. I hear your parents are getting on very well on the Costa. (So that's confirmed, she has been in touch, they've put her up to this.) Very well. I bet they're enjoying some lovely weather, and they won't be missing this snow one bit. How do you have your tea? interjects Dennis. Oh, milk and just one sugar, dear. The kettle utters its electronic whistle, puffing out clouds of steam that subside. Dennis removes a quarter-full milk bottle (is it safe?) from the fridge, then hunts in cupboard after cupboard. Sugar. We don't appear to have any sugar. Or maybe we do, I just can't remember where it's kept. Never mind, dear, I'll have it without, that won't do any harm to my waistline, ha ha. Now tell me: what are you doing with yourself these days? Dennis thinks, starts to formulate ways he might introduce the concept of *World Music Parts 1-25* to a complete novice, fails, has a bright idea, replies: I'm in Retail Management.

This seems to surprise as well as impress her. Retail Management? That sounds good.

He places a steaming mug of tea on the kitchen table in front of Mrs N. She stares suspiciously at an unwashed teaspoon, but does not take it up.

Retail Management! tell me more. Well, there's nothing much to tell … you know SAVERS PARADISE in town? I'm working for them. As a manager? Trainee manager. That's very good, Dennis, there's a future there, in these hard times. Sure is, I was lucky to get it. Your mother said you were trying hard to get in the music business, but I suppose that's very dicey, isn't it? Very dicey, agrees Dennis, dicey is exactly the word, dicey. So this is much safer, oh, I'm so pleased for you. Yes, that's pleasing. And it's a full-time job? Yes, full-time, I work Tuesday to Saturday, doesn't leave much time for my music, which I've been trying to catch up on today Monday. Oh dear, well, never mind, at least you'll have no financial worries, but are you sure you don't need any help, it must be a task looking after the house, and with a full-time job even more so, I could always come in occasionally and help you tidy up, she says meaningfully. Oh no, no, no, Mrs er, I couldn't possibly expect you to do that, although it is very kind of you to offer.

The conversation begins to peter, for want of new stimulus. She has left half her tea to cool.

Well, look, Dennis, I'd better get on, I have lots to do still this evening, got to get my husband's dinner, and you must get back to your music practice or whatever it is you're doing, but enjoy the rest of your evening anyway, and good luck for the rest of the week. Thank you, Mrs er. And thank you ever so much for the tea, dear.

She waddles back down the darkening garden path, and, at the gate, turns to wave, porchlight flashing on her glasses. She will no doubt be reporting to the authorities. Will the report be favourable? Who knows? Dennis must realise in his heart that it will be mixed, but not totally damning – he did get some positive scores in. The snow is beginning to come down a bit harder.

He's relieved to be allowed to get back to his music. Except that, actually, once he's sat in front of the PC he finds he's at a dead end. The magic has gone. Again. And he has come to the end of his respite, and tomorrow is terrible Tuesday. He looks back at what he's done, and now perceives it as egregious noise. A succession of failed attempts, each one the result of a delusion that at last, now, he's solved the problem that made the previous attempt, so pregnant with promise at the time, another dismal failure. What's resulted is a string of shining failures, each having masqueraded in its time as success at last.

From: thegrumpymarxist
Subject: Re: marketing of the moment
Date: 4 March 15:29 GMT
To: NMP Discussion Zone

Are we being a little unfair to Tarquin Smith? For all our many disagreements I do admire Tark's total energy and inventiveness. I suppose my principal disagreement with him, and not only regarding the content of those excerpts from Neo-Marxist Aesthetics and the Marketing of the Moment that we have seen so far, is on the question of *ontology*, on which I believe his position is decidedly problematic. To put it mildly. His fetishisation of the Revolutionary Moment leads him into distinctly dicky areas, arising perhaps from his unstinting belief that the revolution *will* happen in this country, during our lifetime. That is a fatal error from which I think he cannot recover, or if you like a premature gamble that allows the Right too much leeway to jump in with its usual destructive reification. His distinction between the Revolutionary Moment (which apparently is a collectivised moment, or if you like a social and political collective moment of creation) and the Moment of Gratification (which is manufactured by Capitalism, apparently) is just plain weird and unsustainable, I would go so far as to say sentimental were it not that I have too much respect for his integrity. As if knowledge were other than a provisional thing, and the present moment (his, yours, mine) quantifiable, in terms other than a mere listing of its content. I believe that he is departing radically from the truth of Marx by just imitating his (and Lenin's) polemics. That is, he's a *Romantic* in Lenin's sense of the term. Nevertheless, I think it's going too far to cite "grave errors" of ideology, as Fred does in his earlier posting. Wow, Fred, where did that come from, did you never make mistakes? Ideological issues there are maybe – Tarquin's use of Kleinmann is, I believe, a little shaky, leaning heavily on Kleinmann's early works, where he had not fully developed his thought, and I think it is a mistake to use Yundt at all – but it's not altogether incoherent, as some have alleged. And I like the approach to aesthetics, always a tricky area for Marxism, Neo-or otherwise, and his attempt to define a *materialist* poetics, one capable of generating a true poetry for the people, which he also tries to practise elsewhere, in his editing of *Virus* and his own poetry – give him his due. Having said that, he also sticks it to several recent Marxist theorists for elevating a proletarianised art – and this is always a point that is liable to heavy criticism in these circles that we move in, along with his tendency to employ "vitalist" metaphors and his undialectical adulation for cultural forms, like free improvised music, that he approves of. But enough said, there's a lot to chew on here, so let's try and cut Tark a little slack, guys and gals.

From: Steve Chalk
Subject: Re: marketing of the moment
Date: 4 March 22:08 GMT
To: NMP Discussion Zone

Brothers and sisters, I can't believe this, I think it's a scandal that the NMP Publications is even considering publishing this load of wank with all due respect by Comrade Smith. I mean, it's got neo-marxism in the title but does it even represent the views of the Party in any way shape or form? No way! There has got to be some accountability here in my view, comrades. Yeah OK I heard the criticism that I havent read it all, who has the time to read 150 thousand words or whatever it is, I've got a job that takes up all my time when I'm not campaigning for the Party, and my bosses are trying to make me work even harder and at the same time cut my overtime, so I admit yeah I've got limited capacity but from what Ive read online this is elitist bullshit that is not going to advance the cause one jot, I mean poetry and avant garde jazz is going to liberate the proletariat, give us a break! OK he's got a perfect right to his opinions, we live in a free country – supposedly – but I repeat, this would be going out under the name of the Party and NOBODY voted for it, unless I missed something? The bit I just read is all about a book apparently written in the 18th century which was very influential to the structure of Capital though never translated from German, so bully for Smith he's able to translate it for us, and it discusses animals ability to make and respond to art. And then he goes on to talk about where they gave paintbrushes to elephants who, it turns out, make great paintings. Or maybe I'm getting confused with that elephant orchestra? What the hell, I don't know what all that's about and how it relates to the lives of ordinary working people. I have to say that's when I gave up, I didn't read any further. I heard our comrade Tarquin Smith edits a magazine and a small press, well, good for him, he's got his own resources as is well known, so why doesn't he put the book out under his own name or imprint, there's nothing to stop him doing that, but please not using the hard won resources of the Party (because this aint going to make a mint, comrades, quite quite the opposite) and definitely definitely most importantly not in the name of the Party. Sorry, got to leave it there, must get some shuteye I got a hard day ahead, SC

From: Fred X
Subject: Re: marketing of the moment
Date: 5 March 10:42 GMT
To: NMP Discussion Zone

Let me come back on some of the stuff that's been said here, or at least weigh into a discussion that's become somewhat acerbic since my first remarks which were designed to be helpful but may have become distorted along the way. When I said "grave errors" I was trying not to mince my words. I was trying to be precise. Tarquin Smith's error is not in imagining that the revolution will happen in our lifetime, as a matter of fact I very much hope it does. But actually his polemics do away with the need for a revolution at all. Basically, he's saying the revolution is here, we don't need to organise, we don't need to struggle, in fact we don't need to do anything except engage in what he defines as creative revolutionary action or the revolutionary moment or whatever he calls it, which doesn't amount to more than a bit of épataying the Boojwahzzee. Well, we've heard all that before. And does he imagine that his creative activity isn't going to be recuperated tomorrow for profit? This is naïve at best. Above all,

Neo-Marxism needs to have a fix on how Neo-Capitalism works, and Tarquin doesn't get off first base here. Talk about gesture politics! The fact is he effectively advocates just ignoring capitalism as if it will go away if nobody pays it any attention, or will be frightened off by a bit of weird poetry or noisy free jazz. That doesn't mean I'm averse to his cultural theory, and I certainly don't endorse comrade Steve Chalk's workerist prohibitions in this regard either, but it's massively beside the point. Which is that capitalism can NOT be ignored, it needs to be OVERTHROWN. Sorry to be boring about this, but it's a fact. And it's no use expecting this to be brought about in our democracy, so called, however radical one's cultural practice. I mean, show me a country where democracy hasn't failed and I'll start to take that point seriously. Actually, as far as I am aware, democracy has not existed anywhere. There has been no state where the freedom of some has not been dependent on the servitude of others: slaves, agricultural (and other) workers, the exploited in the global south... "majority rule" is NOT a form of democracy. So we can talk about the Authentic Moment or whatever till we're blue in the face (and blue is the appropriate colour) but we all know nothing will do it other than revolutionary political action. And yes, if necessary, I make no bones about this, revolutionary violence. Because "our democracy" will never give access to the authenticity that Tarquin fantasises about, and deep down, I think he knows it, which is why his book is so ominously silent about the topic, for all his weighty discourse about ethics. But it is the moment of armed resistance, whenever that comes, that is the crucial moment, pace Smith. That is the moment that will never be recuperated, the authentic, unmarketable, revolutionary moment, if we can use Tarquin's terms against himself. Until it comes, and it will only come through our endeavours, we are whistling in the dark, friends.

Cheers, FX

We could follow Dennis through his first day back at work, but it would be utterly devoid of incident, if incident is what we crave. Unless of course we had privileged access to his brain processes, imagine that. In regard to these, the inanities of those dull young poltroons in the stockroom (the Trainee Storage Facilitators) are utterly blocked out, nor do the easy, already dated management jargon of Mr Steve Leuchars or the banal tautologies of his bronze-coiffed sidekick play any part. He can't listen any longer to his personal music player while on duty, as he has been reprimanded for this, but no matter: imaginary sounds fill his brain from morning till clocking-off, from one end of each bank of display shelving to the other. It's a whole other universe that might take a lifetime to explore. And so the day passes – without incident – and night returns.

It is snowing quite hard now. He parks the car on the hard standing.

He lets himself in at the front door. The big yellow envelope is back, nestling on the doormat, the worse for wear.

The yellow envelope, damp, crumpled, re-sealed. Tarquin's name, and "Virus" on the front, in Alison's neat, beautifully formed hand, and below it Tarquin's address added in his own scrawl in a different coloured ballpoint ink, and the whole of that crossed out with black felt-tip slashes and his own name and address substituted, in what are recognisably Tarquin's vigorous black uppercase letters – and a jumble of postage and cancellations superimposed, upper right.

Dennis picks it up, takes it into the kitchen, sets it on the table, sits down and stares at it for a while. Then he slits it open. There is Alison's letter, and there are Alison's poems, neatly typed out, one to a page, which he has neglected to read thus far. He looks for a note from Tarquin. There is none. Tarquin has not committed his judgement to paper. Tarquin has left it to Dennis to find a polite and sensitive form of words for the rejection. Tarquin has washed his hands of this whole business, essentially.

Well, returning the packet could provide him with an excuse to go round to the Wellington Estate, to see her again. It will be a few days before Severin is back and she becomes off-limits once more. But on the other hand, he would be the bearer of bad news. How would that go down? That would not reflect well. Best to spin this out a bit. Think, Dennis, for once. For starters, read the poems.

He spends the next half-hour apprehensively doing just this, flicking the corner-clipped pages one by one. Twenty-five of them.

These are admittedly not the works of Wanda Fowler, Occasional Chanteuse of his imagination, rather of Alison Fowler, mother and part-time admin worker at the nuclear power station. But they're not that bad, surely? O my little sapling, with your baby leaves / Soon you will grow to be / A mighty tree ... begins one. That's about motherhood, isn't it? OK, Tarquin would probably hate the invocatory "O". Here's another, this one's called "Masks": I walk my baby around the estate / And all I see is masks of hate / White masks, without eyes / Ashes falling from the skies ...OK, that rhymes, he doesn't like rhyme.

His brain illuminated in several places and racing hard, he crams the sheaf back in the yellow envelope. The stain of rejection must not be allowed to sully Alison/Wanda's glorious eminence, especially not summary rejection – as this is – and above all he, DC, must not be viewed as the agent of such rejection. He could just do nothing for a while, hang onto the poems secretly, but the suspense could prove unsustainable. She would without doubt ask him before very long, I haven't heard from your friend Tarquin yet, have you got any news? and he would be unable to look her in the eye. A holding message, that must be it. One that keeps hope alive a little longer. One that keeps the window open. With the possibility of a promise. The hint of a promise. He could email, but has no email address. He could text, but what he has to say is too complex for such technologies to handle effectively. He can't pluck up the courage to confront her face to face, or even on the phone. What he has to say is, well, could it be summarised? no it couldn't.

He must write it out longhand, and this is what he does: Alison my darling or should I call you Wanda (!), I've got good news, Tarquin is reading your collection. He's too busy right now but he asked me to tell you he really likes the poems and he might consider them for Virus, but it might be a while. It's all a bit complicated, so the best thing is if you want to come round I can explain, it's all to do with the next issue being full up and so on. But I would love to see you again anyway, on our own, if you can manage it. I've done more work on World Music, you'll love this, if only I can play it to you. I feel the touch of your breath (crossed out) fragrant breath, and I long to see

111

you in your furs, like a large cat like an electric battery in the snow, hey, let's go for the nuclear option this time … etc, unfortunately it goes on a lot longer than that, and when he has finished he folds the paper, finds an envelope and a stamp in his father's desk drawer, writes her name and address on the front with a shaking hand, grabs his coat and wool hat, and runs in a frenzy, in the accumulating precipitation, to the postbox at the end of the road.

DC? It's me.

Her voice, faintly, at his bedroom window. Again. At last.

Two days and two nights have come and gone. The Peninsula region is under a thick blanket, more like a goose-down duvet, but the snow has stopped falling.

It's midnight. The scene is set. We are going all the way to the core.

He pushes the pane. Streetlight part illuminates a lovely beast on the path, a creature covered in luxurious animal hides, fire in its lustrous hair. Part of the figure is in deep shadow.

Is that you, Alison?

No reply.

Wanda? Is that you?

Yes, DC, it's me!

Hang on, I'll let you in.

No, no, I can't come in!

Why not?

Come with me!

But … what do you mean?

Come with me, now!

But, but…

No buts, DC, I'm ordering you!

And she opens the animal skins and shows her pale torso, her pale self magically as she is or might be, this is not happening, this is not happening. She whispers. Her skin's flaring in streetlight, the contours of her body modelling the snow drifts, then gone to darkness again. The animal skins close.

This is not happening. This is happening. This is the one upon which the whole piece pivots.

DC, I've longed for you for years, can't you see? she whispers excitedly, absurdly. Come and kiss me, DC. But not yet. Because I'm going all the way, I'm going now. The sound of her breathing is magnified, with maximum gain. The breathing comes harshly, with wave-like regularity, as from a person in the throes of uncontrollable passion.

Wanda, wait for me, please don't go.

I'm going, you're the one, you can follow me if you, if you really want. If you really, really want.

You bet he really. Our hero has raced downstairs stark naked, flung open the parental front door. He's ridiculously tumescing in the blue snow. Wanda is there, a shape in the frozen garden; she extends a slender hand. I'm going, DC. Are you coming with me? Yes, yes. The touch is exquisite, the brief scent.

The two figures are now in the deepest part of the night, the one naked the other swaddled in fur. In the dead fallow. Midnight blue on snow. A huge volume of dark air, seeming to centre on a double pinprick. They move down the road and soon out of the suburbs, their four naked feet crunching softly. They don't talk any longer. Space opens up. They see the tiny buildings that glow on the horizon. The metal of the endless road, shrouded, sparkling. The containing dome of the sky, deepening to black, and beyond. But a sudden clarity too, as if old meanings had been removed, you might say. Their shadows, revealed. No birds sing. No animals cry. Life has been extinguished, we have come to the end of its sentence, whose full stop contains billions of atoms, dormant, awaiting the kick of the stray neutron. The dead cinders. The snow has ceased to fall on them.

Alison transformed to Wanda, clad in musky animal hides, takes nude Dennis by the hand through this transfigured landscape, out of the suburbs, approaching the Wellington Estate, but bypassing it, and onward to where the street lighting begins to give up, into the dark country, joining the road that leads to the Peninsula with its small collection of houses containing sleeping humans and the dead World's End, to the dark beaches with the abandoned fishermen's huts, and beyond them perhaps the drowned town with its heavy covering of sea, to the beginnings of a glow on the horizon. They walk in the middle of the road, avoiding the dirty, piled-up dunes on the verges on either side, but they are in no danger from traffic, because the world has died.

And soon the nuclear power station comes into view, but this is still alive, the only thing alive in the whole vicinity, its great dome and collection of vast, interconnecting blocks all floodlit, up and humming through the night, above the snow line.

He utters an involuntary cry.

She turns and puts a finger to her lips, and then to his. But her beautiful face can't be seen, because of the shadow.

Ahead, topped by barbed wire, the first of the chain-link fences approaches, concrete posts at three-metre intervals, their shadows projecting towards them. The light from many windows blazes beyond. An animal skin drops from the wonderful creature named Wanda onto the snow with a soft plop, but she pays it no heed as she leads the way towards and right up to the fence; we see her smell it although we can't see her wrinkled-up little nose, we see her make to mount or mark it, prowl along its length, left to right; he follows, aghast and bewitched.

There is no break in the chain-link fencing except for a gate. And there is security.

But the guards are frozen in their positions, like uniformed statues. They stare ahead blankly into the night. They have always, and will always stare like this. Their chained dogs, too, are immobilised, or immortalised, their mouths frozen agape. The big gate opens slowly and magically for the two mythical beings that approach it. They are through the gate, and into the beautiful country beyond, which is approached by a snowy corridor.

That none of this could ever be happening must not be allowed to trouble Dennis. What could be in store?

Transformers.

Fences.

Radiation is all around. It comes from outer space, from the sun, rocks and soil, falling out of the air into the milk, grass, seaweed and silt, into the fish and marine life, and the bodies we occupy, an unknowable, generative heat at the heart of cold.

And so they move further in. There is latticework, too finely detailed for any analysis. Steam rising from behind railings, from an unknown place. They come to the second gate. Here, she sheds another skin. They are in the abandoned control rooms, with their mysterious switching and cabling. There is a considerable hum from somewhere, the turbines probably, deep in the bowels of the building. A plastic chair, at an angle, recently abandoned. A starburst of concrete in the ceiling. The third. She sheds a third skin. The fourth. Codes are bypassed, doors slide open silently. A fifth and sixth. She sheds a skin each time.

They are in the reactor containment building. The sacrificial area, a theatre in the round awaiting its audience. Silence of the containment vessels. Their objective has to be the nuclear reactor itself.

The beginnings of a grid, a notation of distance.

Lights in the darkness.

The last skin has gone, and she is revealed.

The void at the centre of an array.

Rods positioned in an array, an impenetrable code. She turns to position her companion, at the core where she might mount him or be mounted, as the whim takes her.

Remains of a code unsolvable by humans. This is a plant that has been abandoned by humans – everywhere, their ghosts stand frozen at the controls.

Pipes in series, leading out into the air, leading to nowhere.

Grids.

Four grids.

The landscape behind a diamond grid. Her voice arises out of nowhere, whispering, but with a considerable echo added.

Come, DC, make love to me.

Her beautiful body, spangled and denuded now of all furs, is spreadeagled over the core.

Fuck me really hard, DC, my love.

Drill down into the zone, and what sound do you hear? Every sound imaginable, from all parts of the spectrum, all melded into no-sound. And we are in the zone.

There is cataclysmic florescence.

A silvered picture of a thorn tree in the desert, mildew at its edges.

Dead husks of sepals, dried petals, traces of organisms left in a bath, transformed, repeated.

From nowhere, from the depths, a huge shudder now starts to build up. We hear cries, howls, yelps of all kinds, faintly at first, then getting rapidly louder until becoming unbearable. And the animals begin to invade the power station – out of nowhere, out of everywhere they make their way through the liberated gates and doors that now stand open, moving towards the voided containment building and the reactor: rabbits, mice, voles and rats at first, then stoats and weasels, foxes, squirrels, badgers all running in through the corridors and up and down ramps and stairs, hither and thither, some having come to life and unstuck themselves from the roads for miles around where the traffic had flattened them, and smooth snakes, adders, lizards crawling out of winter hibernation, and also various forms of bird life clattering their wings at the windows and chirruping, calling and screaming in a loud cacophony, sparrows, rooks and magpies, plovers, terns, herring gulls, black-headed and black-backed gulls, cormorants and shags, all squabbling and making a fearful fuss.

Now it's coming on to morning, streamers of velvety grey disappearing into the horizon, and he notices he's by a brick wall, in the environs of absolutely nowhere, where someone has abandoned an old bicycle under a low-wattage lamp, the air salty, human sounds beginning somewhere. But he is alone; he has no clothes, no companion, neither animal nor spirit. Emaciated vegetation has begun to emerge from dirty runnels of snow. A breeze begins too, from the direction of the sea – that was the source of the smell. More lamps at intervals. Snow streaked with rust. It's bitterly cold.

Wanda, he calls out, Wanda.

There is no reply.

Looming out of slow white dispersal, the great bulk of the power station's mass persists through time as it passes. Light ever so slightly bends around it. We will be into the second half of March, and therefore technically springtime, before anybody notices. But great melts and gluts of rain begin to prevail as the days wear on. Almost unrelieved gloom. Yes, snow has turned to rain, and rain does not cease. In tracts of sodden soil, large numbers of earthworms begin to come to the surface to feed. On the roads, car headlights appear from nowhere for a glorious moment, then fade to the obscurity from which they originate. Booming, and a sudden, sharp bark. From within each dwelling the length and breadth of the Peninsula and its hinterland come domestic sounds, the evidence of cyclical patterns, the usual mental spaces undergoing transformations. It would seem that cases are altered, and constitutions incline to growth. Umbrellas are erected in the estate and in the towns. Many passers-by can be observed everywhere, standing in the rain, shining, drinking it in.

Night falls and day breaks on the estates; nobody can tell the difference. Lights are yellow. Night returns to the broad hinterland, where animals have struggled to survive the long winter, where furred bodies sit trembling, where bad light has permeated every environ. Night returns to the abandoned buildings of the Peninsula itself, on the fringe where the coast crumbles, and has been crumbling for more generations than can be remembered, and will continue to crumble, and occasionally shear, until one day in the far future it will be wholly claimed by the sea. The charred huts above the hump of the beach drip raindrops from their eaves. Those fishermen's cottages that will never be inhabited again await their final destruction. Great depredations have been wrought upon them. Though no bird alive could have pecked its way through those roofs, some surviving small creatures slip quietly in and out of a glassless window, a broken air vent, wherever they can find.

And so at last Dennis does pluck up his reserves of courage. He tries to make a phone call. Her mobile is ringing, his heart is in his mouth. But there is no reply after eight rings, and it goes to voicemail.

Hello, this is Alison.

Her voice! Warm, but rather stilted.

I'm sorry, I cannot take your call at this time. Please leave a message and I will try to get back to you as soon as I can.

Hello, Alison. It's me, DC. I need to talk to you. Please call me back. Not a prob if you're busy... Love you.

Oh god, he cringes at that last. Love you. For god's fuck's sake. Too late, it's done. Click. And he didn't say what he might have said. Perhaps he could try again. Try the landline.

Eight rings, voicemail.

Her voice again! Distorted.

Hello, this is the voicemail of Alison and Severin Fowler. [A babble in the background – Adrian?] I'm sorry we cannot come to the phone. If you have a message for either of us [hesitation] or for Nightmare, please speak after the tone and one of us will call you back. Thank you ever so much.

Alison...

Wait a minute, this is no good, Severin could pick up the message, he can't possibly say what he wants to say. Seconds go by. Feebly, he puts the phone down. Oh fuck, this is even worse.

Hours go by. Dirty snow melts.

Rain returns. Work happens. Stock is taken.

Rain ceases. Car headlights. Silence.

Dennis's heart beats faster. His palms clammy. Dennis tries again.

Hello, this is Alison. I'm sorry, I cannot take your call at this time. Please leave a message and I will try to get back to you as soon as I can.

Alison? Can you pick up? It's DC.... Are you there...? OK, I wanted to say sorry, I sent you a stupid letter the other day, just ignore it. Or just ignore most of it, I mean, Tarquin likes your poems, that's the most important thing right now, but he says to tell you he can't get around to publishing them for a while. Also, sorry if I sounded stupid on my last message. Anyway, I wanted to see you again. Hope you're OK. Oh, and Adrian too, hope he's OK. Well, perhaps you can give me a call back whenever. All right? Bye, Alison, talk to you soon.

So the slow thaw continues to creep across the hinterland. These are the dark days, these are the dog days. The boy is not in good shape; hasn't been in good shape for a while, as we have seen. Seriously thrown off kilter. The great melt is on. There are tiny beads of water on his wool hat as he traverses the intermediate space between his private universe and that of his gainful employment. Yes, his kilter has been compromised. He is neither duck nor rabbit, and possesses little or no consciousness of his situation. Arguably. Let's stay with the problems we can solve. Where is Dennis to go now? For he is stuck in a holding pattern, like those military aircraft, or indeed like the low that hangs over the Peninsula right now and which is responsible for the gloomy, increasingly mild and damp weather that we can expect over the next week or so, according to the models. That's the situation. It's kind of chunky, and not in a good way. Basically, there is a lack of precise data that would lead us to make an informed prediction as to how things might turn out.

Dimly, Steve Leuchars senses this. Hi Dennis, how you doing? All right, Steve, thanks for asking. Everything OK in the job, then? Yeah, fine, no problem. Only you just seemed a little distracted, forgive me for saying. Did I? Yes, just now, you were standing in the aisle staring into space for quite a long time. Oh yeah, I'm just thinking over one or two issues, you know, personal stuff. Aha, yes, I can guess, Dennis, girlfriend problems! [Dennis's wan smile:] Something like that. Girlfriend problems, I remember them all too well! [No response.] They're a different species, you know, women, who can fathom them? [Dennis:] U-huh. [Steve:] Women! but what would we do without them, eh? What indeed. My wife, bless her, makes my lunch every day.

Steve Leuchars lunches every single day on the same fare: two white-bread, cheese and cucumber sandwiches, out of a Tupperware container. They are taken at his desk, in front of his computer. He does not appear to consume any of the produce actually retailed by SAVERS PARADISE, with the exception of two litre bottles daily of own-brand mineral water, which he gets the bronze-haired PA to obtain from the stockroom each morning and line up precisely by the side of his mouse pad. Every five or six minutes during the length of the working day he takes a sip from one of the plastic bottles, carefully replacing the cap afterwards. When the first bottle has been drained of its contents, usually by around 1pm, he replaces the cap for the final time and hands it to said PA for disposal in the recycling. Then he begins on the second. Complete consumption of this second bottle is normally timed with more or less precision for the end of his shift. We don't drink enough water, Dennis. Medical fact. Hydration is crucially important for our physical, and indeed mental, health. Two litres a day, that's what everyone needs, that's what I take. I would strongly advise you to do the same, Dennis.

Yes, Steve.

Well, you can always speak to me if you have any problems, Dennis, my office is always open, as you know. Yes, Steve, thank you, Steve. Women, hah, an unknown country, what was it the Bard said? [Dennis cannot enlighten him on this.] Well, never mind, onward, eh? onward!

Hello, this is Alison. I'm sorry, I cannot take your call at this time. Please leave a message and I will try to get back to you as soon as I can.

Click.

[Pause.]

Hello, this is the voicemail of Alison and Severin Fowler. I'm sorry we cannot come to the phone. If you have... *Hello, Severin here.*

Big shock. Dennis is tongue-tied.

Hel-lo ... anyone there?

Sorry, is Alison about?

No, mate.

Is she not back in from work yet, will she be back soon?

She ain't here any more.

What do you mean?

She's gone. Excuse me, who is this speaking?

My name's DC. I'm, er, a friend of hers, actually I'm calling on behalf of someone else. Another friend. Well, actually, the editor of a poetry magazine.

Oh, yeah?

She sent some poems … well, anyway, you're saying she's gone, she won't be back?

That's correct.

Where's she gone? I mean, I have an important message for her.

She has gone, Severin enunciates carefully, to the city.

The city?

Up to the city. She's staying with friends.

With friends? Do you have an address? You see, I need to talk to her. About her poems.

No, mate. Do you have her mobile?

Yes, I do.

Well, there you are, then.

The only thing is, she hasn't been answering.

Well, she don't answer me, either. So we're both in the same boat. Heh heh heh.

I see. Well, I better try her again.

You better.

So she's left her job, then?

That's correct. She's left her job, she's left me.

And what about the band?

The band? You know the band? She's out of the band, man. Actually, she left the band some time ago. Wanda left the building some time ago, know what I mean? That's got nothing to do with it.

Another thought occurs to Dennis: And what about Adrian, has she taken him?

That's a lot of questions. She has taken my son with her, yes. Do you know my son, then?

I've, I've met him briefly. And what about the dog?

What do you know about the dog?

Nothing.

What the fuck do you know about the dog, man?

Nothing.

You know something about my dog?

Keep away from my dog, Dennis remembers in terror. His fingers holding the phone become clammy. But with an effort he composes himself: I don't know anything about your dog, Severin.

That's all right then.

[Pause.]

Well, says Dennis, I'll try her again. I'm sorry to have inconvenienced you.

That's OK, man. What's the name again?

DC.

That's OK, DC. Yeah, sorry, I'm a bit under pressure here, you know? If I can be of any further assistance....

No, no, thank you. I will try her again.

You do that. Cheers.

Force of circumstance is pushing Dennis, inexorably, in the direction of the city. He will shortly, temporarily, leave the country and the coast for the great metropolis – just as things are becoming more interesting here. For example, herring gulls, which have been scavenging garbage dumps and landfill sites on their winter sojourn inland, are beginning to return to coastal regions to seek out their mates and their familiar nesting places such as on the roofs of the Peninsula's dwellings. Dennis, by contrast, is becoming less interesting as he goes on. His monomania is dull. He has abandoned his music entirely, so far as we can judge. Not that there isn't plenty to be gleaned from the world about him. Trains of nuclear flasks rumble through the night. Soon spring will arrive, and with it the menacing call of the cuckoo, the scream of swifts on their return from unknown regions of sub-Saharan Africa, the cries of scaffolders and the clang of their long poles as building work recommences. News comes from sub-Arctic regions of a beluga whale that has learned to imitate human speech. It may sound more like someone endeavouring to play the kazoo, but we have to make allowances: it is a creditable attempt. But as for Dennis, yes, there is little interest there; the level of interest he manifests or evinces declines in inverse proportion to his increasing state of sexual anxiety. He has been late for work more than once. There have been more telephone conversations since the exchange with Severin.

Tarquin called late one night: Hey, DC, mate, what gives?

Oh hullo, Tarquin, I'm OK, I guess.

Listen, did you return those poems?

Those poems?

You know what I mean, Alison Fowler's poems. Did you get them back from me, did you return them?

Oh yes, I received them, no, I don't think I've got around to giving them back to her.

Well, she's been in touch, and she says you said I liked them.

Is that so? well, I can't remember saying that.

Well, that's what she says.

She must have got hold of the wrong end of the stick, sorry, Tark.

She also says she's living in the city now, I thought she lived down your way.

Yeah, I heard she'd split up with her partner and gone to the city.

Well, it doesn't matter, I just wanted to check it out with you before I talk to her again.

Yeah, OK, Tark, how are you anyway?

Things are very up and down, DC, very up and down.

I thought I might come up for a couple of days, any chance I could doss down at your place?

Yeah, man, there's plenty of room here.

That would be fucking supreme, Tark.

OK.

OK, I'll give you a bell.

It's Friday evening. He really must go to work tomorrow. One last heave, then he has his two days off. But he cannot face it. Especially in the light of one more telephone exchange:

Hello, this is Alison. I'm sorry, I cannot take your call at this time. Please leave a message and I will try to get back to you as soon as I can.

Hi, Alison, it's DC. I heard you split up with Severin. I'm very sorry to hear that. I hope you're all right, and Adrian is all right. Listen, I may be going up to the city to stay with my mate Tarquin, and I wondered if I could come round to see you. I really would like to see you, Alison, I've been a bit upset. Well, I know you must be too.

Anyway, give me a call back.

And twenty minutes later his phone rings:

DC? It's Alison.

Alison ... I'm so pleased to hear from you.

I'm really, really sorry, I haven't been in touch, DC, but as you appreciate it's been a very difficult time.

Oh, I know. How've you been?

Not too bad. Not too bad, DC. And Adrian's fine. I do appreciate your concern.

Alison, I may be going to stay with Tarquin for a few days.

So you said. When is that?

This weekend. Can I come round to see you?

Well, it's difficult, love, very difficult. You see, I'm staying with friends. I don't have my own place.

I really would like to.

[Pause.]

Just for a short while, then. Give us a call when you're here.

And she rings off abruptly. That does it, then. Fuck work. DC is off first thing in the morning.

He is by no means a stupid boy, but he is not thinking. Or his thoughts meander. Look at his notebooks, full of circular diagrams, becoming ever more intricate, leading nowhere.

Alison, in the city, adrift with her child.

Dennis has caught the first up train of the morning; it's not even light yet. There are only two other, somnolent people in the carriage, one reading a newspaper, one reading a novel. When the ticket collector approaches down the aisle, he pays with his father's credit card for a return ticket, which the official dispenses from his tame computer. Have a nice day, sir, he says.

Fields. Fields upon fields come up in the gloom.

Alison, someone she knows very well, someone she knows less well, someone she knows not at all.

His trousers are bulky on the gently bumping seat. The image of his curly head floats in front of the grey, rapidly side-scrolling countryside.

It is a field of force that comes up, spreading out into empty space, keeping everything together. The electrons of his dream, the electrons which are the dream of the nuclear core, keep the air in contact with his clothes and his clothes in contact with his skin. That is what is called music. We think they are touching, but they are not touching, just hovering an infinitesimal part of a micro-millimetre away, exciting the molecules of our own surfaces.

Alison's thoughts, inaccessible to anyone for ever.

Dennis below the slowly lightening sky.

Alison below the slowly lightening sky.

We must now follow Dennis right up to the city, away from his natural habitat. More and more people get on the train. There is an air of great solemnity about them all. Some listen to personal music players, some read, some fiddle with their phones, some merely stare into space. Although it is Saturday morning, they nevertheless have business in the metropolis. Of what sort, we do not know. It is not our business. We do not know where this journey will truly end for any of them.

Industrial spaces begin to scroll past. The drowned towns, the labyrinths. The mysterious toxins in that air. Dennis himself doesn't know where the journey will truly end. But here are the suburbs.

A pale light. Huge buildings. The acid colours of red, green and yellow signals flashing past against pale grey.

Cables and bridges. Urban foxes, dancing cheek to cheek.

Dennis has had to squeeze up, an uncommonly fat woman next to him. A man and a boy wear the colours of a football team.

Alison thinking about her boy.

The great metropolis looms – the greater force-field. Immense buildings studded with flashing windows. There are announcements. Movement has stopped, but there's a tsunami of sound, its detail impossible to fathom. There is a house, somewhere. There is dispersal.

Dennis in the city. Dennis on the bus.

Far overhead, passenger aircraft wend their ways.

Hello, DC, welcome. *Mi casa es su casa.*

Dennis, uncomprehending.

Hello, Tarquin.

The house is large and, on first appearance, gloomy. The tiny front garden lacks the shrubbery of its neighbours. There are some steps up to the front door. The long front room, next to the entrance hall, has half the wallpaper stripped off and appears to be a repository for components of machinery of some kind, including maybe printing equipment.

He has already spoken to Alison. I've arrived! Can I come and see you tomorrow? Yes, she says, and names a time. But her manner is strange – she doesn't want to talk.

DC, Sandra. Sandra, DC. Hello, DC.

Tarquin's glasses glitter. Sandra's glasses glitter. They observe him in a disinterested yet friendly way, as though two aliens contemplating a captive human.

The house is incomplete. There are patches of unpainted plaster, and even of bare brick on the walls. The stairs are uncarpeted. The kitchen, strangely, is on the first floor up. Here's where warmth is concentrated, and where people seem to be encouraged to congregate. Posters for Neo-Marxist events and jazz concerts are on the wall. The iconic Che Guevara image. Various high stools. A stripped pine dresser on which piles of paperback books outnumber crockery. Just across the landing is a spare room next to the living room where he can sleep, Tarquin informs him. I hope it'll be quiet enough, he says, Sandra uses it as a study – she has her desk and a divan bed there, but she won't need it this weekend. So you can leave your bag there now, if you like.

Oh, thanks … is that OK, Sandra?

Perfectly OK, DC.

In the living room next to the kitchen a somnolent person of undetermined gender, who does not acknowledge the three passing through, slumps in a vast sofa, watching daytime TV.

A huge, frameless abstract expressionist style canvas dominates the stairwell space. There are two more bedrooms and a bathroom on the next floor up, where currently unspecified residents and guests may come and go, although the incomplete stairs are dangerous. And

Tarquin and Sandra have their eyrie-complex in the attic.

This is very good, marvels Dennis. In fact, supreme.

It's unfinished business, but it's home, says Tarquin.

Who was that called you, Justine says, was that him? Him? Was that Severin? Oh, no no, Alison shrugs it off, it was just a friend. Only, you seemed a bit upset, that's all. I'm not upset, Justine. Maybe not upset, but, you know, distracted. I know, I need to think, you know, about my next move, I need to, I need space, I'm really grateful to you, Justine, to, I need to…. I know. I need to give Adrian the best possible chance. I know. I need to call my mum. [Pause.] So who was it, then? Who? Forgive me for intruding, I'm just concerned for you, Alison, you don't need to tell me anything you don't want to. He was, like I said, a friend, I think he's concerned about me too, I just don't want it to go any further. It won't go any further than me, Alison. No, that's not what I meant at all. What did you mean? I mean, this guy, DC, his name's actually Dennis but his friends call him DC – apparently – Apparently? Well, he's a really sweet guy, but – But! Exactly, I don't want him hurt. You think you might have hurt him, or you might hurt him? Or Severin, I certainly don't want Severin to hurt him. So he knows Severin? He's … shall we say … encountered him. So he's from down your way? Yes – except he's calling me from round the corner. What do you mean? I think he's followed me, he's staying with some friends nearby. He's followed you! It's OK, I don't think he's a stalker or anything like that, like I said, he's a sweet guy. But he's following you? In a manner of speaking, yes. Does he know where you are? He does now. You mean, you told him? I told him he could come round and talk to me tomorrow. Alison! It's OK, Justine, I know he's harmless, I just need to talk to him, reassure him, explain a few things. Well, it's up to you. It *is* up to me, I can handle this. I'm sure you can, I'm sorry. He's a friend, that's all, he's friends with that guy I told you about, Tarquin Smith, who might be publishing my poems. Oh yes? That's who he's staying over with this weekend. So they're all part of some poetry thing? No, DC's not involved with poetry, he's a musician.

Is that right? He's a composer, used to play me his compositions on the computer, electronic stuff, I've never understood what it was all about really, but it sounded quite interesting. Well, I'll look forward to meeting him. Uh-oh, did you hear that? Sounds like Adrian calling. It is, he's woken from his nap, I better go up. Listen, this DC, or Dennis, or whatever he's called, he won't tell Severin where you are, will he? Oh no, of course not, and I will make sure he understands that, but in any case he doesn't really know Severin, he's only met him once, in a manner of speaking, and that was not in the best circumstances, I'm just frightened though that Severin might latch onto him, so I need to warn him about that too. All right, Alison, don't you worry about anything, you're all right here, I'll be here for you. I'm so grateful to you, Justine. Everything will work out. I'm sure it will ... OK, OK, Adrian, I'm coming....

She is wearing the exact same outfit he remembers from his first ever visit: the black crew-neck jumper, the jeans, the fluffy slippers. But her red hair seems somehow faded; it no longer has quite the lustre he recalls, as though the saturation has been dialled down considerably. Also, she seems smaller, somehow. Not that he is fully conscious of all these changes; the mental processes devoted to such perceptions do their work in the background as she ushers him in, her smile wan, her movements slower and more deliberate than maybe was the case before. Consciously, we may rashly surmise, Dennis desperately wants it to be all right, and therefore it *is* all right. Of course it is. So he edits the rest out. That's maybe what's happening.

Hello, Alison.

Hello, DC.

A kiss on the cheek, a too-quick withdrawal.

This is ... different, he says, for want of a suitable opening.

Her little laugh is as pretty as ever, but superficial, slightly mechanical.

It's *all* different. It's not my fault. I wish.... She gestures helplessly.

I came on the bus.

Oh yes? Would you like some coffee, DC?

Sandra put me on the right bus. Yes, please. I find it all a bit confusing.

Sandra?

Tarquin's girlfriend.

Oh, yes. I'll be back in a moment, then.

While she is out, Dennis, seated awkwardly on the arm of a chintz-covered armchair, his boots planted firmly, squints round at the room. The curtains are half-drawn, so that it seems twilit, although the morning outside, he knows, is pearly with light. Some brightly-coloured children's toys litter the floor, reminding him again of Alison's home on the Wellington Estate, but there is no evidence of music here. In the corner, a wide-screen TV is on, with the sound muted. His gaze is pulled to it, as though by powerful gravitational force. A young man in a dark purple shirt with a logo on the breast pocket is pictured against a pale, lime-green background lifting a morsel of food on a fork to his lips. His lips move, his eyes become briefly unfocused, then he looks at the camera and speaks. Cut to a close-up of four sprigs of asparagus arranged exactly parallel to each other on a white plate. Orange sauce is poured over them. Now an older man in a dark suit speaks to camera in front of multiple screens on which garish logos transform and explode. A glass-panelled door repeatedly opens and closes; credits begin to roll, too rapidly to be properly read. There then follows a montage of quick-cutting images: a grey woman in the snow; an oblong cardboard box on a domestic doormat; a notebook computer, its screen scrolling; swinging gently in a yellow-netting hammock, a reclining young woman looks at a mobile phone; a very young child removes the box; graphics show TV screens within screens within the screen he is looking at, all revolving at different rates; a girl in funky clothing opens and closes her mouth repeatedly while sitting on a doorstep, maybe singing; she is abruptly joined by a young man, whereupon they gaze into each other's eyes; a cartoon archer lets fly; mobile phones twirl in space, followed by the manufacturer's logo and purple and red price tags; an entire city is consumed and destroyed by flames within seconds; massed police cars move out from their parking places, the crimson and blue lights on their roofs flashing; a golden single bed revolves; a toy orang-utan performs a cartwheel; everyone in the family has a go at the cardboard box. Now a young, orange-tanned, blonde woman in a flowered blouse, with black-painted fingernails, beams at the camera, followed by a close-up of banknotes being stacked on a green-covered table. Two other women are shown, and appear to have a conversation. Cut to a collection of china dolls with pink cheeks.

Alison reappears with a tray. I've forgotten how you have it, DC. He tells her.

The sleeves of her black jumper are rolled to the elbows, exposing her slender forearms as she serves him his coffee. There is what looks like a bruise on the right arm.

Oh, you've hurt yourself.

She pulls the sleeves casually down to her wrists. That's nothing, a slight accident. So how have you been, DC?

Dennis considers. Up and down, I guess. Job's getting me down. I took a day off without asking yesterday, so I expect I'll be in trouble about that.

I'm sorry to hear that.

Yes, adds Dennis, it's pretty grim stuff, that supermarket business.

I left my job at the power station, reveals Alison.

Oh yes?

Yes, I couldn't stand it any more.

I know what you mean.

Day after day, you know.

I know.

And the horrible weather didn't help.

Yes, it's been awful, hasn't it? That snow. It's still hanging around in the country, it's gone all slushy.

Oh really? well, here in the city it's pretty well disappeared.

Yes, I noticed. So you're living here now?

Well, just for a little while.

This is a friend's house?

Yes, Justine has been very kind.

Is she an old friend?

Yes, I've known her since school, would you believe.

I've lost touch with most of my old schoolmates.

That happens.

I'm still in touch with one or two from college, Tarquin, for instance.

I think friends are so important, don't you?

Oh yes, I think so too.

Justine has been very good with Adrian.

So is Adrian around?

Yes, Justine has taken him out for a walk in the buggy, give me some space.

That's good.

And so on, and on, the seemingly endless exchange of banalities continues as they sip their coffee. On the TV screen, perceived only subliminally if at all by the pair, an older man wearing rimless, crescent-shaped glasses, a tweed jacket and a bow tie has now taken centre stage; he appears to be jesting with a line of silver-haired men and women all wearing identical red T-shirts. They laugh in unison. Objets d'art of various provenance flash onto the screen. The conversation, though, is starting to wind down, silences are beginning to intervene and to lengthen, and it is only a matter of time before one of them will have to cut to the chase.

Dennis is incapable of doing so.

It falls therefore to Alison to make the move: Look, DC, I need to say something.

[Pause.]

She continues: I probably won't have a chance to see you much anymore for a while. I'm planning to move up north.

Oh, yes?

Adrian and I will probably be moving in with my mum. She's got the space for us, and I can get a job up there.

Perhaps I can come and visit you, suggests Dennis brightly.

No, I don't think that would be very feasible, you know what I'm saying?

Why?

[Pause.]

Things went wrong between Severin and me. Things had been

131

going wrong for a while, actually.

I sort of guessed. Well, I spoke to Severin.

You did?

I phoned you at home, and he answered. I was trying to talk to you about the poems, you know, the poems you sent to Tarquin. Anyway, he told me you'd left.

Did he say any more?

Not really. He seemed a bit uptight about the dog. What's happened to the dog?

Cuddles? I'm afraid Cuddles died.

What happened?

I don't want to talk about it.

[Pause.]

You know there was that business that night a while back, when he went for me about the dog…

I know, I know. This has got nothing to do with you, believe me. And listen, don't get involved with Severin.

I didn't intend to. I just wanted to let you know about the poems, that's why I phoned.

I understand.

Does he, does he know about us…?

No, of course he doesn't, are you crazy! He'll never know. How could he know?

I don't know.

Listen, I've got a confession to make, DC, I got in touch with Tarquin. I found a phone number for him, I was so excited that he might be considering my poems, which I think you mentioned in a voicemail, or was it in a note, that I had to talk to him.

He did say.

I told him there was no hurry, my poetry is not at the front of my mind at present, what with all this business, but I wanted to give him my new contact details for the future.

What did he say? asks Dennis in some trepidation.

To tell the honest truth, he seemed a bit … cold.

Cold?

Yeah, not very forthcoming.

He's a bit like that if he doesn't know you. Either that, or he talks non-stop.

He seemed annoyed. Although he did agree I could go round to see him. You see, I have some amendments, I've changed one or two of the poems. I thought I could take the new copies round.

He's got a lot on his mind too, Tarquin has. Political problems.

I'm sorry that I didn't tell you I'd contacted him.

That's OK.

And I'm really, really sorry I've been out of touch. It's been horrendous. I haven't felt like speaking to anyone. I'm sorry, what can I say?

OK. But, Alison....

Yes?

We get on very well, don't we?

Yes, of course.

I want to help you. I hate to see you in trouble. I can help you.

That's very sweet of you, DC, but I don't think you really can.

We're friends, aren't we?

Of course.

And we're ... more than friends.

[Pause.]

Aren't we?

[Pause.]

I want to understand you, Alison.

There isn't anything to understand.

I want to understand.

There really isn't.

But we made love – twice.

Once.

Twice!

Once.

Was it only once?

Yes, DC, only once.

Sorry, I must have miscounted. I enjoyed it.

So did I.

I love you.

No, you don't.

I love you, Alison.

No, you don't, DC, you don't know what it means.

Severin, recognisable from his shaven nut and leather jacket, has been seen walking his dog along the coastal dunes, where it glints. But that can't be right, the dog's dead. The shade of a dog? Not for nothing has this been called the most haunted coast in the country. A grieving wind whispers at its fringes. (It grieves for all who have met their end here.) Wires hum. Ice crystals form between the sand-grains. The alchemist goes forth, alone except for his shade. The huge world outside, stirrings of life: pair of shelduck, one redshank, flocks of ringed plover, little egret, cormorant spreading its wings on a half-submerged post among the grey waves, greater black-backed gull, many herring gulls, a pair of mallards. Severin's heart wrenched out of his chest; beyond that, everything is obscured. Severin, playing the acoustic guitar tuned to an open D chord, now alone in his empty house. Break it up a little. Severin, ostensibly at war with the obvious, yet shackled to it. Severin, involved with exogenous and discontinuous events. CDs deployed as spangly bird-scarers. The Beast rings on his mobile. Fuck off, I ain't talking to anybody. Come on man, let's have a little jam, it'll do you good. No, fuck off. I'm not in the mood. Not in the mood, what sort of talk is that, sir? Yeah, well, maybe I will be next week, who knows, but right now I'm just hacked off, you know what I mean? Ice cream chimes. I mean, ice cream chimes, in fucking *March?* Severin, floating. Anyway, it says no dogs on the beach for 558 metres. *That* precise. Severin is having his brain done in today. Roses are falling from his mouth, wild and shocking. Like a record that's stuck, remember that? You mean, vinyl. He takes three herbs every night, and a little shot of heroin, and he uses comfrey cream for massage, or used to, when she was around. But she's gone now, the fucking chanteuse, and stolen his son. So no more. Ice crystals form between Severin's white blood-cells. So the missus left? She left the building, man. Heh heh heh. You'd think he'd be in seventh heaven the way he'd been going on. Got to do something about it, though. There's no money coming into the house. The band has no more gigs scheduled now till the autumn. Supposed to be recording, but that's beginning to look dodgy now. So what's the use in jamming? Come on, that's stupid, it's all about the music. Play in the local pubs? Not that desperate, surely. The dog died, that's all. Hey missus, my dog's got no nose. So how does it smell, then? Terrible! All right, maybe he'll call the Beast back. Severin, endorphin levels all over the fucking shop. Hello, Beast? Severin, drunk on really poor vodka. Yeah, maybe the old ones really are the best, or maybe it's all the same fucking shit and always has been. Severin, G minor, C minor, D seven, over and over again. Severin, in little flurries as the charge comes in clusters, its triggers firing independently and simultaneously. Severin, with nowhere to go and going fast. Heh heh heh.

The night matures, and grows more fragrant; Sandra has lit some morsels of frankincense in a brass bowl, also some coloured candles. This is Jess, sorry didn't I introduce you before, says Tarquin, Jess, DC. Hey Jess, says DC. Jess is Chairperson of the Marxist Transgender Group, adds Tarquin. Pleased to meet you. Jess grunts non-committedly. I think it's time to break out the wine, don't you, suggests Sandra brightly. She returns from the kitchen with an assortment of glasses. DC sinks into the enormous sofa that maybe can be dated to the Cretaceous period. Already he feels this place is familiar: the damp stains on the far wall to his right, the TV, the sound system (some free-improv is on, sax and percussion mostly, but at a very low volume), the musical and political posters tacked to the wall opposite him, the inlaid North African goblet drum in the corner, the rugs, the gaps in the floorboards.

The front door can be heard to bang, there are footsteps on the stairs, the room door opens and in comes a sturdy, dark-complexioned man with a neatly trimmed black beard and a multi-coloured woollen cap, which he doffs. Hey, Hassan! Tarquin is in jovial mood. Come and join in, Sandra's just opening the red wine – if your religion doesn't preclude that! I can become infidel for just this evening, beams

Hassan. I thought you became an apostate *every* evening, remarks Sandra. Hassan, who has sunk to his knees on an industrial bean-bag, roars with semi-maniacal laughter. Ha ha, he goes, ha ha. Hey, meet DC, says Tarquin. DC, Hassan's an artist, he also lives here. Hey, Hassan. Hassan salutes.

This is fucking supreme, comments Tarquin, turning up the volume on the sound system. A tenor sax squeals beyond the top of its range. Come on Tark, not so loud, some of us want to talk, commands Sandra. Tarquin's eyebrows knit, but the volume swoops down again. Hassan is rummaging in his coat, produces a small tin which he opens. Jess has his/her eyes closed. Wine is poured into glasses. You know, says Tarquin to the world at large, DC is a musician.

Oh yeah, says Hassan, who is now busy rolling a joint on the floor, what kind of music you play, DC?

I'm a composer, actually, explains Dennis, I use electronics on sound sources that I record from the environment. I'm working on a piece called *World Music Parts 1-25*.

So this music has 25 parts? says Hassan. Wow. How many parts you already done?

I'm working on Part 13, or I was before I got interrupted by personal stuff, but I work on all the parts simultaneously really.

Wow. Hassan licks the carefully assembled array of cigarette papers. I also, I work on different art projects, all the same time.

Simultaneity, asserts Tarquin ponderously, is the condition of our epoch. The linear narrative is finished. And we are living in the present moment. Which reminds me –

Epoch? exclaims Sandra, rolling her eyes, what kind of language is *that*?

Hey guys, wait for this. I am Hassan-i-Sabbah!

Which reminds me – what was that you were saying about light cones, DC?

Eh?

When we were talking, that time on the Peninsula, you said something about the present moment being impossible because of light cones not intersecting, you remember? What the fuck did you mean by that?

The joint is now lit, and circulating.

I didn't say the present moment was impossible, I said it was impossible to share a moment.

So how the fuck do light cones come into it?

It's all to do, explains Dennis, with Special Relativity. There's nothing esoteric about it, it's been known for over a hundred years. You know about light cones?

Yeah, sure … well, not exactly.

It being so highly unusual for Tarquin to express doubt, everyone's ears prick up.

Dennis: So the light from the sun takes eight minutes to get to earth, which means the sun is eight light minutes away. So if the sun went out it would be eight minutes before anyone here noticed the difference. [He takes a drag on the joint and passes it on.] Now, if you plot the sun's movement through four-dimensional space-time, the light expanding away from it can be represented in three dimensions as a cone shape, and it's only at the point the earth passes through this cone, which is eight minutes after the event, that any information, including light, can be transmitted to us.

Tarquin: Say again? A three-dimensional cone in four-dimensional space-time?

Yes, that's a way of representing it.

So you're saying if the sun went out now –

No, that's the point, there isn't a universal now. And that goes for us here too, separated in space by infinitesimal fractions of a light second.

Wow, says Hassan through a cloud of smoke. Supreme!

Tarquin: So that's your position, DC?

It's not a position, it's a fact. Einstein.

But we are sharing this moment.

Are we?

We are in a collective situation.

Are we?

Jess opens his/her eyes, accepts the joint. S/he says: He's right, Tark. That's a significant anomaly. You'll want to re-theorise that.

Tarquin is silent.

The musical background ceased some time ago. Hassan has picked up the drum in the corner and is gently tapping his sturdy fingers on the stretched skin, in an asymmetric rhythm. A candle gutters. You gonna play that bongo for us, Hassan? asks Sandra.

Is not bongo.

Dumbek, says Dennis, who is on a roll now, it's a dumbek. A North African drum.

Dumbek. Hey, this guy knows his music, Tark.

Tarquin is silent.

Hassan drums. A panorama of Old Arabia passes before their eyes: mysterious, cedar-clad mountains, unfathomable deserts. Camels, maybe.

Fucking hell, Hassan, that dope is powerful, remarks Jess.

Like I say, I am Hassan-i-Sabbah, the Old Man of the Mountains! Dennis now notices Hassan wears a bulbous turban, and a large, curved scimitar at his waist. Respect! I am mathematician, artist, scholar. I am one badass! Ha ha! And assassin, adds Sandra. Yeah, also! A quick flash of steel, a rapid cadence. He ceases drumming.

Sandra: Did you manage to see your friend, then, DC?

Alison? Yeah. She's not in a good way. She left her husband. She's got the child with her. But the dog died, apparently. Oh yes, says Sandra, what was that dog's name again? Cuddles, says Dennis. *Cuddles?* Everybody but Tarquin roars with laughter. I'm sorry, says Sandra, spluttering, I really really shouldn't laugh. I really really. Dennis says: That's OK, I didn't care about the dog.

Tarquin breaks his unaccustomed silence. You want to forget about her, DC.

I can't.

You got to move on.

Well, maybe.

Her poetry was crap, anyway.

That's not appropriate to say about DC's friend, protests Sandra.

Well, I've got to say it. I'm sorry I put you in that position, DC, I should have replied to her myself. Respect to her, and I'm sorry about her problems, and I hope she gets through them and all that, but she couldn't write poetry.

You're talking about her in the past tense.

So should you be.

Wow, says Dennis, leaning back into the puffy Cretaceous sofa, this house really is unfinished. What do you mean? asks Sandra. Dennis points upward. There's no fucking ceiling! In fact, there's no roof! I can see through to the stars! They all look where he's pointing. They are racing through space at close to the speed of light, the four of them, separated from each other by infinitesimal fractions of a light second. Their light cones, past and future, intersect in real time. The house is a three-dimensional diagram of four-dimensional space-time. It folds neatly into a three-dimensional representation of the city, perfectly detailed. All interacting like ripples in a pond.

Yeah, them fucking stars, says Hassan, pointing at the ceiling which isn't there.

But we're seeing them as they were thousands and millions of years ago, says Dennis, from deep within the bowels of the sofa.

Ha ha, laughs Hassan. Space-time curves gently into him. Jess closes his/her eyes again. A sparkle on a wine-glass follows its geodesic. But does consciousness exist?

Will you be staying another night, DC? asks Sandra gently.

No, I've got to be getting back in the morning. I got work on Tuesday. I already missed Saturday without telling them, so I'm already in the shit.

Sandra: Are you sure? Will you be all right?

I'm sure. I got to get home.

Where is home, laughs Hassan. Where is home? Ha ha.

As Dennis's train approaches the Peninsula region once again, industrial structures can be observed in every direction; grain silos, cranes and harvester hangars mark the return of the familiar hinterland, which in essence is no more than a vast factory floor. So the functional buildings and flat, naked fields, furrowed in straight lines with caked ice and solidified mud, spread themselves on either side, falling just short of the unadorned horizon. Power cables, giving off their almost insensible and beautiful vibration to the land around, hang between the giant pylons that stride from their unseen point of origin, their vanishing point.

With a heaviness in his step Dennis returns home, if home this can be said to be. And can it? Must it? For how long?

The storms of early March would appear now to have ceased, and the dark clouds no longer mass at the horizon. The weather is static. There is black, rough scurf on the land, and charcoal grey begins to turn lighter and more luminous in the sky. At the abandoned train station, echoes return the cries of a distant pack of boys, not as adroitly polyglot as may be heard in the city, just that bit rougher-hewn. Three rooks wheel around their usual spot over the rugby field, calling raucously from time to time, seeking the juicy and well flavoured morsels that have eluded them for most of the winter. Their beaks are milky, and their legs dusky; they once procured the greater part of their food from the whitethorn hedges that no longer exist, but they still build on the line of high trees that can be observed at the far end of the pitch. Food will soon burst through the surface of these territories. Above the cloud, an aircraft's phased roar drifts across the stereo picture – a background of high frequency rural sound sources in the elastic air, always emerging. A series of cold turbulent weathers has interrupted the winter migrations, depriving martins of their nests and infecting the normal haunts with desolation; but now a period of relative calm can be expected. A great ash-coloured cloud once moved a mile or more in a moment, but is now gone. Those strangely prolix sounds are carried by the tides and prevailing breezes from distant regions. Soft tissue decays. Teeth, tongue, lips, hooves remain. We can begin to expect the vernal migrations. Towards evening, which comes all too soon, suddenly unseen flocks make a loud bleating noise and a drumming or a humming. They express complacency in what seems the language of fowls. The tumult is pert, and petulant. Loud and exquisite underground drainage-system sounds are fed from resonating sources. In the villages, house sparrows build under the eaves but their conversation is deadened and confused with other utterances. They frequented sinks and gutters in hard weather, ambushed by predators as they picked. Notes like the whetting of a saw begin around the same time. All these sounds, which obey the laws of chaos, which are in the neighbourhood of havoc, may still be filtered, processed and reused at any time. That is to say, they are the available resources. The graceful movements presaged by this mapping display a strange ferocity. Along the banks, open stomachs of woodcocks and snipes are found in their nests with their soft mucus, among which lie many pellucid small gravels. Muscular gizzards have ground the pebbles into various and changeable appearances.

But darkness does quickly fall on all this.

And so as night again approaches, nuclear waste flasks are shunted slowly on creaking and squealing wagons from the bowels of the power station onto the lonely branch line, where they pause for some hours, through the long, dead silence, protected by high chain-link fencing on either side and under floodlights, as always awaiting their locomotive; preparatory to their long journey north for the reprocessing, during which they will lend a fearful new rumbling to the liturgy of nature.

4

ac/dc

Four, five, six tiny black dots start to come into view, far out over the sea. Perhaps they are migrating birds. They hug the horizon. But they do not exhibit bird-like behaviour. And it's not the right time of the year for migration.

They come closer. They can now be identified as aircraft. Military aircraft. As they approach the coast, they begin roaming in stereotyped patrolling patterns. The rumble of their engines can now be heard. They are over land. Now they roar overhead, following each other at regular intervals, emitting Doppler-shifted sound.

Fathoms of heavy water, as well as centuries of slow time, cover the drowned town below.

The aeroplanes drown the peal of the church bells.

News comes from far away. The noise of winter ice cracking on the Neva in Russia. A young couple, and the ebbing of passion in their relationship. Strange things happen when we get unusual weather. We shall be coming up to the vernal equinox shortly. Are the snowdrops out? What of the lambs? Are they being born? How will they fare?

These questions, and certainly their answers, are drowned out by the sound of the planes.

Sea temperatures remain extremely low. There is climate mismatch. We have evidence that invasive plants, such as purple loosestrife *(Lythrum salicaria)*, whose flowering is flexible, benefit most from abnormal weather patterns.

The sacrifice begins.

Finny lived in a town at the bottom of the sea. It was like our own town in every respect, except that it was at the bottom of the sea, with all that that entails. Hey Finny, respect, man. He lived on boy and chips. Mmm, delicious. Some of his friends were humble krill (have you met the krill? marvellous people!). Everything was wet in his town, even the air, which strictly speaking was not air at all but water. Water is the basis of all life, we're all 98% water, this is a fact. That's ironical, isn't it? Water forms the basis of irony. Well, at any rate, it licks iron and makes it rusty. Everything's rusty at the bottom of the sea. Even the church bells. Rusty aeroplanes fly at the bottom of the sea; round and round they go. The sounds they make cannot be heard by a human being, but Finny was not human, he was a fish, of course. High fins, man. In the town, many of the houses had been abandoned. The streets were submarine beaches, where Finny could play all day long. One day, Finny met Fanny. Well, that was quite something. It changed his life, forever some say, though forever is really too long a time to think about. Fanny was kind of enticing, her scales were edged with crimson fire, her gills were soft and wavy. Together, they swam between green wrecks, in an intricate watery dance that had no end. Several other people and important fish warned Finny not to get too infatuated with Fanny, including Barnacle Betty, Turpin & Turpin, and Mr Steve Leuchars. Would you step into my office a minute, asked Steve Leuchars. Fanny sang songs about other seas, far away, where the conditions were very different, and Finny had been entranced for quite some time. Finny knew very little about the world in different seas, let alone above the sea, on what was known in ancient legends as "dry land." In fact, Finny knew very little at all. Barnacle Betty disapproved of Finny's lack of political awareness. The Trainee Storage Facilitators sniggered behind his back: Ooh, he's for it now. Yes, Steve, said Finny, though in reality he was still thinking about Fanny and the musical bubbles she blew. He had been absent without leave. A little chat, promised Steve. Fucking hell, thought Barnacle Betty, though not of course in so many words. This all took place in Call Me Steve's cave. Steve had two plastic bottles of air on his desk in his watery lair, from one of which he took the occasional gulp, in between remarks. Ooh, the boy, said one of the Turpins, I believe I seen him before. The other Turpin nodded sagely. Now, how long have you been with us, said Steve, checking the facts against documents on his desk, about a month, I reckon, that's right, how do you think it's been going? OK, I guess, said Finny. Well, that's as may be, said Steve, but it doesn't seem to me you're entirely happy with your work. I'm not? (The Trainee Storage Facilitators were giggling; the fish with the bronze fins was tut-tutting.) It seems to me, continued Steve The Big Fish Leuchars, that *I'm* not entirely happy. You're not? No, I'm not. Let's see, the attendance record, that's not great, is it? In a month you've had two, three days off sick, one day absent without leave, several days recorded as "late reporting for duty", also sundry other unexplained absences during the working day – this is not good. I'm sorry, Steve. Steve blew a big bubble that drifted languidly to the ceiling of his cave, blb blb. The tolling of the rusty bells from the wreck came in through the window. Steve Leuchars did have a shark-like demeanour, Finny thought. Fat Fish with gaudy stripes swam past the window, peering in, trying not to seem interested. Now, you're not even halfway through your probationary period, but already I sense maybe you're not as cut out for Retail Management as I previously thought, is that the case? I don't know, Steve, what do you think? Well, I have a feeling, a *growing* feeling, that this is indeed the case, so therefore in view of that I'm really sorry, I've had a good long think about this, but I'm afraid we're going to have to let you go. So spoke Steve The Shark. I'm sorry about that too, Steve. It seemed that Finny's talents lay elsewhere: exploring wrecks pitted by erosion, perhaps, burglarising them in a burglatory way, or licking algae off street corners, or swimming with cuttlefish and untutored sprats through kelp forests, or indeed dancing unashamedly with the krill, outwitting the Turpins, the Trainee Storage Facilitators, Barnacle Betty and many others. But where was Fanny in all this? She was nowhere to be found. Round and round went the rusty aircraft. So this is the story of Finny and Fanny. Blb, blb. Their hilarious adventures under the sea, blb, blb, ulla blb, und dull in der doons. Under the ever changing sea, where nothing makes sense in such beautiful ways, maybe the story will begin again.

Well, the upshot is that the very next day newly liberated Dennis is found once more sitting at his computer, in the parental home, trying to get back to his real work, which is of course *World Music Parts 1-25*. For a while, he has unconsciously adopted the idealistic view, bolstered by his own descriptions and accounts to other people, that the entire work already exists at least in rough draft; but in fact he now reminds himself, to his dismay, that large sections are still only there in the form of scrappy notes he has made, exhortations to self and half-baked (as it seems now) ideas. In effect, in his head. And the array of raw sound files is not as organised as it might be, so there's work to do sorting and classifying. A tangle of disconnected wires. It is heart-sinking time.

So he navigates away from where he should be, electronically tacking against the prevailing currents.

Would you step inside a minute, Dennis?

No problem, Steve.

There are currents or vectors that, fight them though you may, take you where you didn't want to but had to go. Or else where you wanted to but didn't have to. Maybe it adds up to the same.

He has found an online video, very poor in quality, not on the official Nightmare website. Taken by a fan maybe, on a phone or suchlike, at a gig somewhere, and posted independently. Poor lighting levels, rapid, jerky panning.

I sense maybe you're not cut out for Retail Management. No, Steve, you're damn right I'm not, so what can we do about it? Well, Dennis – may I call you DC? – well, I have the utmost respect for you creative types, as you know, I think if there was any justice you should be *funded* to do the important work you do, and leave the essential but humble tasks of Retail Management and suchlike to unimaginative dullards like myself. I rather think you've hit the nail on the head, Call-Me-Steve, why don't you have another swig of water to replenish your vital hydration systems? I will, then, Dennis, I mean DC, now, perhaps we can talk about some kind of financial *accommodation* that will permit you to continue your real work unhindered by any necessity to restock shelves and check sell-by dates?

It's in a club somewhere, cramped stage, the equipment all jammed together. Low lighting levels combined with high saturation. It's a version of "Bitch of Vienna", and there on stage is Alison, in her Wanda guise! Her hair is abundant, rich vermilion, her skin white-flares in the spotlight, deep shadows engulf her eyes, she holds a heavy duty mic to her vermilion lips. She wears a red dress slashed off the shoulder.

Ha ha. In your dreams, DC, howl the juvenile jerks in their matching uniforms.

So let's get back to reality. Your record since you've been working here is frankly poor. I won't mince my words. Very poor. Oh, do you really think so, Steve, I've been trying my best. Is that so, let's see, in the month you've been here you've had two, three days off sick, several days recorded as "late reporting for duty," also sundry other unexplained absences during the working day – this is not good – and now to crown it all one day absent without leave, without any explanation whatsoever. What-so-ever. I've had some personal problems, Steve. You have a big problem now, Dennis, because absence without leave constitutes Gross Personal Misconduct, do you know what that means? I have a vague idea, Steve.

Alison/Wanda's vermilion lips caress the mic. You'll come to me in the end, she croons, 'cause I'm no friend, 'cause I'm the bitch you want.... Electronic white noise from the Beast's keyboard mimics the rising tide of erotic longing that engulfs Dennis as he watches the screen, entranced. His hands move to his aching crotch.

I'm afraid we're going to have to let you go.

The camera zooms crazily into Alison/Wanda's beautiful, impassive face, her engorged yet perfectly formed lips, the flash of her teeth. Dennis has, we regret to report, unzipped his trousers. Let you go. Let's see, a month's salary, and, as a gesture only, because we're not obliged to, a further two weeks' pay in lieu of notice. Yes, yes. Dennis needs to relieve his frustration and put an end to his longing.

Drums thrash mercilessly, guitar squeals, bass thunders. Whip-pans reveal the jerky movements of an ecstatic student audience.

The phone is ringing.

Dennis shudders; he has come all over himself. He badly needs the services of a paper handkerchief or two.

The phone is ringing.

We are Nightmare! Thank you and goodnight! [Applause and whoops.]

Dennis becomes vaguely aware that the phone is ringing. It goes to voicemail.

Hello?

[Pause.]

Hello? Is Alison there?

Oh my god, thinks Dennis, it's him.

Is there anybody there? Can you pick up, please? Is Alison there?

Oh my god. [He recognises the voice. Definitely. Meanwhile he can actually see its owner, the bullet head onscreen, flaring badly.] What the fuck does he want?

Hello?

[Dennis trembles; seminal fluid dribbling, settling, starting to evaporate.]

OK, this is a message for Alison. Can you tell Alison that Severin rang? I just want to know that she's OK. I'm not threatening her, or nothing. Also that my son is OK. All right? If this is a mistake, and Alison is not there, can you please call me back, and let me know, and if you happen to know where she is can you let me know that?

[Pause.]

OK?

[Pause.]
OK, cheers.
[Pause.]
[Click.]

See, there's an impressive array of tinned and preserved food, pilfered from SAVERS PARADISE and now all stacked up in his mother's pantry, row upon row, column upon column. He could hole up here in the family home almost indefinitely! Civilisation is already starting to break down outside, freak weather events are occurring, petrol has run out, there are feral Trainee Storage Facilitators roaming the abandoned streets and roads and fields, but he'll be all right here, board up the windows with a few two-by-fours from his dad's shed if necessary.... Embalmed in aural amniotic fluid like a perfect distillation of real time spelt out according to tidal patterns, a complex of womb sounds an electronic pacifier forming those cyclical patterns in his mental space. Run it as a simulation, the windows shut, the underground drainage system below resonating.... But if there was a meltdown.... He turns on the light, gazes upon the gleaming pantry stash. Well, you'd have to monitor contamination somehow, but the tinned food would probably be OK. What about the water? Need to rely on bottled. Steve Leuchars would have said you need two litres minimum a day, you don't have enough, no chance. But Steve Leuchars talks bollocks. You don't need nearly so much. Get fluid intake from baked beans, etc. Dig an artesian well under the house? There are various possibilities. Look it up online. But come on, there won't be an online world! The darkness of unknowing is all around. Digital failure kicks in as beacons go out in the dream time. The ice is breaking up. Or the electricity will fail, so you won't be able to access it even if it still exists somewhere, or the music, for that matter. Sound installations may well be the way to go. He was right in a way, you don't need the computer. Acoustic sound events, making a shining path through the dark wood of unknowing. Memories of gulls over the dump, black earth, luminous eyes, tumbled squawks obliterate a leaden silence, and you're drinking from cans and listening to booming systems looping exultantly and so very bizarrely in which fluid is detailed and polyrhythms are buried in the trees; there'll be new ways invented to capture this at the top of the range while deep below the gongs boom. It's a periodicity to be listened to in real time, a ceiling of complexity, a universal structure. A white head gleams. Break up the furniture for firewood in the meantime, you don't need it. A very battered yellow envelope sits upon the floor, amid the other mullocks. Kiss me, DC, she said. And he did. The sound of glass shattering. The end of the world. But it won't be, it will just be the end of a particular civilisation, which was built on phony principles anyway. A new one will arise, in which, yes, sound installations will be the thing, people will get in tune with that, supreme. People or newly intelligent animals, entirely new species that will take over. Fucking supreme. Make a better fist of it. Her neat handwriting: Tarquin Smith, Virus. Eventually, you'd be able to grow stuff again. Adapt to the floods. Live underwater. Intelligent fish! That will take time, you wouldn't live to see it of course, but the music will live on; that will never come to an end, expanding forever in an information cone in four-dimensional space-time. In the meantime, live on corned beef, baked beans, tinned tomatoes, rice pudding, plenty of uncontaminated nutrients there, even if they are only SAVERS PARADISE own brand, maybe a few root vegetables grown under secret poly-tunnels, survive until the conditions are right again. Anyway, work on the music for now, that's all that matters, stop all this wank. Lay it down for future generations, for when they re-invent electricity or other as yet unknown harnessings of energy and information....

Next morning, out of the blue, what do you know, the phone rings again. Dennis, startled and then anxious, hovers over it, like a kestrel over a roadside field mouse, but without nearly as much confidence; indeed, let's revise that comparison, it's as if the rules of thrall are reversed, that is, the raptor's in thrall to the rodent. He lets it go to voicemail, anyway. As soon as the outgoing message finishes, the voice says:

Hello?

[Pause.]

Hello, this is Severin. I wanted to apologise for my call yesterday. It was all a misunderstanding, I got confused…

Now Dennis gathering up more in the way of *compos mentis*, bravely decides to take on this particular challenge rather than continue to be in such ridiculous thrall to it:

Hello Severin, yeah, this is DC.

Oh, DC, how you doing, man?

Not so bad, and yourself?

Yeah, up and down you know. Listen, you know the message I left yesterday, I wanted to apologise, man, I was a bit confused.

That's all right.

Only, I was going crazy trying to contact Wan- … I mean, Alison, and I got your number somehow mixed up with another one.

No problem.

You're the composer guy, right? You live nearby? I think Alison mentioned you when she was talking about her poetry.

Yeah, that's right.

Sounds like you're doing really supreme stuff, man.

Well, that's very kind of you.

I'd like to hear your shit sometime, I really would, once I get out of this fucking awful situation I'm in, you know what I mean?

Any time, Severin.

I tell you what, I'd like to apologise properly for any grief I caused you, I'd like to buy you a drink.

You don't need to do that.

Yeah, just to make amends, clear up any confusion, like. How about I buy you a quick drink at the World's End? Tomorrow?

Uh-huh?

Tomorrow, OK? At the World's End, man.

Even the sound of turf growing may be filtered so it resembles a monstrous small portion of antiphonal material. Then at a given location a tin can rattles in a trancelike space. The possibilities are endless, even if the furniture is impossible to reproduce at present. Voices, and the vexations they cause, melt into memory and become like talking drums, simulating troughs of arcane noises in the garden. And you can get a purity of tone and sustain it over some distance, even across the sea, you can hear individual bird species like the fucking lark ascending into the cosmic soundtrack, giving the illusion of swelling, travelling backwards, graceful movements like this, and subtle variations close to body cellular level. He is like a child with a brand new toy again thinking on all this, and how he might achieve the necessary manipulation. He imagines strange and artificial echoes trunked over distances. He imagines the sounds of food and perversity, moments of utter strangeness in the dark. He picks up more vocalisations, swarms of aether talk, filters them using post-production floaters within the information sea. Sound like swarms of demonic geese and shrieking rooks. All of this quite fluid and quickly travelling to the farthest reaches of the hinterland....

Dennis, I'm just ringing to let you know –

Hi, Mum. Sorry I let it go to voicemail, I was afraid it might be someone I didn't want to be bothered by.

Oh, hello. Actually, Dennis, I didn't expect you to answer. I was intending to leave a message in any case, because I didn't want to disturb you. I thought you'd be at work.

I'm, I'm, flusters Dennis, I've taken the day off today.

I see. So how are you getting on with that job of yours?

It's OK. It's moderately OK.

The house all right?

Oh yeah, fine.

I heard there was some bad weather. But you didn't phone us, so I hoped no news was good news.

Sorry about that, I've been very busy, you know, what with work and all that, and time just slips by. Yeah, we had some snow, no real problems. Everything's fine.

Central heating working?

Yes.

That's good, then, dear.

How are things on the Costa?

Well, that's what I was ringing about. Your father's not too well.

Oh, I'm sorry to hear that, Mum.

It's all right, we're coping. It's his usual problem that's come back. But the medical facilities are very good here. So we're going to monitor the situation over the next three or four weeks and see how he feels, and it's possible we might return after that.

Oh, right, I thought you were there for another two months.

That was the plan, dear, but we'll see how it goes. Most likely we'll be back in a month or so. Of course, it depends on the weather there, too. If this winter drags on beyond March ... but then, the weather here has been rather disappointing too.

I thought it was warm?

Rather disappointing recently. Very dull and damp it's got. And the law and order isn't what it used to be. Do you know a girl tourist was raped in the town?

So I believe you told me the last time we spoke, Mum.

Did I? Well, do give us a ring from time to time. The mobile's working now, so ring us on that.

I will.

You're all right for money, I expect, now you have a job, so don't max out Dad's credit card, as they say!

I won't.

Car all right?

Oh, yes. I use it for driving to work, that's all.

Well, I won't keep you. Lots of love.

Love to Dad, Mum.

That's definitely him, sitting at the inglenook table in the World's End, exactly the spot where he'd first seen him, arguing with – with *her*.

Over a month ago. Now on his own. His white bullet head gleams. Actually, in some lights it looks grey and bony, a light grey part-fuzz on the skull-shaped skin, then just shining nakedly a bit when he turns, recalling briefly the bleached-out glare of the skin tones in that video. Wearing black leather, cradling a pint. And also the tiny gleam of the earring at his left ear. But he looks strangely smaller and less threatening than he'd remembered. More compact, if you like.

But it's definitely him.

Unzipping his bomber jacket with his left hand, heart pounding, Dennis steps across the lounge bar, proffering his right. Severin half-rises. Hi, I'm DC, says Dennis. Severin, says Severin, and clasps hands, palm to palm. Can I get you one, man?

A pint of beer is delivered for Dennis. The two sit across each other at the table.

Neither seems to know how to start the conversation.

Hey, DC, finally ventures Severin, how's your music going?

Oh, pretty good, says Dennis, after a bit of a hiatus while I was doing this supermarket job, which really made it difficult for me to work.

Yeah, day jobs are a fucking killer.

Well, I don't have it any more.

So you left the job?

I got sacked, actually. I was deemed unsuitable for Retail Management.

Heh heh heh.

But I'm really getting back to my music now. What I do, I call it World Music because it comes from the world and goes back into the world. I record sounds digitally, might be birdsong or machine noise or conversation, I've been trying to get sounds from the power station actually, whatever, wherever, then I mix them, manipulate them –

Wow, supreme. You know, Alison used to work at the power station.

I know.

I'd really like to hear some of this, man. I've been wanting to use more sampling type noise type stuff in the band's music, you know my band?

Nightmare?

Yeah, right. I'd be fucking *agog* to hear some of this. We could work together!

Dennis becomes excited: Do you really think so? I've listened to Nightmare a bit, I think I could really contribute.

We're kind of influenced by the Velvets, thrash metal a little but more intelligent, you know, art-rock, blues, but I'd like to take it further out, really left-field stuff. Stockhausen. You know Stockhausen?

I'm aware of him, yes. I did a music degree.

That's fucking amazing. Wand- ... I mean, Alison, she was in the band for a while. Chanteuse. I got her writing lyrics. I'm shit at lyrics. I'm fucking useless at lyrics. Maybe you could get some of your poet friends involved as well?

That would be, yes, that would be possible.

Trouble is, Alison never really *got* the band., you know what I mean? It could have been so much better.

I'm sorry you and Alison have –

Yeah, well, it's all history now. She had a good voice. But she really fucked me over, man.

Did she now?

Oh, yeah. She's left me in the shit.

How's that?

Well, first of all she decamps all of a sudden. Taking my son. I have a son called Adrian. [Dennis nods.] Well, we both have. She just ups and leaves. I know we had arguments, I know I had problems with the dope and so on, but I've been trying to resolve them issues, I thought we were on the road back, next thing she ups and leaves without saying nothing, takes the kid with her. But not only that, I find she hasn't been paying the rent for months. I always let her do those sorts of things 'cause I'm fucking useless at them, you know, administration. Anyway, she hasn't paid the fucking rent for fucking *months*, man, I never knew! And she disappears just as the house is about to be repossessed. Which she never told me about. There's no money in the budget, I can't do nothing about it. I can't pay the arrears, which are, like, monstrous. The money from our last tour, such as it was, is all gone. They're coming to repossess the house next week.

You're kidding! exclaims Dennis.

No kidding. She left me in the shit, the fucking bitch, excuse me. Fucking Bitch of Vienna, right. Sorry.

So what are you going to do?

Barry said he'd put me up, Barry the Beast, you know, heh heh heh. Keyboard player in the band.

The Beast of Babylon, remembers Dennis.

Yeah, the fucking Beast of Babylon, heh heh heh. He's a good mate, Barry. But unfortunately he can't do it just yet. He's got major building works in his house, and his in-laws staying and whatever, blah blah blah, so he says he can stash my gear in his lock-up for now, but I won't have anywhere to sleep next week. I'll be sleeping under a fucking bridge, man. Or on the beach.

You can't do that!

Might have to. Might have to. For a week or two.

I could put you up, blurts Dennis, just for a short time.

No, no, couldn't put you to that trouble, man. You don't know me.

Just for a week maybe, if that helps. My parents are out on the Costa and I'm looking after their house. You could have their room.

[Pause.]

That would be supreme. That would be fucking supreme.

They're probably coming back in three or four weeks. But I could put you up for a week, if it would help. Two weeks max.

That would do it. That would really do it, says Severin, clapping Dennis on the shoulder. Barry should be able to take me in after that. That's all I need.

Consider it done.

You're a fucking mate, DC. And you know what, we could work together on some music in that time, 'cause we ain't got anything else to do. Heh heh heh.

Supreme, agrees Dennis, slightly shocked at what he's committed to.

The pint glasses have been drained.

I promise you I won't cause you any trouble, says Severin.

I'm sure you won't.

I can pay you rent for two weeks, that's not a problem, I just can't pay what the arrears amount to on our house.

Well, that would be helpful, but whatever.

I owe you another drink now.

No, no, it's my turn.

No, I insist, man. I'm really grateful. This will really get me out of a hole.

When Severin arrives on the doorstep off Barry's van, he has with him just a guitar case, a practice amp and a large carry-all on wheels. The rest of his gear is in the van, he says, to be transported on to Barry's lock-up for the interim. Hey, DC, this is Barry, Barry, DC. Barry shakes Dennis's hand vigorously. He is taciturn, but not particularly beast-like. Hello, Barry, says Dennis, and to Severin: I'll show you where the bedroom is, you should be OK for a week or so. Fucking fantastic, says Severin. OK, man, I'll leave you here, says the Beast gruffly, cheers. Cheers, they reply in unison.

Barry's van departs, and Dennis and Severin are alone together.

A routine is implicitly yet swiftly established. They rise late, each in their own room. Breakfast is ad lib, every man for himself. Work follows: Dennis in his room, at the computer, Severin in the paternal bedroom or in the living room, with his chosen guitar, a semi-acoustic cutaway Gibson, gorgeous in its subtle sunburst goldenness.

Hey man, says Dennis on the way to make some coffee, I love your guitar. Yeah, this is my favourite axe right now, says Severin, in black T-shirt, sitting barefoot on the sofa. He fingers a rapid series of soft, unamplified arpeggios, his forearms, Dennis now notices, deep blue-grey, heavily disfigured by tattoos. His shaved head glints in the morning light coming in through the curtains.

Dennis hands him his coffee.

You sure I'll be all right here, man?

Yeah, yeah, my parents aren't due back for another three, four weeks.

I'll give you some money for the week, no worries.

Thanks, I appreciate that, you know, my ex-employers have promised me a month's wages plus two weeks in lieu of notice, but so far I've seen absolutely fuck-all.

Yeah, no surprises there, fucking profiteering bastards, you got to fight for every penny. Day jobs, who needs them?

Severin, I got to go out to the corner shop for a pint of milk, you want anything?

Nah.

They are both sitting in Dennis's room, looking at the computer screen.

Dennis recapitulates: You see, the raw sounds come *from* the world, then I make them *into* an imaginary sound world. It's a process of transformation, I suppose.

I like it, says Severin, I like it. Puffs a small cloud out. He is smoking a roll-up here, knocking the ash into a small tin of the kind he keeps his plectrums in, because Dennis has expressly forbidden him to smoke elsewhere in his parents' house.

There's 25 parts to this piece, I haven't finished it yet. This one's kind of interior, like ultramarine sounds, different shades coming up. Like being inside a sea of sound, you can imagine your body becoming lighter.

They listen. Supreme, is Severin's opinion.

The climax to it is number 13, which is the centre of the piece. It's a huge arch structure, the whole thing, and this is the centrepiece, a bit like Bartok's arch structures, you know Bartok? [Severin nods, stubs his butt out in the tin.] But I want to include samples from the nuclear power station in this one, which is difficult to do. I asked Alison, actually, if she could take the digi recorder in, but she never got round to it.

Oh, yeah? She never told me about that.

I think sounds change consciousness. If you can talk about consciousness, which is controversial.

This is fucking conscious music, man.

Listen to this one, it's originally starlings but slowed down like a

158

hundred times, sounds like Tibetan Buddhists across a huge distance of mountain ranges. You know, the chanting, the big horns. Driving away spirits with special bells and such like. It becomes kind of an empty big sound.

Wow, fucking starlings, you wouldn't have thought it.

Yes, it changes the experience of duration, you see.

How long will this whole piece be, then?

Dennis thinks. All 25 parts? About four, five hours. Maybe six.

Can you do this in real time?

What do you mean?

Change the sounds, you know, do that transformation thing, like in a live situation, a gig situation?

Yes, I could do I guess, but I'd need the right gear.

We could get you the gear, man.

It's three o'clock in the morning, and Severin is suddenly hungry. In the kitchen, Dennis makes coffee and heats up some baked beans. He finds a few slices of white bread in a polythene bag with the delicate greenish beginnings of mould round the edges, but they are all right toasted. Severin plays a chord sequence on the Gibson. This is a song I just started writing, man, he says. The words go: don't you know my name? you fucked my name, you fucked my name. I'll change them later, he adds. I like that, says Dennis.

Noon is waking up time.

Dennis stands in the bathroom scouring his gums.

Herring gulls bleat over the town. Switching modes within unending duration. The clatter of the refuse trucks. In real time? We are here and we choose our harmonies from the ambient sound. My harmony is not your harmony. What is real time? Like reflection in the mirror, looking at yourself as you existed a fraction of a nano-second ago. Got to tell Severin that. John Cage, did he mention John Cage? Nothing is impossible, nothing can be known.

He can hear Severin in his parents' bedroom, playing the same chord sequence. And his hoarse voice: You fucked my name, he's going. You fucked my NAME.

Later that day they are back at the World's End. Dennis insists on buying Severin a pint. You're giving me rent, Severin, it's only fair.

You're a fucking gentleman, beams Severin, heh heh heh.

So where are we going with this?

Could be going anywhere. Heh heh heh. Anything's possible.

Everything's uncertain, says Dennis, I can see that.

What kind of gear would you need?

To go on the road with the band?

Yeah, maybe this autumn we'll put together another tour, I want to completely revamp Nightmare. Post-Wanda, you know. I've wanted to get more into that big ambient noise for a while, but more subtle, you know what I mean, not just the white noise Barry puts out on the keyboard.

Well, I'd be happy to work with Barry.

Not everybody is.

Severin removes his leather jacket, lays it on the chair back.

You know, they are truly awesome tattoos you have, comments Dennis, indicating his forearms.

Yeah, thank you.

Where'd you get them done?

Severin names an establishment in a nearby seaside town. Why, you thinking of having some done?

Might be.

Well, this guy's the business. Really good. Really recommend him.

Did he do Alison's tattoos as well?

Beg pardon?

Alison's tattoos.

What the fuck do you know about Alison's tattoos?

[Pause.]

Sorry, I just couldn't help noticing she had like a small blue bird on her arm –

Tattoos. You said tattoozzz.

Severin's face has suddenly gone rigid and hard; he is not looking at Dennis but staring out the window. Dennis's face starts to feel clammy.

I just … sorry, I didn't mean anything, I just assumed she had other –

Severin's gaze has now moved in to focus hard and still on Dennis.

You shouldn't assume, man.

Sorry. Didn't mean anything.

Dennis notices for the first time how blue Severin's eyes are. Ultramarine.

Severin's voice has suddenly got very quiet:

That's OK, man.

[Pause.]

Severin looks away again, and continues: Well, you have a think about the kind of equipment you might need. Hardware, software, you know.

I will, Severin. This is very exciting.

Let's have another drink, man.

Hello Mr Chaikovsky, how are we this morning?

Dennis smiles: We? I'm OK. I don't know about you.

I beg your pardon?

By the way, it's Chaik-owsky. Not –ovsky.

I'm so sorry, Mr Chaikowsky. Please take a seat, I'll be with you in a moment.

Beige woman in a beige setting. Very peaceful here. Doffs his wool hat. Palm fronds and daffodils. Two other people waiting.

Mr Chaikovsky.

Dennis returns to the desk.

Now let me see, you're requesting a Rebirth interview?

Well, explains Dennis, I'm not sure what the procedure is, but I want to go back to where we started, because my employment didn't work out.

I'm sorry, the notes say you've had your Rebirth. You can't have another one, it's against the rules. According to the notes, we did in fact find you employment, Mr Chaikovsky. SAVERS PARADISE, Trainee Replenishment Executive, that was it, wasn't it?

No, no, that's what I'm trying to say, the job didn't work out, I'm unemployed again.

I see. We haven't had the paperwork yet, then. So did you resign, or were you dismissed?

We … parted by mutual consent, explains Dennis. It wasn't the right job for me.

Well, that makes it a bit difficult. Rebirth is not an option now.

I'd like to go back on Citizen's Allowance.

Citizen's Allowance isn't an option either. You see, Mr Chaikovsky, Citizen's Allowance is only paid for a limited period now, to enable you to find a job. We do our best to get everyone into gainful employment.

So I can't go back on Citizen's Allowance?

If the employment doesn't work out, for whatever reason, then you used to be able to go on to a second Rebirth automatically, but unfortunately the rules have changed, and that's not allowed now.

So what am I supposed to do?

Let's have a look at your options, Mr Chaikovsky, says the beige woman, returning to her computer screen.

I mean, I haven't got a job and I haven't got any money.

She taps away at her keyboard, scrutinising the screen.

Mr Chaikovsky, I think the best I can do is offer you a Reassessment appointment.

What's that mean?

If we put you in for Reassessment, well, that's a discretionary option we've introduced for when things have not worked out for genuine reasons. In other words, if there are extenuating circumstances we might decide to give you a second chance. We would need to have a report from your employers, and weigh up the situation.

How long will that take? I haven't got any money, as I explained. My employers said they would pay me off, but I haven't seen anything yet.

These things take time to come through. But I can offer you a Reassessment interview, let's see… [she peers at the computer] … ah, that's good news, day after tomorrow, is that all right?

Yeah, I suppose so, I'm not doing anything else.

Nine o'clock in the morning? Lovely!

She taps at the keyboard some more and a piece of paper slips out of the printer.

Here you are, Mr Chaikovsky, all the details are on there.

Reassessment interview, day after tomorrow, nine am.

Thank you, says Dennis.

Have a lovely day, Mr Chaikovsky.

I need to keep off the Funny Powder, you see, mate, and *this* kind of helps. Severin indicates the open can of lager he holds in his hand. Found it in your pantry, hope you don't mind.

Oh, that's OK, says Dennis, I nicked a whole load of those from SAVERS PARADISE before I left. You're welcome, help yourself.

I already have, says Severin, thanks, man.

It is 11 o'clock in the morning of the fourth day of Severin's sojourn when this conversation takes place.

The Funny Powder, says Severin, taking a swig from the can, is the bane of my fucking life. But I ain't going back to it.

OK, that's good.

You know, says Severin, I'm getting on real good with that new song I'm writing. I'll play it to you later.

I'd like to hear that. [Pause.] Severin –

Yeah?

Do you think we might get together with Barry to talk about my input to the band?

Do you think we might *what?*

Talk to Barry. You know, about how we go forward with my joining the band.

[Pause.]

Man, you don't want to talk to Barry.

I don't understand, Severin.

Severin mimics him: "I don't understand, Severin." [He takes a huge gulp of lager, and it foams round his mouth.] Listen. Barry's a fucking *animal*. *That's* what you gotta understand. The Beast of Babylon, heh heh heh.

Dennis naturally finds this disturbing.

Well, he seemed all right to me when I met him the other day. And he's storing your stuff, and he's going to be putting you up in a week

163

or so.

Is he? Is he?

Well, I hope he is. You can't stay here, my parents will be returning.

Yeah, your parents, your parents. I forgot. Your fucking parents. Listen, DC, Barry will eat you *alive*.

Well, how are we going to work together then?

A demonic gleam comes into Severin's ultramarine eyes, and he raises the lager can like a trophy. Puts on a stupid Germanic accent: Ve vill find a vay! Hah!

They are in their separate rooms. Dennis is lost in an ocean of sound, darkly reverberating from unfathomable depth, mood music from another planet. There are shocks of unimaginable bass power coming up from the nether regions every now and again, interfered with by layers of gamelan-style middle region loops, modulating ever so subtly. He has to admit this is very good, he really is getting somewhere with it. Bubbling up into an enormous crescendo, a simulation of a vast conception of space-time. He sculpts the sound slightly, replays it. The range is potentially from 20 to 20,000 Hz. Here it comes again, as the sub-woofers kick in. Supreme. Just a little more tweaking. A third attempt then, but this time something's different, there's an interference he didn't intend, a sharp treble clangour, where did that come from? No, it isn't emanating from anywhere within his system, it's outside; he pauses the playback, the ambient sound dies instantly but the clangour continues. It's Severin in the other bedroom; he must have turned the volume on his practice amp up to max and beyond. Now he can hear Severin's hoarse vocal too, You fucked my name, You fucked my name, Don't you fuck my name, over the repeated guitar riff…. It's time for a break.

The day goes by. It's grey outside.

Dennis is in the kitchen, pangs of hunger having driven him here in search of something which might be eaten quickly. Something with a high salt content, like crisps. Even SAVERS PARADISE own brand crisps would do.

The door opens abruptly, and Severin enters, his eyes glazed. Hey, man. He is holding in his right hand, forefinger knuckled into the opening, an empty milk bottle. In his left hand is a lit roll-up.

Hi, Severin. Sorry, you know I asked you not to smoke in here.

Hey, aycid-easy! says Severin, smiling vaguely.

What was that?

Nothing. Severin puts the fag to his lips, and the coal luminesces briefly.

Sorry, Severin, my parents will smell it, they'll give me hell.

I was just finishing it, man, protests Severin, his words slurring. Look, I'm putting it out. OK? He stubs it onto a plate conveniently positioned on the work surface. He lifts his right hand, with the finger crooked into the rim of the milk bottle, and smiles again, enigmatically. He dangles the bottle, wiggles it slightly.

Dennis stiffens.

You all right?

I am, asserts Severin slowly, in perfect control. And he brings the bottle round in a long slow arc and deposits it on the kitchen work surface. Then again the ghastly smile, staring straight at Dennis.

How you getting on with your song? asks Dennis.

Severin spreads his tattoo-stained arms: Just fine. I'll play you the whole thing soon. You got any more beer?

In the pantry. Help yourself.

Dennis is back in his room, feeling vaguely sick. He has no stomach to do any more work, anyway. He takes his boots off. Perhaps he will get into bed and read, even though it's still insanely early. There is a book on chaos theory he has been looking forward to. Or just lie on the covers anyway for a bit.

Severin is back in his (Dennis's parents') room.

After a while, Dennis hears Severin plug the guitar in again. The composition performance recommences. The guitar riff has changed slightly. Now there is a definite modulation into a related key.

Dennis lies on his back, staring at the ceiling.

Severin's new song appears to have acquired a chorus, or a bridge, or something. Dennis can hear a new refrain over the changed chord sequence:

Hey, aycid-easy!

Is that what he said in the kitchen?

Hey, aycid-easy!

What the hell does that mean? Aycid-easy?

And then again: Don't you fuck my name! You fucked my NAME!

Lying on his bed, Dennis begins to tremble.

You fucked my NAME!

You kicked my DOG!

Dennis sits bolt upright, his skin prickling. You kicked my *dog?* Is that what he's singing? Surely not?

This is not good. He goes to his bedroom door, presses his ear against it.

Is it: You kissed my hog? Maybe that's what it is.

And was that: You [something] my life? You saved my life?

But now the guitar fades away, and Severin has gone silent. Peace returns. The tiny sounds of the house – slight creak of the radiators, rattle of a window-frame – take over.

Night falls.

A feedback banshee wail from the farthest depth of the world sound spectrum wakes Dennis suddenly from his dreaming. He sits bolt upright in bed. He looks at the dim blue face of the clock radio in the darkness.

It is three o'clock in the morning.

It dies, and a clangour immediately begins, an electric guitar riff on a familiar, descending chord sequence. It fills the house. And then the voice, hoarse, with an urgent and yearning sub-quality about it:

You fucked my NAME!

You kicked my DOG!

Over and over again. The chords jangle for a while; and then there's a modulation, and they tumble in an immense and awesome cascade into a new sound-world, and the vocal returns, with a sneer in it:

Hey, AC/DC!

That's what it is.

Hey, AC/DC!

Hey, AC/DC!

He is being called – summoned.

Fear paralyses him, and the sweat starts to break.

He snaps the light on.

He gets up, puts on his dressing gown, goes to the door and opens it. The noise immediately multiplies in volume. He steps along the dark landing to his parents' bedroom; he can see a line of light at the bottom. He listens at the door to the ferocious, continuing guitar riff.

He takes a deep breath, opens the door.

Severin is outlined by the bedside lights, sitting on his parents' bed cradling and strumming wildly his guitar.

Fucking hell, Severin, it's three o'clock in the morning!

Turning to look at him, Severin does not cease his playing. He is entirely and voluminously enveloped in what looks like a huge fur coat. Mostly he is shadowed, but the lighting frames the silver outline of his shaved skull, glints on his earring and also picks out his eyes; there is a kind of band of light across his eyes, it seems, which have turned from ultramarine to jade. And they glint, too – you would have said there were tears in them, but that's probably a trick of this lighting.

Hey, AC/DC!

I mean it, Severin, I'm just so fucking tired and you woke me up.

Hey, listen, man, says Severin, I finished the song.

His words slur – he is clearly out of his head. He gets off the bed, stands unsteadily wrapped in his fur, the guitar strapped to him, the lead snaking down to the amplifier, his feet bare on the carpet.

Can you play it to me in the morning?

I'm gonna fucking play it NOW! roars Severin. Heh heh heh!

And the song begins:

You fucked my NAME
Don't you fuck my NAME
You fucked my NAME
Don't you fuck my NAME

Hey, AC/DC!
Hey, AC/DC!

You kicked my dog
You fucked my wife
You've been a cunt
For all your life

Hey, AC/DC!
Hey, AC/DC!

You fucked my dog
You kicked my wife
You've been a cunt
For all your life

Hey, AC/DC!
Hey, AC/DC!

It stops abruptly, the guitar's reverberation hanging in the air for some moments before dying away. Dennis, in his dressing gown, remains rooted in horror to the bedroom's threshold. Severin grins malevolently. You like it? You likee da song, AC/DC?

I'm not so sure about it, stutters Dennis.

You're not *sure* about it? I think it's fucking *brilliant!*

Severin unstraps the guitar and lays it gently against the wall. The fur parts as he does so. Dennis can see that he is naked underneath.

I think it's the best thing I ever wrote, man!

If you say so.

And, continues Severin, slurring, I owe it *all* to you, man. I owe it all to you. He opens the voluminous fur coat fully, revealing his stringy white body underneath, networked with old scars. His penis is half-engorged. Dennis stares, horrified. He has never seen anybody else's erect penis in real life. If this is real life. Furthermore, tattooed around the groin in curlicued and shaded and gothicky lettering, is the unmistakable name: WANDA. Dennis looks away with a shudder. But Severin seems unconcerned. Hey! he shouts, as if an idea has just occurred to him, let's have a drink, man! Let's have a drink to celebrate! Let's have a drink to celebrate me finishing the fucking *song!*

No thank you, says Dennis.

We've got to, says Severin, staggering, almost falling over under the weight of the sagging fur coat, but picking himself up at the last moment, celebrate the completion of a fucking *work of art!*

I don't want a drink. It's three in the morning.

You've drunk with me at three in the morning before, man.

I've got to be up early, Severin. I have a Reassessment appointment, or whatever they call it, in the morning. I need to sleep. Got to be there at nine sharp.

Cancel it!

What the fuck are you talking about, how can I cancel it?

You *cunt*. Well, *I'm* going to have a drink.

Is that Alison's fur coat?

What?

The fur you're wearing – is it Alison's?

This is the genuine Wanda fur. Thee gen-yoo-wine. Wan-dah. Look, feel the quality!

And he shrugs off the glistening grey fur altogether from his body, gathers it in his naked tattooed arms, takes three steps towards Dennis and thrusts the heavy garment in his face. Dennis recoils. The fragrance of the fur is unmissable and exotically familiar, and mingles with the odour of Severin's body. He is enveloped in it. He feels a mixture of longing and revulsion. Severin releases his grip, and the fur slides to the floor between them, brushing against his dressing gown as it does so.

Wanda, repeats Severin, now stark naked, the wonderful Wanda. You know her so well, don't you? Don't you, DC? AC/DC?

She's gone, mutters Dennis.

Yes. She's gone. And now Severin's ultramarine-into-jade eyes really do seem to brim with tears. And I'm back on the Funny Powder. It's all her fault. She should have punished me. But she didn't punish me, she wouldn't punish me, man, she just ran away, the fucking slag.

That's unfair, says Dennis.

Oops. An impish grin steals over Severin's face, twelve inches from Dennis', and he puts his fingers to his lips in a girlish gesture. Sorry. He whispers in a child-like voice: Don't tell her I said that, she'll be very,

very angry. Heh heh heh.

I can't tell her anyway, says Dennis, because she won't see me. She won't have much to do with me any more.

Same here. Same here. So we're both in the same boat. Both in the same boat, rocking on the same sea. Up and down, rockin' and a-rollin'. Just a-rockin' and a-rollin'.

Suddenly, Severin grabs Dennis's right hand with his own and clasps it.

So you see, all that's left is the two of us, man.

He stares right into Dennis's eyes, but it's as if he is not really looking, as if he is gazing into another reality that is only partly Dennis. My head's not good, he says. I fucking hate the Funny Powder, you know, but it's my only friend at a time like this.

I'm your friend.

Really? Severin releases his grip. His eyes become even more glazed, unfocused.

Yeah, I'd like to help you.

Naked scarred Severin suddenly embraces dressing-gowned Dennis with his long, wiry arms and holds him tight.

Dennis smells Severin's perspiration, feels Severin's bulky penis against his abdomen, and goes rigid with horror.

Really? You really wanna help me?

Well … up to a point.

Heh heh heh, goes Severin, releasing Dennis again. Up to a point. Heh heh heh. That's very good, man. That's ver' ver' good.

I think you better get some rest, Severin.

Good idea. Fucking great idea. My head's not too – He staggers to the bed, slumps onto it.

I'll see you in the morning.

But Severin, white body crumpled, appears to have instantly fallen asleep, and is starting to snore gently.

You see, he explains, what I'm after is a materialist aesthetic. An aesthetic that owes its presence to the day to day, to the living conjunction of ordinary people in real time, and not to the dead past. An aesthetic that is *created* daily by acts of political commitment, by, if you like, collective action – that is what's real. It might manifest in poetry, or music, or whatever. Do you follow what I'm saying?

Yes, she nods, doubtfully.

And this happens moment to moment, a shared aesthetic commitment.

I see.

Now, you mentioned my friend DC, well, he objected to this on some rather technical grounds. He denied there was any such thing as a shared present moment. What he was saying was, and I think this is rather specious, that because the flow of light, ergo information, is not in fact instantaneous, therefore there cannot be a shared present, we are all trapped in what he calls self consciousness, and so on and so on. Well yes, in a technical sense he might be right, but the fact that information transfer is not in fact instantaneous doesn't mean anything in the real world. But what DC's formulation does do is act as a metaphor, right, the shared moment doesn't exist, OK, but what a dismal, individualistic universe it conjures up. Individuals in the dark, unable to communicate in real time. Atomised individuals! What kind of a world view is that? How can it ever advance human consciousness, how can it even contemplate the overthrow of power, the emancipation of the collective human imagination from the ruling class that has enslaved it? No, DC is seriously deluded in this regard, I'm afraid.

He seems like a nice guy to me.

Yeah, nice guy. But lives in an atomised universe of his own. Then he starts going on about murdering old ladies –

Oh, he'd never do a thing like that!

– I don't mean he would, no of course not. But he has no social intelligence. Not politically conscious.

I think he's quite innocent, really. So do you think poetry awakens consciousness, is that what you mean?

Only in so far as it awakens a collective, political consciousness, which is all that exists. In other words, class consciousness. Individual consciousness, what I referred to as self consciousness, well, that's illusory. Individuals may take part in aesthetic action, which creates the collective consciousness that drives social and political change. Vis-à-vis poetry, that's what I mean by materialist poetry, poetry that *truly* serves the people. I don't mean infantile agit-prop doggerel, I certainly don't mean comforting nostrums or greeting-card clichés or half-remembered and ossified so-called "classics" recycled in such a way as to prop up the ruling power structure, or whatever, I mean the poetry of true innovation, of the politicised imagination, made of words, as Mallarmé said, words liberated to charge the ... excuse me, I have to take this call.

For Tarquin's mobile phone has just trilled insistently.

Hello, Sandra?

Hi Tarquin, just thought I'd give you a ring.

Hi, how's the conference?

Averagely boring.

Did you give your paper on Paydushkova yet?

No, not yet, that's tomorrow. I don't have anything to say, actually, just wanted to touch base and hear your voice....

Yeah, well, OK, listen, can I call you back, it's just that right now –

Are you doing something?

Yeah, I'm right in the middle of a discussion –

Are you with someone?

Just one of the comrades, you know ... listen, I'll give you a call right back.

No problem, Tark, I'm here. Bye, love you.

Love ya.

Tarquin ends the call. Sorry about that, friend of mine. Where were we?

Look, I really don't want to take up your time, I only came to give you the updated manuscript of my poetry collection. I'm really grateful you're considering it. I'll be on my way now.

No, no, please stay, Alison, I'll make you a cup of coffee.

Well, that would be very nice, thank you. Only, DC said you were interested in my poems.

Did he, did he? Well, you know, there's a lot here that's very promising. Very promising.

Really? You really think so?

He is in big trouble. It's coming round again. The big nothing. Excessive feedback. He's in a feedback loop. The alchemy doesn't work any more. The drugs may not. She was the only one who could have helped him, the slag. With the red and with the lips and in the rain and in the snow and in the blood flowering. Five days, and he's close to blowing it forever. This house is so oppressing. But this is such an unfortunate incident. She's a big cat. He hates her majesty. But yes, she's gone. He's got to blow it up. The cunt. You fucked my NAME, Don't you fuck my NAME, You fucked my NAME, Don't you fuck my NAME, Hey, AC/DC! Hey, AC/DC! You kicked my dog, You fucked my wife, You've been a cunt, For all your life, Hey, AC/DC! Hey, AC/DC! You fucked my dog, You kicked my wife, You've been a cunt, For all your life, Hey, AC/DC! Hey, AC/DC! Fucking great song. Fucking great song. That is Severin's considered judgement. Anyone would fall down at the feet of that song and lick it all up. The cunt doesn't think so. He should be so grateful. He should be fucking grateful. That he is the inspiration for Severin Fowler lead guitar and vocals grappling with the demons like a hero. He has a right to luxuriate in his wife's absent compulsion. The blackness, which is the absence of colour. The torment he has to go through, the cunt knows nothing about that, what does he know? What does he know about cruelty? What does he know about fucking beauty? The cunt comes in, can you turn the noise down please, like a schoolteacher. This is a fucking *masterpiece,* schoolteacher. That is Severin's considered judgement. My wife, my life. Her green eyes filled with tears. The slut. But he was her dog, and he obeyed her. And *his* dog obeyed him. And the cunt's like the dog's dog. That's the hierarchy. The cunt's just a pervert. But the alchemy, can it still work, can the blood still flow? Or can it flower? (Can still write a great song, that's for sure.) But I just don't care, he says to himself. I just don't care any more. Sailing the darkened seas. He is a very distinguished gentleman. Heh heh heh. But the cunt, he is in big trouble. He is in bigger trouble than me, determines Severin. Because

I'm closing in on don't care any more, that big sea. Hey, don't you fuck my name, he says, I'll teach you. Remember when she returned with the ropes. My wife, that is, he says. His wife, clad only in spangles of light, commands her servant to fuck her. Boy, you been a naughty boy. Slash and burn. The cunt knows nothing about all this. He thought he had my wife's beautiful body under *his* command, what a cretin, she's way better than him, she would eat him alive. The whip, the steel, slicing through flesh. Big nothing. It all happened a thousand years ago. And when you're in the sea of don't care any more, then all hell breaks loose. Punishment. The cunt doesn't know anything about punishment. He'll find out one day. Very soon. The rose, the thorn. Blood flowering. Steel. Excessive feedback. Steel on the flesh. Flood tide on darkened seas.

From: Fred X
Subject: Re: Re: Re: marketing of the moment
Date: 26 March 18:43 GMT
To: NMP Discussion Zone

I think we need to put this thread to rest if that's what you do with threads, I don't know but anyway what I mean is I think all that needs to be said about Tarquin Smith's book has been said by now. Sorry I'm a bit rushed, but I've got just one final final comment. I stand by what I said earlier, which is that Tarquin in the course of a very commendable but ultimately misguided attempt to reconcile his aesthetic position re poetry re music re art with Neo-Marxism commits grave errors of thought. The substitution of the politics of transgression for those of class struggle, and so on, etc etc etc, we've had it all out ad nauseam, and I really really don't want to go over this old ground over again, I've said my piece, basically. However, I do want to conclude by taking issue with something Tarquin said yesterday in this space about the question of language, and what I think he calls negative endorsement, which turns out to be a kind of poetic babble which he claims "undermines" the discourse of capitalism, well, I think it does no such thing. Coherent language matters because people matter, in my view, the working class need in their armoury to have the ability to think and make meaningful utterances about their lives and experiences, otherwise self liberation, that is, class liberation, cannot be possible. I don't know why Tarquin valorises a kind of "poetry" which seeks to violate even more relationships (there are oodles of examples, which he quotes in his book, or else you can look in the output of his Virus magazine or Virus press). If Neo-Capitalists disregard the integrity and meaning of human communities, as I think we mostly agree they do, then it ill behoves Neo-Marxists to disregard the integrity and meaning of human language which is the rightful expression of such communities. Tarquin has a perfect right to insert his viral expressions into the body politic, but to claim revolutionary validity for this activity, to claim that it advances the overthrow of capitalism in any way is just extraordinarily untenable, imho. Let me make it absolutely clear, there's nothing wrong with Tarquin making the kind of art he does, and theorising an aesthetic out of that, or the other way around, whichever it is, it's a free country (ho ho!) but it's the claim that such activity or such a theory is actually a theory or praxis of revolution, that will advance the interests of the working class and usher in a Neo-Marxist future, well, that's what sticks in my craw. But hey, Tarquin has his Virus so he can always publish this massive and in many ways very impressive book himself, I believe he has the means to do so. Sorry to go on so long, I've had my say, that's it.

Cheers, FX

From: The General Secretary
Subject: Tarquin Smith's book
Date: 26 March 18:57 GMT
To: NMP Discussion Zone

Comrades –
I really need to intervene in this discussion, which has gone on far too long and is distracting us from other pressing issues. Brothers

and sisters have made various references to what has been described by some as "grave errors" in the writings of our friend and comrade Tarquin Smith. In terms of the ideology of the Party, I would prefer to term them "irregularities", but that is of no moment. What I would like to make clear, and I'd like it to end the discussion, please, is that Tarquin's book as it stands has in no way and never has been accepted by NMP Publications for its programme. I think there have been certain misunderstandings about this, perhaps triggered by an injudicious remark made to Tarquin by one of my colleagues some time ago. That was clarified recently when my colleague became aware of the misunderstanding and wrote to Tarquin, pointing out that there had been no such acceptance, based on the existing draft he had seen, and that the clear intention had been to invite Tarquin to make some major revisions, following which a decision would be made about the acceptability of his text for our list of publications. It has also since become clear, and comrades will have read this for themselves, that Tarquin is absolutely unwilling to revise his text in any meaningful way. You might say he's dug his heels in. That being so, I cannot see how the NMP can sanction his book. It is patently obvious that NMP Publications exists to disseminate the ideology of the Party, and while Tarquin is perfectly free to take issue with some aspects of that ideology, which after all is always the subject of discussion, in accordance with our dialectical and democratic processes, he cannot expect the Party simply to endorse his political-aesthetic theories by issuing this book on his behalf.

I hope that does indeed clarify the issue once and for all, and I would also respectfully hope that this protracted and sometimes unseemly correspondence can now be brought to an end.

From: Tarquin Smith
Subject: Re: Tarquin Smith's book
Date: 27 March 03:22 GMT
To: NMP Discussion Zone

I am, as you know, saddened by the response here from several comrades, but especially so by the knee-jerk reaction from our General Secretary to something which might have been adequately resolved by the good old dialectical processes he alludes to. I have always been partial to fruity discussion – this doesn't bother me – but I smell here an end-of-sale auctioning off of allegedly stale produce surplus to requirement, an attempt at clearance or ethical cleansing that I fear will have a bad outcome for all of us. Yet I hold to my ethical – and aesthetic – principles. I submit that everything I do is poetry, and therefore politics. Poetry, that is, which by its very form exposes or critiques the capitalist structures of social and political power. That I have always shunned easy populism is true, but this is scarcely a crime in the face of a cynical "popular culture" that encodes in its narratives the rapacious interests of cultural proprietors, dead and undead, a usurped authority that is always a trick perpetrated on the imaginative bodies of living people. Whose authority? That is what poetry, as I understand it, questions. It maps strategies of disguise and desire. It refuses to replicate. It opposes the marketisation of every instant of time and replaces this with authentic living moments of shared intervention. It rejects "the creative industries" and "corporate culture" and "cultural products" through its bodied, incontrovertible presence. It creates reality. It beautifully advocates the refusal of false authority. It reclaims sexuality for its awesome cognitive maze. It substitutes the word uttered in real time for the capitalism-logos-logo, yes, the utterance for the "brand". It champions the ridiculous sublime. Unexpected juxtapositions, random associations, sex-positive ejaculations, dark-feminist cries, all participating in the outing and discomfiture of bourgeois market morality, the unseen and creeping carcinoma of our so-called civilisation, metastasing into every cultural body on this planet. For all this I have been accused of idealism, of bad faith, of betrayal of the working class, you name it, when the truth is diametrically opposite, I am advocating a poetical politics, or a political poetry if you prefer, which exposes passively received previous thought, which actively engulfs life, shatters language in order to remake it in the image of the desire of the people, and, finally, exults in the wreckage of capitalism and the triumph of the collective imagination. For this, I am deemed guilty. Well, guilty I may be, but only in the eyes of the transmitters of dead memory narratives of the ruling class on the one hand and arid, dated workerist fantasies on the other, both sides working ultimately, whether they know it or not, in the service of profit and of those who would profiteer. I could say more, much more. But I see that I have come to the end of this particular line. I wouldn't mind if the scrapping had been uniformly conducted in good faith, but no, people I had previously regarded as my friends and comrades in struggle have joined in the kicking. In particular, Fred, who had previously identified himself as a supporter, if qualified, of some of my positions – and the toss of transgressive v class struggle politics is one I can at least endure to argue – now actually repeats some of the unwarranted slurs I have had to put up with for a while. He asserts, for example, that I could easily publish my book myself (and therefore have no need of the Party's organ of communication), as "he has the means to do so." What does this mean? Ostensibly, he is referring to my own small press operation, which issues "slim volumes" of oppositional poetry from time to time, and a very occasionally appearing journal – though it would be madness to expect this outfit to undertake the publication and distribution of such an admittedly massive work as the one under discussion. But no – behind those words – "he has the means to do so" – lies a snide reference to my economic situation, one which has been repeated behind my back again and again, the implication being that I come from a privileged position and *for that reason alone* I am to be shunned or sneered at. The truth is that I came into a relatively modest inheritance a while ago which enabled me to set up my press and also to purchase the somewhat rickety inner-city property in which my partner and I now live, and which I have put entirely at the service of comrades for some years now, offering a space to work and live to countless brothers and sisters both within and outside the Party, while my partner and I earn the means for the ongoing and perhaps never ending process of refurbishment, which we are trying to undertake in a politically ethical fashion. It is true that my paid toil to help finance this involves freelance shifts as a working sub-editor in a number of editorial settings, and yes, that includes the office of a very well-known journal servicing the capitalist finance industries, but these are the necessary realities and contradictions of the working lives of most of us, and will continue to be so until the advent of the revolution we are all hoping for and expecting. I therefore bitterly resent such insinuations that I lead a privileged existence, especially from those whom I had previously considered my friends. But clearly, and I admit it freely, I am running out of friends here. Now the General Secretary has seen it fit to "clarify the issue". Well, that is his privilege, and I must defer to it. But I assert that my position has been rendered untenable. He has made it public that my ethics and aesthetics are at variance with those of the Party. It's there in black and white now. I seem to have been backed into a position where my resignation is an unwanted yet inevitable consequence. I have been driven into this corner where it appears I have no option but to resign – with a heavy heart – from the Neo-Marxist Party. I maintain that I have, in effect, been expelled, that this is a case of, if you will, constructive expulsion. Comrades, you can draw your own conclusions, but rest assured that, however it is interpreted, I will not trouble you in this forum any longer.

Yours in revolution,

Tarquin Smith

It is just gone eight-thirty in the morning. Dennis is sitting at the kitchen table nursing a slowly cooling cup of coffee. On the table lies a kitchen knife, a dark stain on its blade. It is not clear how that got there. On the wall, the clock ticks audibly.

There are slow footsteps on the stairs, and his heart misses a beat. The door creaks open. Dennis is relieved to see that Severin is back in jeans and grey T-shirt, although his feet are still bare. The T-shirt has a stain on the left shoulder. Severin's eyes are bleary, his chin and scalp grey with stubble.

I'm sick, man. Severin slumps suddenly on a kitchen chair opposite Dennis. He rests his temples on his fingertips.

You look it. You want a cup of coffee?

Nah.

[Pause.]

I have to go soon, Severin.

What? I'm *really* sick, man. I didn't sleep at all all night.

You need anything else before I go?

What the fuck? Where you going?

I told you. I have a, what d'you call it, Reassessment appointment at 9 o'clock. Dennis looks at his watch. I have, like, 20 minutes to get there.

You can't go, man! You can't leave me!

I have to. I need this Reassessment interview, it's my last chance. I've got no job, no money, this is the only chance to get back on the dole.

You'll get money, didn't I say I'd pay you rent?

This is the other thing, this isn't working.

What? What's not working?

You can't stay here.

What the fuck you talking about? I got nowhere else to stay!

Severin, I've got to go. I'll be back soon, we can talk.

Severin reaches out and grabs Dennis's wrist, pins it to the table (Dennis recoils), gazes into his eyes, but once again as if gazing into elsewhere, and utters in a low and oleaginous voice: I'm really, really sorry, man. I'm sorry if I've caused you any inconvenience. But you gotta help me. I'm sick.

Dennis has never really noticed before that the dense grey mess covering his forearms is composed not just of intricate tattooing but also of intermingled scars and small bruises of variegated colouring. And now, by contrast, a tiny red trickle appears on his upper left arm from under his T-shirt sleeve.

Hey, Severin, you're bleeding.

Severin dramatically rolls up the sleeve to the shoulder. He exposes a recent transverse cut that is starting to weep blood again. He stabs his right forefinger at it.

I did that for you, man.

What do you mean?

To show you how sorry I am. To show you how really, really sorry.

You're nuts.

I really, really apologise for all I done, that's what *that* means, that's fucking genuine *remorse*. That's what it *represents*, you see what I'm saying?

Dennis stares at the bleeding cut in horror, then glances down at his watch.

Severin, I'm already late, he says, standing up in panic.

I need you to stay, I need you to stop me doing … things I'll regret.

Fucking hell, Severin. [Dennis is already putting on his bomber jacket, pulling the wool hat out of its pocket.] Listen, I shan't be long. I'll be back soon, we can have a good talk.

You fucking cunt!

Don't abuse me, Severin. [Dennis is at the front door, Severin staggering after him.] Just stay cool. Half an hour, that's all it'll be.

What the fuck am I going to do, whimpers Severin.

Stay cool, OK? Put something on that cut. There's some plasters in the bathroom cabinet, I think. I'll be back.

He's outside, shaking, slams the front door behind him.

There is a second crash.

The lozenge shaped pane of crazy glass in the middle of the door has shattered. He surely didn't bang the door that hard, did he? But there is a white fist in the middle of the lozenge. The little shards are all over the doorstep like diamonds or snowflakes. Key trembling in his hands, barely able to fit it in the lock, he re-opens the door feverishly, pushes against a weight. Severin, can you let me come through?

Severin makes way. He has slumped to the carpet, one T-shirt sleeve rolled right up. There is blood smeared on his left bicep. Bright, fresh blood has started to appear on his right hand. His eyes have gone from ultramarine to black.

You smashed the glass! With your fist!

Don't you ever call me nuts, he moans, wagging a finger.

Don't call me a cunt.

They are in the bathroom. Dennis is frantically searching the medicine cupboard while Severin sits on the toilet seat holding wadded toilet paper to his right fist. Heh heh heh, I punched the fucking glass out, don't worry about it, man, I'll pay for the damage.

You sure as hell will, mutters Dennis.

I'm in a bad place, man.

We both are – hey, I've found them, here's some plasters.

Least it wasn't my left hand, so long as I can hold the fucking plectrum, heh heh heh.

Just put that on, stop the bleeding, wait, rinse it under the tap first.

Let's be mates again, yeah? have a drink together, oh, by the way, did you know you were out of beer?

Out of *what*?

Just thought I'd mention that while I remembered.

Listen, Severin, you're lucky that wasn't more serious, just stick that on.

Yeah, can you cut it for me, please, I've only got my left hand?

The bleeding is inexpertly staunched. The cut on the shoulder appears to be already congealing.

You made me miss my appointment, says Dennis.

Make another one, man, ring them up, tell them your grandmother fell down or something.

Fuck off.

Yeah, recapitulates Severin, I'm in a bad place, I'm sick. I gotta get out of this. I gotta get out of this situation. Wanda was the one who kept me on the right track, she was the only one could tell me what to do, and now she's fucked off. It's all my own fault. She's fucked off with the kid. I wanna see him, I wanna see my boy. Adrian, his name is, you know. He's my boy, but she's taken him away from me. I was a good dad. I was capable of being a good dad to my boy, only some issues that I have got in the way. Wanda, she just fucked off, but I just wanna talk to her, you know, man? I just wanna say I'm sorry, I'm really sorry. I wanna start all over again. I wanna speak to her, but she won't speak to me, no way. You know, I think she blocked my number, man. Hey! You think I could call her from your number here?

Even if you did and she answered, says Dennis carefully, she'd probably put the phone down as soon as she heard your voice.

Yeah? What do you know about it? Wanda – she's the only one who can make me do the right thing. I forgive her, why can't she forgive me? Hey listen, man, why don't *you* phone her?

What?

Why don't you phone Wanda, I mean Alison? Tell her I'm in a bad way.

Why should I? It's got nothing to do with me.

Fucking hell, all you gotta do is tell her I need to speak with her, tell her I'm sick, tell her I need to speak to the boy. A boy needs his father.

It won't do any good.

How the fuck do you know? You don't know nothing about it!

Severin, the thing is, you've got to leave, you can't stay here. I can't have you trashing my parents' house.

Yeah, OK, OK, I said I'd go, just as soon as Barry can take me in. Next week.

Sooner than that.

Listen, you try Wanda, I mean Alison, try and get her to talk to me, then I'll call Barry, see what his situation is.

Dennis considers this. OK, he says.

They are in the kitchen again. Dennis dials Alison's mobile from his.

It goes to voicemail – he holds his hand up. Hello, this is Alison. I'm sorry, I cannot take your call at this time. Please leave a message and I will try to get back to you as soon as I can.

Hello, Alison, he says, it's DC, sorry to bother you, but I've got Severin here, he's in rather a bad way and he desperately wants to talk to you. Please can you do me a really big favour and call me back on this number? Hope everything's OK with you, bye.

Is that all right, Severin? asks Dennis, ending the call.

Yeah, yeah. She knows what I've been through. You don't know.

I'm beginning to get a sense of it. So you're going to call Barry?

Yeah, yeah. I've got big substance abuse issues, man, all sorts of issues, you don't know fuck all about it.

I don't want to know.

Nah, of course, you don't wanna know, you're just paranoid about your fucking *parents,* that's all.

Well, it's their house you're smashing up.

OK, OK, I said I'd pay for it, didn't I?

So are you going to fulfill your part of the bargain?

What?

You said you'd ring Barry.

Yeah, yeah, I'll ring the Beast, don't you worry about that.

Dennis's phone trills.

That'll be her! says Severin animatedly, that'll be her calling back.

Hello? says Dennis.

Hello, Dennis?

Hi, Mum. Sorry, I was expecting someone else.

Dennis, I'm really sorry to call you on your mobile, I know you'll be at work and I hope this isn't inconvenient, but I needed to talk to you rather urgently.

Oh, what's up, Mum?

Don't be alarmed, everything's under control, but your dad has been taken ill. It's a recurrence of the usual thing, once again. Don't worry, everything's fine, but we decided to come home early, that's all.

Early? How early?

Well, I'm sorry I didn't call before now, but we're at the airport.

Airport? What airport?

The airport, dear. We're waiting for a train to bring us home. We should be there in a couple of hours. Are you all right, dear?

I'm … I don't know … you can't –

Is everything all right?

Yes, it's just that … I need to tidy up the house a bit –

Dennis, your voice sounds rather strange. *Are* you at work?

I'm … I'm just feeling a bit off colour, I took the day off.

Oh, I'm sorry to hear that, dear. Well, listen, if you're not at work I did wonder if you could possibly do us an awfully big favour and bring the car and meet us at the station, but on the other hand if you're unwell –

No, no, I'm fine, Mum.

Oh, if you're sure you're well enough. I'd really appreciate that. We'll give you another call when we're approaching the station.

Yes.

Dad sends his love.

OK, lots of love … look forward to seeing you.

Dennis ends the call. You heard that, Severin?

What?

It's my parents.

Yeah?

My parents will be here in two hours.

You're kidding.

I am not kidding, you've got to go NOW.

What the fuck do you mean, man? I got nowhere to go!

This is a fucking EMERGENCY!

What you mean, emergency? You don't know nothing about emergency!

Severin stands upright suddenly, accidentally jerking the kitchen table; a mug that has been standing on it slides to and smashes on the floor. You don't know nothing about it. I'm fucking HOMELESS, man. You don't know what that means. You and your fucking college friends, you have NO IDEA what that means. Your parents will always bail you out, you know what I mean? My parents abandoned me, I've had to fend for myself all my life, yeah? I've had to make something of myself, I ain't got nobody to do it for me, fucking AC/DC or whatever you call yourself. You don't know nothing about that. My *life* is a fucking emergency, you selfish cunt.

Don't you, repeats Dennis weakly, call me a cunt.

Trembling with fear, Dennis is to be found in the downstairs toilet, wherein he has bolted himself. He is sitting on the lid, head bowed, hands pressed to his ears. The sounds he is trying to block out are of shattering, maybe glass, maybe something else. And banging – repeatedly and rapidly, as of a fist on a door. The house shaking. And shouting – screaming, even. Perhaps furniture being overturned? A hideous crash – from upstairs – then silence, then another crash, and another, and another. Dennis's eyes are closed, also. Heavy footsteps, a door banging again. A bumping sound.

Then silence.

Uncanny silence. Meanwhile...

What does it mean, it means nothing. Nothing means anything. The cunt means nothing to him, hurt the fucker. Beautiful as a plaster Venus. The rope round his/my neck. The big nothing. Just hurt him, but cunts like him will always survive, they got all the connections in place, so they need their faces ground down, into the mud or whatever, they need the fear to be stuffed into their fucking faces, till the connections break and it all becomes as meaningless as anything else. Fuck him. Fuck him. Smash it all up. That'll fucking teach him. Smash my/him/herself up, all of it, just to show I'm serious, that this ain't just another stupid game in an eternity of stupid games, just put an end to all that fucking palaver, all that world shit that nobody believes, just smash smash smash all the pretending all the what do you call it pretentiousness. Beautiful. Then there would be the punishment. Wanda, she's the only one who can punish him/me, the one true saviour, the only one who understands and can punish absolutely mercilessly. Yeah, punishment. That would be beautiful, nothing else. Nothing else would.

Some of this is inside the head, some outside. It is not possible to determine the difference. Hey, fucking beautiful.

But silence now.

Dennis remains in the downstairs toilet.

Alison is in the bathroom upstairs, her beautiful face close to the mirror; she is carefully putting on eye-liner, transforming into Wanda. Alison/Wanda, in the blink of an eye.

Unbearable silence. The hideous noises are replayed inside the silence. They are a distant, ghostly echo.

Alison/Wanda in the bathroom, at the mirror. Alison/Wanda, the same old ritual as before. No, it's not. It's not Alison/Wanda, her thoughts, inaccessible to anyone. It's Severin, clad in Alison/Wanda's slash-cut red dress, standing close to the bathroom mirror, carefully applying eye-liner, mascara, his hands barely trembling, one hand disfigured by several layers of a band-aid strip stained with dried blood; or you might say it's Severin/Wanda, a new hybrid being

186

conjured into view but not Dennis's view because Dennis sees nothing of this, Dennis's eyes are still shut, in the toilet below. And Severin/Wanda is also humming softly to him/herself as s/he works, humming maybe the riff of that new song s/he was so proud of a thousand years ago, yes, s/he can still do it, but it's meaningless now, which is beautiful.

Beautiful. The End.

Half an hour has gone by, and there have been no more noises in that time, except the tiny, familiar, peaceful sounds of the house. And maybe distant traffic.

Trembling, his heart beating rapidly, Dennis unbolts the toilet door.

Sunshine pours through the empty starburst of the front-door panel and falls into the hall. It is a lovely late morning.

Perhaps he has gone. Perhaps it's all over.

Dennis stands, undetermined, in the hall a long time, close to the front door. He has his phone with him. He could phone for help of some kind. Or make a bolt for it. Which is it to be?

But the nightmare may be over. He gazes up the stairs. He grasps the banisters with a clammy hand. Still no sound.

He feels sick, a profound sickness he has never experienced before.

Dennis is ascending the stairs, slowly, one step at a time, ready to turn tail and hurtle down and out the front door at the least provocation. Even though he has clutched in his right hand a kitchen knife.

But everything continues to be peaceful.

Dennis has reached the landing. The door to his bedroom is ajar. He pushes it.

His room has been wrecked. The window glass is shattered; some object has clearly been hurled through it. The bed is on its side, the many things that had been left on it spilled onto the floor. The desk the computer had been on is also on its side, and along with everything else Dennis's computer is on the floor, comprehensively smashed, shards distributed randomly, logic board naked to the world. Next to the computer is the sunburst sheen of Severin's Gibson guitar, also irrevocably broken, the wood split in several places, six released strings snaking in all directions. It takes time for the evidence to register in Dennis's paralysed brain; the separate parts just do not cohere into a meaningful narrative. We may surmise, on his behalf, that the guitar has been used as a weapon to attack the computer, but this hypothesis does not immediately occur to Dennis; in fact, does not occur until much later.

All he is thinking is that *World Music Parts 1-25* has vanished forever from the world that gave birth to it. This isolated thought comes to him in an entirely logical fashion, even though nothing else so far has made any sense, even though a theory of cause and effect will take an extraordinarily long time to assemble itself within him.

Still clutching the knife, he withdraws back onto the landing. He glances across at the door of his parents' bedroom – which is also ajar. He approaches, inch by tremulous inch.

From within, a flash of red through the crack. But still no sound.

He pushes the door.

Lying peacefully on his parents' double bed is Severin, partly clad in Alison/Wanda's red dress, as seen (thinks Dennis at once) in the video. Quite still. Is he alive or dead? Perhaps neither – he is inscrutable. His eyes, open, kohl-framed, indigo as globes of lapis lazuli, stare at the ceiling as though in puzzlement. His jaw is grey, spangled with shiny drool that has also stained the dress, and his scalp also grey. The little gold ring nestles in his oddly delicate left ear. Where the gown fails to cover, part of a network of ancient, livid scars is visible on his naked white skin.

A hypodermic needle glints in the morning sunshine that comes in through the window – still attached to his disfigured right arm.

And now through the window also, the only sound to accompany the tableau: a faint squalling of inland gulls.

Dennis contemplates all this with awe, as a pilgrim would pay homage to a legendary, much revered icon or relic suddenly encountered at last, after years of unrequited fervour and long travel.

He drops the kitchen knife to the floor. He fumbles for his phone, and dials the emergency number.

There are sirens. And blue and red lights flashing. A small knot of people, neighbours and strangers, has assembled; they stare uncomprehendingly. Please stand aside, ladies and gentlemen, there is nothing to see. Dennis has been asked to step outside the house, and is in the company and care of a woman police officer in the front garden. There is a police car and also two ambulances parked in the road, paramedics in olive-green uniforms rushing back and forth with resuscitation equipment. More police arrive in a second vehicle. Garish fluorescence: bitter yellows, oranges, greens. Radio traffic bristles. A rumble crescendos to a clattering roar as a helicopter passes overhead. Subject is male, white, in his late 20s or 30s. He has been identified by the principal witness as Severin Fowler, that is S, E, V, E, R, I, N, Fowler, formerly resident on the Wellington Estate, Peninsula region. Subject has distinctive tattooing to the forearms and lower torso/groin area, earring in left ear. An ash-grey cloud starts to move across the sun. It can be verified that Severin has removed himself, he will play no further active part in this narrative, barring recollections and observations by other players alluding to him from time to time. Subject was found by the witness at approximately ten-oh-five this morning in a lady's dress lying on the bed in one of the bedrooms of the property at this address. Hello? Yes, copy that. That's been confirmed. There are recent lacerations to the left shoulder and right hand (a dressing having been applied to the latter), which may or may not be relevant to the enquiry, and also evidence of healed and partly healed lacerations to the body, clearly sustained some time earlier, in various parts of the torso and on both arms. Subject pronounced dead at the Incident location by paramedics, waiting to confirm that. Hypodermic syringe observed still attached to subject's right arm. Medical evidence at the scene suggests narcotics overdose may have been a key factor; clearly, an inquest will be necessary. A bladed object, possibly a kitchen knife, was found on the floor of the room where the subject was discovered, with evidence of bloodstaining; this has been taken away for analysis. Witness is named as Dennis Chaikovsky. -Owsky. Excuse me, sir? Chaikowsky, not -ovsky. Correction, Dennis Chaikowsky, that is, Dennis with two Ns, surname, spell that, C, H, A, I, K, O, W, S, K, Y, that is, Charlie Hotel Alpha India Kilo Oscar

Whiskey Sierra Kilo Yankee. Is that correct? Witness is resident at this address, the property he says belongs to his parents. No, they are not in residence apparently. Dennis, Dennis, what *is* going on? Excuse me, madam, can you stand back a moment, please? Pink-rimmed glasses flashing, iron-grey hair. Hello, Mrs er. Dennis, are you all right? Yes, thanks, Mrs er, I'm OK. You look terrible! Dennis's legs have suddenly fatally wobbled and lost their ability to support him; he has sunk down to his haunches against the garden fence, the woman police officer looking on the while, her hands laced in front of her. His face is grey. I just had a little problem with a, with a visitor. Mrs N reaches out and squeezes his hand, gazing into his eyes. You're not hurt? No, no, I'm fine. Excuse me, sir. Blue and white ribbon POLICE LINE DO NOT CROSS is being unwound and stretched to start to form a boundary around the premises, cordoning it off from the public. Excuse me, stand back, please. Dennis, was he an intruder? Sort of. Dennis, shall I phone your parents, oh, Dennis, whatever will they think? No need, Mrs er, they'll be here very shortly I believe, they're on their way back from the Costa. Yes, I know, was it a robbery? No, no, nothing like that. An Incident has occurred, that's all we can say at this time, madam. An Incident? An Incident. There is nothing to see. Oh, Dennis! (Mrs N has started to cry.) Some of the people who stopped to watch have moved on, but others have now joined the throng on the pavement outside the front garden, so that the general spectator count is up, if anything. The earlier sunshine has gradually given way to cloud, and the gloomy prospect is now enlivened solely by the ubiquitous fluorescence of the lights and liveries of the vehicles. The helicopter in the sky makes another pass overhead. Paramedics prepare one of the ambulances to receive the stretcher. Dennis's phone trills. Hello? Hello, Mum? Hello, dear, we're on the train, we're nearly at the station at last, and looking forward to seeing you again, are you able to pick us up in the car in about ten minutes? No, sorry, Mum, I'm in no, I'm in no position, no position to, er, to do that. Dennis, are you all right? I'm, yeah, I'm fine, I'm just having a little problem here. Dennis! are you ill? No, no, it's just the policewoman won't let me go right now, it'll be a few minutes yet. The *policewoman?* Dennis, what on *earth* is going on, has there been an accident? You might say that, Mum, but don't worry, I'm fine, Mrs er, Mrs, your friend is here, look, I think it would be best if you got a taxi when you get to the station, is that all right? Dennis, you're frightening me. Let me talk to your mother, Dennis, puts in Mrs N, who has dried her tears. He hands the phone over to her. Excuse me, Mr Chaikowsky, can you remain here a few moments longer, a detective will want to be asking you a few questions. Thank you, sir. More siren noise swells. A third ambulance roars to a stop, lights flashing. Excuse me? Male, name of Severin Fowler, please confirm that he has been pronounced deceased? That's Sierra Echo Victor Echo Romeo India November. The siren has stopped. A police photographer is now wandering around, apparently taking pictures of the shrubbery. Furthermore, evidence of considerable damage to property in an adjacent room, no, sir, I'm sorry, you can't go back indoors to collect anything, please be patient. Also noted that the front door glass panel has been punctured from the inside, glass fragments observed on the doorstep. Another siren, distorted, which stops suddenly in mid-phrase. A third police vehicle has arrived, flashing blue. Here's the detective inspector now. Deceased's next of kin? One of the ambulances revs up its engine and starts to reverse into the road. It encounters an approaching taxi cab. All three police vehicles continue to flash blue. The taxi draws into the kerb a little way up from the house, and two figures, a man and a woman, are seen to get out while the cab driver goes round the back to extract luggage. Meanwhile, the ambulance accelerates past it and away. You may be asked to accompany us to the station, sir, please be patient.

Turpin & Turpin, purveyors of the finest fruits of the sea to denizens of the Peninsula and the Wellington estate, are frying once again tonight. Cod, haddock (plaice while you wait).

Turpin shuffles back and forth, tending to the illuminated deep fryer. So what was all that palaver yesterday, then?

Mrs Turpin: That'll be the Chaikowsky boy in trouble.

Oh, yeah? I heard they was back, the Chaikowskys.

Oh, they're back. Back from the Costa. They found the boy had ruined the place. Ruined it. And what he'd been getting up to, I don't like to say. Fanny who cleans the pub was telling me all about it.

Oh, you had it from Fanny?

Yeah. She seen it all. Police was involved, ambulances.

So what happened, then?

He had some mates round, low life. Was like some orgy, or sum'n. Bloke from the Wellington estate was found dead, apparently.

Found dead! Who was that, then?

Yeah, been taking drugs and that. Dunno who he was, the bloke what died.

Never liked the boy. Getting involved with all that business. Don't know what his parents were doing, I thought they was decent folk. He was poking round here some time back, weren't he? Asking after old Mrs Stevens what passed away. What was he wanting with her? Hello, then, what can I do for you?

Finny has come into the shop. Medium cod and chips, twice, wrapped up, please.

Medium cod and chips twice, right away.

Mrs Turpin: Dunno who he was, all I know is he was overdosed on drugs or something.

Finny: You talking about the Chaikowsky affair yesterday? That was that Fowler from the Wellington, what's his name, Steven Fowler or something. He'd had a big bustup with his wife, she left him, took the kid with her.

Turpin, attending to the order: Ah, Mr Fowler, I remember him, skinny chap with a shaved head. Never thought too much to him. He were civil enough, though. Moosician, I think he was. You can never trust 'em. So he got involved with the Chaikowsky boy?

Finny: I reckon the boy was involved with his wife. But they say he was dressed up as a woman.

Who, the boy?

No, this Fowler. So they say. That's how they found him. They're all mixed up with each other.

Mrs Turpin, grinning through her thick glasses, remarks: You can never get down to the bottom of what goes on these days!

Finny: You're right there.

There is a respectful silence while they contemplate this wisdom, and while Turpin waits for the chips to turn gold in the bubbling fat, blb blb. The shop windows are all steamed up.

There you are, then. You want salt and vinegar on that?

Please. Thank you.

Thank you, and a very good evening to you. Bye.

Mrs Turpin: There was helicopters and everything.

Turpin: Drugs. They're all on drugs these days. Drugs and, what do they call it, free love!

Ah, nothing comes free, blb blb blb.

No, you're right there, flb blb blb blb, ulla blb.

Flb, ulla lollobollolla.

Glb a-blb, yer li'l flb blb-boy, never did like the boy.

Blb, blb.

Blb.

When does night cease to be, and where does dawn start? Where does an event end, and the next one begin? But there are no events or incidents, only endless flux. A thin strip of light cuts the rim of the sea. There's glossy, flat sand at the waves' edge. And the waves continually move in, in corrugated lines, a long shadow at the base of each and white flecks of foam appearing at their peaks; and one after another with a low crash each flings itself at the sand and the packed shingle above it, pauses, then withdraws with a lengthy hiss before the next starts to arrive. The rhythm is slow; it does not vary.

Flat fingers of sunlight penetrate the clouds at the horizon. They make the outline of the distant nuclear power station glisten. An area of high pressure is approaching the Peninsula. The forecast is for colder, clearer weather. It's going to be a quite beautiful day.

5

the poetry reading

At last, springtime begins to make inroads along the coast. Under the deep indigo of the April sky, the sea turns golden brown; white butterflies skip against and before and above it, zigzagging hither and thither in the salty air. The water warms up. It hisses on shingle.

Inland, there is new growth.

From its hollow, the skylark breaks cover, scenting as it runs. Now it begins to give voice. Anxiously profuse and unpremeditated is its song as it mounts the air, making its delivery while soaring almost vertically above the nuclear power station on a complex pattern of quickly beating wings. Its utterance is powerful and varied. It ascends into the cosmic soundtrack.

The skylark. At last. It's the appropriate time.

It is said to have jealous and combative manners.

So the day declines, the light becomes dimmer. A soft boom in the dusk now grows to a roar. Black aeroplanes appear on the Peninsula's horizon: one, two, three, four, five, six, following each other at intervals, in loose formation.

They circle the vast dome of evening air once, and begin to come round for a second time.

Now they are flying low overhead – no longer featureless dots. Bigger than the mind's eye could have conceived, they reveal themselves as dark, complicated military aircraft – bombers – with quadruple white lights on each raked wing, powerful searchlights sweeping a path in front, red tail-lights blinking. They appear to be following a set flight pattern. One sweeps by, then the next, and the next.

Giving the great illuminated castle of the nuclear power station a wide berth, they roar low over the Peninsula settlement, crossing the Wellington council estate and the scattered houses on the country road. To anyone on that road, ant-like figures of pilot and co-pilot are just discernible for an instant in each cockpit bubble before the shadow screams overhead and is gone.

Their little helmeted heads move from side to side. They can see everything that goes on below.

And then they return a third time. Again, they come in low; it seems as though they are flying under instructions to cover methodically every square metre of an invisible grid thrown over the thawing territory around the plant. A frenzy it might seem from the overwhelming power of the performance, but this is no carnival. Not a chance.

It is overwhelming and unbearable.

But at last the aircraft recede, noise dying away slowly, until once again they are only visible as pinpoints of light wheeling over the dim horizon to seaward. Half-moon to the south, stars coming out. There will now be a shorter space for human reflection and recuperation till dawn returns.

This year, all along the coast, the horned poppy is flowering exceptionally early. On the sandy seashore, it spreads its branch-like stems, its thick, blue-green, roughish leaves. The papery yellow flowers start to unfold, throwing off their sepals.

Not far behind, above the sand and shingle, bird's foot trefoil and sea-kale will push out their flowering stems.

Already buttercups, marsh marigolds and coltsfoot have spread over the inland pastures, adding their yellows to the mix. Pale lilac lady's smock lies upon wet ground.

The vole ventures timidly into this hazardous environment. The kestrel takes the vole. A flock of Brent geese in V formation crosses from right to left over the sea, apex pointing away from the estuary that lies to the south. Beetle turns over a stone; curlew arrives from warmer climes, and takes beetle. It glides by day, and by night seeks a nest in a hollow, north of the Peninsula. Unfreezing. Gnarled, mossed wood, rutted mud. There are many blackbirds, thrushes, redbreasts, chaffinches, hedge sparrows. Redshank too on the marshes, and, flying inland to pick at whatever they can in the fields, flocks of herring gulls. Sedge warblers arrive, and early swallows on the wing, following cattle. Martins build tiny mud houses in the eaves of the Peninsula's dwellings. Sounds and movements forgotten for a season now return. Geese on the ground, honking, clip pastures. The curlew hunts for worms.

The skylark observes all this from a height of a thousand feet. Wonderful in ascending, it hovers over the mouth of a funnel of air, secure in its improbability. It obtains a view of the hinterland on the one hand, and the dunes and the sea on the other. Signs of the new season gleam from afar. Now is the time for fieldfares to travel, exposing themselves to still cold seas. Little detached parties give voice. Owls hoot in B flat. Sundry different notes proceed from different species, and also feed back from the echoes of rainsqualls too brief to have consequence, harpsichord patterings on the homes of tree-beetles, polyrhythms retained by depleted foliage in the ghost of beech woods' leafless armies, before the sky clears again. Over landfill and black earth, over luminous watery eyes, the herring gulls tumble and loop exultantly, their squawks obliterating a leaden silence. Youths drink from cans and listen to booming in-car systems. The mornings remain rather chilly, with the wind in the north-west, but the tenor of the weather for some time has been quite other. Corrugated, galvanised zinc structures stand rugged and broken, with their fluted, variegated sides exposed to chemicals. In this irregularly flat country, anything can be an eminence. The season builds in ten days, or a fortnight. All that clamorous hooting appears to come from the woods. The owls have fledged. It looks a different game now, a renewed struggle for survival. Returning swifts, swallows and martins will soon swell in numbers, feeding on gnats and flies, and will make use of a placid, easy motion, in a middle region of the air, or will settle on the ground or paths, skulking and collecting; or the whole day will be spent in skimming. They are endowed with architectonic skill. The old holes are forsaken, and new ones are bored. Banks are perforated throughout. The dung of their nestlings will be enveloped in jelly. Many rush forward to be fed. A harsh, screaming note is produced, as they dash through the air. Carbon is fixed.

In time, fields will turn bright yellow with the flower of oilseed rape. On the estuary, their images reflected in solid, glossy, olive-green mud, a squadron of terns will bicker. A lone peregrine will dive into a flock of shimmering knot. Roses will bloom in the untidy back gardens of the Peninsula. Horrid wasps will torment children.

Clouds will indubitably have a silver lining. Electric fences will hum. A tower, studded with satellite dishes, will buzz. A solitary horse in a field will neigh. Noise of a power saw. The slow turn of the sprinklers at the sewage treatment plant. A distant tractor. Widgeon drakes with buff heads, whistling. Molehills and piles of dung. The wind howling through the marram grass above the dunes. A rare meadow fills with ox-eye daisies and red clover, and six black aircraft drill the air in formation above it.

Actually, they are bumble bees.

The sun becomes bright, and almost warm, coming through the skeleton trees in perfect flakes. Every great disparity of size and kind occurs. Vagrants come from the east, rushing in clear light. On elevated stations, trees distil vapour, running the ruts through with water. Heliotropes are constructed. Dews prevail. Leverets are cherished. Earthworms fill chasms. Torpid insects awake.

(Nine months hence, the fields will have been ploughed up once more; the lark's skull and matchstick bones will feed the frozen tilth below another winter.)

In the Chaikowsky residence, the atmosphere is not good, it has to be said. There isn't much in the way of conversation. A massive programme of cleaning and tidying has been instigated. Some debris has been transported to landfill. Glass has been repaired, at a nominal cost to Dennis's entirely theoretical credit balance. There was the highly embarrassing business of the credit card statement, unexpectedly showing (among other unexplained debits) continuing payments to two internet porn sites. (How did that happen? I have no idea, it must have been an accident. An accident – twice? I mean, I didn't realise it was going to be debited, I thought it was just for security.) And the drinks cabinet, by the way, almost entirely denuded.

On the plus side: a bewilderingly well-stocked pantry.

Fragmented slices of white bread lie along the length of the garden path. They never say anything, I'm so fucking nervous I just can't stand it, he says – he's on the phone (no computer, no internet, no email) as he walks up and down the path, out of earshot of his parents. In the front garden, but no way home. A male blackbird in the early morning, song of, that is – a specific pattern, but without meaning. We are so used to these incidental sounds that it seems inconceivable, you know what I'm saying? I can't stand meaning anyway, he says, I never could. Just attention, to the thing. Get rid of peripheral vision, securely fix the attention, remain still. That's all I ask for, he asserts. It seems after all no magpie or blackbird has taken the gift. Already, cautiously, they are flying back and forth from the telephone wires to their next demolition job, and each time they leave others land to take a break. And there's no way home from here. No way: processed bread marks it. Already we are thinking of springtime in the city. Aren't we? Today, Dennis says, renewing a conversation, I saw it all in a different context: a suspension across dissonant chords, OK, and all the rest of that blah, but … stupid woman, doesn't she know it can be harmful in the wrong context, for example when passed from the adult's beak

199

to a brood of nestlings? Bread, I'm talking about. Oh well, what does anyone care? What's the matter with me, they're thinking. OK, you could say I screwed up pretty comprehensively. Inside the house, the atmosphere is frozen, it doesn't even count as atmosphere, it might as well be fucking Mars. Nobody will talk to Dennis, least of all his parents, though that's the least he cares about, when everything has been lost. Everything. On the other hand. On the other hand, what did it all add up to? Who. Am. I. Fucking. Kidding? What was it all about? It's all cheap tricks, that's what. You could buy an airforce with the money that's been made from such cheap tricks. Big fucking nothing, I'm so fucking nervous, you know what I mean.

He ends the call, in despair. He opens the garden gate, embarks along the footpath, heading for open country.

Coltsfoot is a wild flower that's taken to the big nothing with consummate ease. A tough underground rhizome that can regenerate whole plants from small fragments. You have to admire it.

We saw it on the coastal sand dunes.

But in a sheltered fold, laced with terrible frustration.

It erupts through asphalt everywhere.

So this morning, for want of alternatives, he's decided to go for a walk into the woods – one last glimpse of that deep hinterland stuff on a cold blue day, before he heads for the city. There is ditch after ditch after ditch to be negotiated, but soon he's out of everybody's earshot. He dials another number as he crosses a field.

Yeah, hi, it's me, DC.

Hi, how are you mate?

Not too good.

You still want to move here?

Yeah, soon as I can, get a job of some kind.

Well, there's a room vacant whenever you want it, you know Jess moved out.

Yeah, I appreciate that, Tark.

How was the inquest?

Fucking nightmare, they really gave me the third degree, as if I hadn't had the third degree already from the police, I mean it was the fourth degree if you like.

Really?

Well, you know, the detective had me in the station for three hours, fluorescent lighting and all that, finally I thought it was finished with, but then next day he hauled me in a second time, asked me the same questions over and over again, can you explain this, can you explain that, tried to make me sign a statement full of bullshit.

Bastard!

Yeah, he'd prepared this statement, already written in plod-speak, about how there'd been a struggle during which I'd knifed him, because you know my fingerprints were on that knife, but then so were his, and it was a fucking kitchen knife after all, I mean my *mother's* prints would have been on it too, anyway he said I would be doing myself a favour by signing this statement, which basically said "during the struggle, acting in self-defence, I struck Mr Fowler on the shoulder", but I said no way, that's not how it happened at all.

So you didn't sign it?

Damn right, but then the police brought it all up at the inquest again, they were obsessed with this, and my parents were sitting there on the visitors' benches listening to all this, but eventually the coroner believed my story I think, anyway the verdict just came out as accidental death by overdose.

Fucking hell, that's awful, DC.

Well, it's all over now, I've just got my parents to deal with.

And did you go to the funeral?

Did I hell, that's the last thing I'd want to do, I couldn't have faced any of it, I couldn't have faced *her*.

She would have been sympathetic.

Maybe, but I just wanted to forget about it all after I offloaded the rest of his stuff to Barry, you know, Barry the Beast or whatever he's called, the keyboard player in Nightmare, he came round, and I asked him what would happen to the band, but he said that's the end, the band couldn't continue, *he'd* been the creative genius, that's the term he used, creative genius, but that basically he had screwed up his marriage, he had screwed up the band and everybody in it, and incidentally he had screwed me up too, so I shook his hand and that was the end of that.

The conservation area. Coltsfoot in the verges, and where the ox-eye daisies decided to implode. And a carpet below the trees of baby bracken shoots forcing their foetal curls up through the earth.

The woodland is mixed coniferous and deciduous, with plentiful examples of Norwegian spruce, Scots pine, holly, larch, beech, silver birch and other species. This is chiefly managed forest that he walks in, the aboriginal oaks and yews having long disappeared. Birdlife is abundant. Pleasant hilly woodland trails are offered for the benefit of visitors. There are intervals of sandy soil where little grows.

So, as he walks in his zipped bomber jacket down the sandy path between holly and conifers, he notices up ahead, apparently parked at the trailside, perhaps left for half an hour by weekend ramblers, a small car. Other visitors, he'd have thought, on this fine, early spring Sunday afternoon, would have given it little more reflection than that. But as he gets up closer to it, he begins to realise this is no parked car. It's the ghost of itself, thoroughly rusted, and utterly burnt out.

Close up, the reality becomes even more manifest. He comes to a standstill. No, it isn't parked – it has been there for a very considerable time.

The upholstery within is all gone, it is indeed a mere shell of rusted metal, a hollow enclosing a broken floor. The tyres are long gone, and the thing rests on its corroded axles. The engine is exposed by the absence of a bonnet, a black, complicated mess that has profusely leaked.

He contemplates another quasi-religious icon.

With a shudder, he leaves it behind, and continues his walk.

A hundred yards further on, though, among the trees, he comes upon another similar vehicle, in the same state. With mounting dread, he circles it, meditating in reverential silence for some minutes. Looks back along the trail to the first car, the first enigmatic marker. Then happens to look ahead and, how could he have missed it, a third, immediately apparent in the middle distance: this time a burnt out van. Big one, like a Transit or something. Dead. A scorched smell mingles with the sour, clean scent of pine needles.

Big fucking nothing, and he's so fucking nervous again now.

He leaves the straight path at once and almost immediately finds himself out of the trees and on a broad stretch of sandy wasteland. Dazzled after the forest gloom, he peers. There are pylons, and power cables linking them, buzzing softly against the broad sky. It goes on forever, this prairie. Small items of abandoned furniture and pieces of coal are dotted among the system of ditches that permeates the space. The ancient, white sun shines on all this. And that faint buzzing the whole time. It's too exposed.

Despite the superficial warmth, he shivers, craving the shelter of the wood again. So back by a different route, and into a shaded labyrinth of undulating, hilly forest paths. But from behind the trees now arises, looming closer and closer still, a sinister communications mast, ramrod straight and studded with dish antennae. It is a major source of buzz. What, he wonders, is it surveying? Whatever, it is *bad* sound.

And also now beginning in the distance and coming closer, a tenor roar of low-capacity engines that waxes and wanes.

In that same distance then the intermittent sight and noise emerges of motorbike scramblers flitting between the trees: young men bouncing up and down the hillocks, dodging the saplings on their little machines. And, as he walks further, more of those cremated, corroded vehicles appear – first in ones and twos, then dozens of them: tumbled singly in gullies between tree-roots; four of them nose to tail in a death shunt in a clearing; one completely crumpled against a tree; all of them empty shells. Moreover, now individual auto components are also revealed here and there, dismembered, posing as human body parts. Occasionally a complete, intact bumper in a bush; many hubcaps discarded on the grass. And the beercans, everywhere, generations of them scattered between the shrubs and in among the baby bracken: some shiny and only recently dented and vented; others beginning to acquire skins of corrosion; some at last, the oldest, completely rusted, as unrecognisable as ancient fossils.

The palpable silence of their presence, against the background coming and going whine of the motorbike scramblers, the communications tower buzzing all the while: it's more than he can bear.

It's time to go home, if he could find his way there. If he could remember, or if not, if he could invent the way. Pieces of bread as markers! The need to panic is at all costs to be resisted.

Coming back through the open area, he passes a man loading logs onto a small truck, who stares at him for some seconds without acknowledgement – but he braves the stare and, further along, finds a bridge made out of logs, car tyres, oil cans and other detritus across the biggest of several muddy pools. He skirts the olive-green, still water. Pure chance brings him to the original trail. You are now, he reads thankfully, leaving the conservation area. Please take your litter with you.

Back near the exit, comparative quiet. An alleged hotel and a golf club that looks completely deserted. Sounds from the housing estate up ahead. No birds sing.

The white sun sinks to the horizon.

Sunset – here it comes: a killer cortege of terminal colour, blood-orange leaking into a milky sea stretched across a vast backdrop of absinthe and petrol blue. But Dennis has now left the conservation area, he's leaving the country – soon he will be safely out of it.

Night falls.

A 1200cc hatchback, headlamps blazing and loaded with youngsters, roars through the gate and up the trail, leaving sandy clouds in its wake. There may be four or five individuals in the vehicle, at least one of them a girl. A young man is hanging almost completely out of the front passenger window, maybe sixteen years of age, belching virtuosically, waving his beercan like a weapon or a trophy in one hand, the other arm stiffly held in the air, the whole effect defiantly cruciform.

Who was that cunt we nearly ran over?

Was it the new bloke?

Nah.

Yeah, the junior manager. Friend of fucking Leuchars, you know, at SAVERS PARADISE, until he sacked him.

Who's he?

The bloke what put the –

– cunt into country, yeah, I know.

Ha ha.

Who, Leuchars?

No, the bloke what was sacked. Chaikowsky, his name is. You know what happened after that?

No, what?

You didn't hear about it?

No, for fuck's sake tell us.

It was all in the paper. Turns out apparently he's a fucking *gay*. He was having a relationship with that Severin bloke, you know, the guitarist from Nightmare who killed himself with drugs, and they was both found dressed in women's clothing.

That's disgusting!

Was *that* the bloke, then?

Nightmare – they was quite a good band, are they still going?

Yeah, that was him, just walking along the path, just now. No kidding! It was all in the paper, he got away with it.

The forest is dark. The cows have come home.

The car's engine is a symphony of revs. It bucks and prances on the trail's humps before leaving it entirely where the trees thin out, and heading for open country. The sound echoes in the gathering night.

You fucking moron.

You yokel! Ha ha!

Excuse me, there are ladies present.

Where?

Ha ha!

The car, expertly driven, whirls in an arc around the rim of a depression, then makes for a gap between two beech saplings, which it momentarily illuminates with its headlamps – and bisects them perfectly. Very hard to see by now. Loud cheers for the driver's expertise. Go-o-oal!

Onward.

Oh fuck.

There's a fucking HOLE there!

Whatever takes your fancy.

Suddenly, the vehicle is out of control. A tremendous jolt as the stump of a tree in the middle of the hollow takes all the speed out of it at once. And then there is silence. And a pool of light in the darkness.

The twin beams of the headlamps have come to a rest.

Fucking hell, Wayne, what was all that about?

They climb out one by one, those in the rear via the hatch. Fun and games. Nobody really hurt. Now get this.

Smell of petrol in the night. That pool of illumination, and the darkness all around. The screech of an owl. Fucking scary stuff.

One, possibly the one who had leant out of the passenger window, has a party trick he wants to demonstrate. It involves lighting a match and simultaneously flicking it forward. The first time, it doesn't work at all, the match doesn't even light. The second time it flares, but immediately dies. The third time a firefly arcs into the air. The sixth time it lands perfectly and catches the dark pool of spreading liquid. Another cheer goes up. Some moments elapse. Get back, for fuck's sake.

Flames are licking round the carcass of the hatchback. And then, with a rush, endstopped by an explosion – and a cry of joy, fucking supreme! – up it goes, a huge, hot orange beacon that conquers the darkness. Yes! as one, in triumph, they punch the dark, shimmering air. Four or five of them, lit up. It's hard to make out exactly how many, they glimmer so. But do any of them feel, in their moment of euphoria, that the victory is hollow, that somehow, once again, they have not quite acquired the validation that could never be theirs, that consequent upon being observed? We don't know: it's too dark to see into their several and collective consciousness, the four or five of them. That is, if they exist at all.

The bonfire rages. And of course it does give their position away to the countryside for miles around. So they, too, have to get out of here sharpish.

At night, the neighbours used to say, we would see the flames. Every weekend it's been happening, they grumbled, and nobody does anything. The authorities ought to do something about it, it's a disgrace.

The game is thrown open at last.

Nevertheless, it is a good half-hour before the first, distant sound of a helicopter can be heard, before its searchlight starts to pierce the gloomy heathland. By that time, the young adventurers are back in the anonymity from which they emerged – scarpered, the lot of them, well gone.

Sandra, I don't understand, says Tarquin, what all the suspicion is all about, I really don't.

So when did it begin?

When did what begin?

You know.

No, I don't know what you're talking about. I've been put in some very unfair positions just recently, especially by some elements in the NMP, when all I'm doing is, I'm just trying to, like they say, speak truth to power.

Oh, speaking truth to power, that's what it's about!

That's what I try to do.

You don't even know what speaking truth means. Let's leave power out of it.

I'd like to end this conversation, please.

Did it begin when I was at that conference?

What, the conversation?

Don't be so stupid, you know what I mean.

I was just trying to talk about ideology.

Really?

Power. What it comes down to – but there's no such entity as "power", is there? Only the specific power that one human being, at a specific time, has over another. I don't believe that, he says. But he will have to admit he's in danger of being outflanked here. He takes off his glasses, and polishes them studiously.

Or love, same thing.

Or *love*? Sandra, what are you talking about?

She persists: So it all falls to pieces.

You don't understand. You don't understand the need for ideology.

Tarquin is in dismissive mode. As usual. She really cannot take it any more. Dismissive, perhaps and particularly because she is a woman? He would, of course, be the last to allow that.

You're so dismissive. It isn't, perchance perchance, because I'm a woman?

Come on, Sandra, give us a break.

Per*chance*?

No, of course not. I mean, I'm *not* being dismissive. I'm hearing what you're saying, you know what I mean? This is all I need, after I resigned from the fucking NMP.... Anyway, what do I care?

You didn't jump, technically, you were pushed. For "irregularities."

OK, for, so to speak, "irregularities."

He flings himself back on the mattress, depositing his glasses on the side table, rubs and pinches the bridge of his nose.

Sandra: So to speak. And speaking of which –

[OK, here it comes.] I am *not* being dismissive.

This is the question of –

Of Alison?

Yes. Thank you.

So?

So, did you fuck her?

What kind of a question is that? What d'you want me to say? What can I say, Sandra?

What can you say, I don't know what you *can* say, Tarquin. Update me. I was only away just over a week, and since then things have gone from bad to worse. Did you?

I think you're insulting her, actually – she's a sensitive woman. Anyway, I agreed to publish a couple of her poems, and that's about it. I have to admit, I took pity on her. She's vulnerable, she's been through a lot, all that business with leaving the husband, and then you know what happened to him, that ghastly business with DC, what a nightmare ... I mean, she has needs –

So you fucked her?

Whoa. I offered her friendship. When she needed it.

Friendship of a *very special kind*.

Maybe. What d'you mean?

What do I mean, what *you* mean is you fucked her.

I'm sorry, I am very sorry Sandra, I am not participating in this conversation, not on those terms. You know, it's all about respect.

How many times did you fuck her?

For christ's sake, can't a person care for another person when they're fucking *vulnerable*?

Are you still fucking her?

[Pause.]

No.

That's it, he's off. He's out of the Peninsula hinterland. He rides the train back to the city now, the reflection of his face superimposed on the side-scrolling landscape, reading a paperback on black holes and strange particles. The car journey to the nearest station was endured with little conversation. One huge rucksack, one wheelie case, the rest to follow. A brief peck on the short station concourse. His mother: You be careful now. (Whatever that means.) Give us a ring when you're settled in. A manly silence from his father. No allowance, no wages, no dole. A bundle of nothing. Enough cash for a taxi at the other end.

He rides the cold slap and surge, his white shanks dangling in the endless wave motion. He is the classic duck of coastal dunes.

Somewhere, there are larger movements.

Light is forever receding from us, as are sounds.

And in the sunlight he is a beautiful metallic green.

He is neither a duck nor a goose.

He fails to reconcile dualism and reductionism.

The waves on the grey waters are phase-locked oscillations that, following period-doubling, may become turbulent (chaotic).

He walks purposefully upon the grass.

Whistles.

Rabbit corpses litter the road.

There will be difficult times ahead – you bet.

A quantum origin for consciousness?

Moulded from red plastic.

He is sociable, usually seen feeding on mud or sand flats, pools or shorelines.

The more tractable problem of cognition?

He is clubbed to death for his skin.

He achieves consciousness.

This arises from his strange habit of nesting underground, often under an old hayrick or in a disused rabbit burrow.

Neither a duck nor a rabbit.

You're back!

It's Sandra who opens the front door. I heard all about it!

Did Tarquin tell you?

I heard there was a bit of a problem.

You could say that.

You poor thing, I can hardly imagine. Tarquin's out, he'll be back this evening. He's doing a shift at *Lucre*.

Uh-huh, goes Dennis.

Do you want a glass of wine?

Yes, please.

You can put all your bags and stuff in what used to be Jess's room, it's going free.

Thanks, Tark told me about that.

Dennis dumps his things. They share a bottle of red wine. I would have kipped down anywhere, to be honest, says Dennis, just to get away from the family. I'd have bunked down in your workroom like before.

Well, as it happens that's not available anyway. I'm sleeping there full-time.

Oh, yes?

Yes, Tark and I had … a bit of a disagreement. We need to cool off.

Oh, I see.

They settle in for the rest of the day. Sandra is at her laptop, writing. As the light starts to close in, Dennis slumps in the sofa, sips wine, remains restless, continues reading about black holes and strange particles.

Hey, DC, my man. Hey, Tarquin. Tarquin unexpectedly hugs Dennis, strange body language for the big man. How you doing, Tark, says Dennis, when he has recovered from the surprise.

Tarquin says: Not so good, in fact. Really been tested to the limit, you know, big ructions in the Party, I've been, well, I've been stabbed in the back, it's fair to say. People I'd classed among my friends, and even among the few dozen readers of my work. Then [lowers his voice – Sandra is in the next room] problems closer to home, but I'll tell you more about that. You know, it's all politics, it's all fucking politics, it's not surprising, people will be on the lookout for their own best interests, vying for lebensraum in the goddam hothouse, or nest of snakes, whichever metaphor you prefer, but anyway I'm busy trying to revise the book, I'll get it out somehow. Don't you worry about that. Just been doing another day shift at fucking *Lucre*, I hate it really, but got to make some shekels, it's not as though I'm a man of property, as some people allege. So I'm subbing articles about managing hedge funds, ha ha! How's that for your dramatic irony? But the book, yeah, there are one or two conceptual problems, it's fair to say, so I'm working hard doing a bit of rewriting, you'll be able to read the results pretty soon, I'll email you the revised file, oh, sorry, that reminds me, you haven't got a computer any more, have you, you've been through the mill somewhat, as well, haven't you?

Dennis says: I lost it all, man. Computer, external disk backup, all trashed, my work all gone. *World Music,* twenty-five parts. More than seven hours of finished or near complete music. Two or three years' solid work. All gone. Smashed it all using his fucking guitar as a club, can you believe it. The external disk, apparently, he chucked through the bedroom window, it was found in the garden later. Everything smashed. Then there was all that having to deal with my parents, you know, they thought their bedroom had been defiled, didn't even want to sleep in it at first, but there wasn't an option, and they blamed me for everything, well, they were right, it's all my fault, I was being stupid, I just didn't mean any harm, I was trying to help out someone in trouble, but what good does saying that do? So I've got no money, I need to find a job soon, I really appreciate having a place to stay while I sort myself out, it's been hell at my parents'. I haven't even been able to *think* about my music since it all happened.

Wow, I didn't fully realise all that. Did you have any other backup?

Not an adequate one. Some raw files on CD, some fragments of first drafts on another portable drive somewhere. The digital recorder's still functioning. But the software's all gone anyway. And yes, I no longer have a computer to run the software on anyway, and no money to buy another.

You know, that reminds me, I had second thoughts about –

What?

Never mind, I'll tell you another time. Anyway. Yeah, even Sandra's turned against me now.

What's that about?

Ideological dispute. About the nature of personal relationships. All very messy. But you'll be all right here, you can stay as long as you need.

Thanks. You know, I've been thinking, I really should go and see Alison after all, before she goes up north to her mother's. See if she's all right.

[Pause.]

I wouldn't do that if I were you, I really wouldn't.

It's about closure, you know, narrative closure.

No such thing. No such thing as closure. There's only endless dialectic. Anyway, I think you still harbour hopes about her, well that's not good, it's not productive.

No no no, not at all, I just, I just want to make her aware that I care about her, that I'm there for her if she wants.

There? Where?

There, man. Wherever.

I really wouldn't.

You've always been very insistent about that, haven't you?

Listen, Tarquin says, you need a bit of distraction, DC. I'm going to hear the poet Tom Raworth read tomorrow night, and also to sell copies of the new issue of *Virus,* which has just come out. Really good issue. You know Tom Raworth's work? Great poet. Why don't you come along?

Yeah, well, I might. Though I don't have much money.

I'll buy you a drink.

How will we get there? Underground. Look, says Tarquin, I have to go on up ahead, I'm involved in organising it, you see. Collect copies of *Virus* from the printer. Get the bookstall sorted. Hassan will go with you.

Black holes and strange particles. Hassan grins.

Is Sandra not going, then?

No.

Hassan: We have four, five, six stops. Then we walk. You OK?

Yeah, OK, Hassan.

Fucking supreme!

The evening arrives. Hassan walks jauntily, chatting the while. DC, you no like living in country? My parents also live in country, very nice place, palm trees, olives, I go there sometimes. But the political situation is, you know, like you say, *dodgy*. So it's not good. You OK?

Lovely, Hassan. Actually, it's pretty dodgy in the country where I come from too. I much prefer the city.

Here is subway.

The mouth of the underground railway station exhales heat and the hint of exotic stenches on this spring evening. Commuters are still emerging from it into the glow, pausing to gain their bearings, then setting off in the various directions of their homes – but their stream would have dried considerably since about an hour ago. Already, the news vendor is starting to pack up his stall. Posters warn of the terrorist threat and the need for vigilance.

Hassan stops in front of one poster, chuckling maniacally. It depicts in comic-book cartoon style a Bruegel-like, densely populated cutaway overview of this subway station, or one like it, with security measures highlighted for reassurance at all its various levels, inside and outside – the platforms, concourses, escalator shafts, passageways and tracks arbitrarily terminating in abrupt fashion at the edges of the picture.

Security! exclaims Hassan.

Dennis nods.

Look! [He jabs his finger at the picture.] There! and there!

Dennis contemplates the places he has indicated, the chasms at the cut-off points of tracks and stairways, the endpoints of the particular world, or slice of a depicted world.

Where is the security? demands Hassan. He laughs again. Where is the security!

That's very funny, Hassan. Very good.

You buy ticket, orders Hassan. I have pass.

Dennis buys his return ticket and they descend the escalator. Hassan knows which platform, so he can drift in a dream in his wake. After five minutes' wait in silence on an almost deserted platform, punctuated only once by Hassan repeating "Security!" and snorting with laughter at the memory, there is a muffled rumble that rises to a roar, and a train, blazing with light, emerges from the darkness.

They travel the six stations as far as the stop nearest to where the poetry reading is to take place. Dusk is well advanced when they emerge. Dennis takes a step into the road without looking, is almost mown down by a passing taxi.

Where is the security? he smiles at Hassan.

Who roars with laughter all over again.

They enter the pub, which feels quite down at heel. The floorboards are stained, evidence of generations of spilled drinks. Sections of (also stained) patterned carpet are kept in place by rods of dull brass. Dennis is oppressed by the heavy, dark wood of the bar and the various floor to ceiling pillars round which are affixed long mirrors and circular ledges for depositing one's drink. Three or four small groups of men in business suits, and the odd woman, at the end of their long day, stand around drinking; one man laughs self-consciously at a remark by a woman he is ensconced with. It feels very much the end of an evening, though another is surely about to begin. But there is no sign of any poets, or of the kind of people who might have come to hear poets. It is upstairs, says Hassan, it must be starting. He indicates an obscure staircase. No obvious sign or poster proclaims any poetry reading.

Yet as they ascend the stairs, a faint hubbub can be heard. Across a landing, a lighted doorway, bodies moving, voices. Another, secret world. A corpulent man in a beard and dark, stained T-shirt beckons Hassan in. Hassan says: I am sorry, we are late. Then the man asks Dennis:

Are you a concession?

I'm unemployed, confesses Dennis.

The man names a modest price of admission, which Dennis manages to produce, and he is in.

The upper room is small, and oppressive. The lighting glares but, paradoxically, it seems very hard to see anything. There are too many people in it, and yet, at a swift count, their objective number is not large. Most are already seated, on an ill-assorted selection of plastic and wooden chairs, arranged on the dark carpet in concentric arcs focused on a small round table at a corner of the room, on which reside a glass of water and a digital recorder plugged in via an extension cord to a wall socket. Some of the audience are carefully picking their way to a vacant seat. One nearly trips over the trailing electric wire, and there is nervous laughter. Dennis spies Tarquin, glasses glittering, seated by another, slightly larger table at the back of the room, on which are crammed piles of what must surely be poetry books, pamphlets and magazines, including possibly copies of the latest issue of *Virus*. One or two people are inspecting this merchandise. Tarquin nods briefly at him across the room. Hassan is engaged in conversation with a cadaverous man with a naked, domed forehead, long hair and a beard, somewhat resembling Shakespeare. Dennis finds a vacant seat at the edge of the small throng and sits down. The hubbub begins to die. The poetry reading is about to begin.

The first bearded man who had taken his money moves to the centre and starts to introduce tonight's poet, Tom Raworth. His voice is sonorous, his remarks measured and complimentary. Dennis notices that the chair beside the small table with the glass of water is now occupied by an older man with a florid complexion and a greying moustache, in an open-necked check shirt worn over a white T-shirt, who has deposited a sheaf of paper on the table – and he assumes this is the poet being introduced, which is indeed correct. After a while, the remarks have come to an end, there's a ripple of applause, and Tom Raworth begins to read from his manuscript. He reads briskly.

The reading gives Dennis an opportunity to begin to take stock of his surroundings. Glass cabinets on one side of the room house mouldering, leather-bound volumes. The wallpaper is gold and white stripes, and the walls are dotted with framed prints: engravings of castles, a portrait of some ancient queen or other royal personage. The audience is predominantly male, in shirtsleeves, T-shirts or sweatshirts, but includes some earnest looking women, similarly dressed, and one rather large, jolly one in a voluminous skirt. A young man in the front row with floppy hair leans forward intently, his elbows on his knees and chin cupped in his hands, eager to catch every word. There is no gap in Tom Raworth's rapid-fire delivery, but the cadences jostle within it. Dennis's gaze drifts along the front row, and then along the next – absently, he is counting the heads. He notices that all the chairs have now been occupied, and indeed the audience overspill has been obliged to find accommodation on the low window ledges and (*oh, my god,* starts Dennis, it's her!).

Sitting on the window ledge, unmistakably, legs dangling in jeans and a white chiffony top with a sort of black waistcoat worn over it, dusky strawberry-blonde hair (no longer lustrous red) bunched at the back, is Alison. When did she arrive? Has she been here all the time? She is intent on watching the poet. Has she seen Dennis? He quickly averts his eyes, then has another surreptitious look to make sure, then looks away again. His heart rate increases. The flow of words obscures it. There is no content to the moment. It ebbs away. But a residue of reality hangs. He looks at his shoes for five minutes. He is hyper-aware now, not only of the poet's voice, with its embedded cadences, but of all the minute shufflings and other sounds from the audience and the room: the hiss of trouser material as someone repositions their leg, the regular, slightly asthmatic breathing of an older man at the back, the rustle, and the creak of the little round table as the poet shifts a page, the tiny consistent buzz of a lightbulb; and beyond the room, the faint noise of canned music from the pub's main saloon below penetrating through the now shut door. It has also become very hot. He's thirsty.

Abruptly, Tom Raworth's voice ceases; and, after a brief, pregnant gap, there is extended applause. The corpulent bearded man gets up: Thank you very much, Tom, there will now be a short interval of about fifteen minutes, during which you can replenish your drinks at the bar, he says. *Please* can you take your empty glasses downstairs, oh, and there's a bookstall over there, please do buy books, which includes the new issue of *Virus* which I heartily recommend.

Audience members step gently past Dennis, who remains fixed to his seat.

When he looks up, most of the audience has gone downstairs. *She* has gone. Three or four people remain hanging round the bookstall, aimlessly picking up publications and putting them down again. Tarquin comes over and sits next to him.

All right, DC?

Yeah, OK.

Want me to buy you a drink?

Yeah … well, thing is, I can't buy you one in return. Bit short.

That's all right, don't worry about that. Let's go downstairs.

Did you see her? says Dennis.

Who?

Alison!

Was that her?

Yes. I couldn't believe it!

[Pause.]

Oh, by the way, I meant to give you this.

He thrusts into Dennis's hands the latest *Virus*. He seems uncharacteristically nervous. Dennis fingers the magazine vaguely. It is more smartly produced than he remembers previous issues being. Perfect bound, a collage illustration on the cover, reproduced in colour, and a good hundred pages of content. Beautiful fresh print smell.

Looks supreme, comments Dennis.

It's for you. Complimentary copy. Come on, let's go downstairs. These people aren't going to buy anything from the bookstall.

Most of the throng are clustered in the saloon bar now, buying or consuming drinks, chatting and laughing. By now, nearly all the business people have gone, and the pub is given over to the late evening shift, the poetry crowd. Dennis is seated at the fringe of a small group, Hassan among them, that has collected around Tom Raworth. Just a mineral water, he mumbles, in response to Tarquin's prompting.

You sure?

To his relief, there is no immediate sign of Alison. He begins to wonder whether he really did see her. Hassan is saying: When I come to this country, only five years ago, I know only one word of English.

What was that? asks a girl with black pigtails and heavy-rimmed glasses.

"Fuck".

There is general laughter.

But I study English, continues Hassan. At first it's very easy, then it's very very difficult. I love to hear about the meanings of words, and the history of English words.

"Fuck" has a long history, I guess, says the man who looks like Shakespeare.

Yeah, where does fuck come from? demands Hassan.

More to the point, puts in Tom Raworth suddenly, where's it going?

People laugh again. Tarquin returns from the bar with Dennis's mineral water, and joins the group. What happened to your girlfriend, has she gone? asks black pigtails/ heavy-rimmed glasses, and then, when she sees Tarquin's face, Oops, sorry.

Where does *any* words come from, marvels Hassan.

They come from everywhere, says the corpulent bearded man, his beard frothing slightly from his beer.

Tarquin, beer in hand, nudges Tom Raworth: Tom, this is my friend DC, Dennis Chaikowsky. He's a composer, staying with me at the moment.

Tom Raworth leans over and shakes Dennis's hand politely; there is a friendly twinkle in his eye. Hi, DC. What kind of music?

Oh, you know, unnamable, says Dennis, flushing with embarrassment.

Sorry, stupid question, apologises Tom Raworth. That sounds like the right answer, though.

Hassan is on a roll: I find English spelling difficult. Ridiculous! So I just spell how I like!

Then you should have lived five hundred years ago, says the bearded poetry reading organiser. They didn't have spelling in those days.

And everyone spoke whatever language took their fancy, remarks Tom Raworth.

The fifteen minutes, more like twenty-five, are up. They file back up the stairs to the poetry room.

What did she mean, whispers Dennis to Tarquin, "your girlfriend?"

Oh ... she was talking about Sandra. Touchy subject at present.

Where's Alison?

Has she gone?

Can't see her now.

Probably went home.

They are arranged in their seats again, and the second half begins. There is now a gap on the window seat where Alison had been. Tom Raworth begins: *stock / irises forward / from power points / won't be housebroken / won't come / to commands / brother / and sister wolf / throat to throat / a friend / in a heavily padded suit...* Now Dennis, still sipping his mineral water, in which the ice cubes have long melted, is paying more attention – or at least, half of his mind is, the other half is somewhere else – and he registers a modicum of anxiety, even fear. His consciousness of the poet's voice flicks off, then tunes in again and tracks it for a bit: *motionless / facing left / sun high / to his right / behind him / nothing has moved / not a wave / not a thought in his head / frame him / in walnut / store him / in the attic / as tastes change / and plastic / replaces wood / metal / cloth / who will program program / when program programs you?* It goes very fast. It seems always as though any instant there is to be a revelation, a resolution, but each potential resolving re-dissolves into a new meaning, or set

219

of meanings, or potential meanings that leave the old ones behind, before themselves receding into the immediate past and vanishing. When the reading comes to an end (Tom Raworth's face is even more flushed than before, but he beams jovially) it is as though everything has been said and yet everything remains to be said. A generous wave of applause concludes the evening. Goodbyes are exchanged. Dennis shakes Tom Raworth's hand once more, and thanks him.

On the subway home, with Hassan and Tarquin, the latter carrying a plastic bag of unsold Viruses.

Hassan: You are a bit quiet, tonight, Tark!

Tarquin: Oh, you know. Bit fucking pissed off.

Dennis is reading his copy of *Virus* as the train rattles along. To his amazement, "Alison Fowler" is listed on the contents page, represented by two poems.

And so conversation has petered out by the time they reach Tarquin's house. The place is dark, the first floor spare room door is shut; Sandra has already gone to bed. By herself, presumably. Hassan says: I got to go to new studio tomorrow, guys, good night. And disappears upstairs. Dennis and Tarquin sit in the kitchen. Tarquin puts on coffee. So, what did you think of it? he asks.

What?

Tonight.

Dennis: He was great. I liked him. Kind of ... supreme.

Then he adds: So you did use her work after all? Tarquin is fiddling with the mugs; he doesn't reply. Then mumbles: God, I don't know if I should be having coffee at this hour. You know, I've really had some bad dreams recently, man – you still want some? Dennis remains silent, perched on a kitchen stool, flipping through the freshly printed pages of *Virus*. He's figured it out now: he used two of the shorter poems from her *Country Life* collection, the minimum he could have got away with, probably calculating they were the least objectionable, little descriptive vignettes that are unlikely to offend anybody's intelligence too much, mainly because they won't be noticed. It's a balancing act. But the signs are it hasn't worked out particularly well. That, at least, is not entirely clear; but what is beyond dispute is that a cold and clammy feeling has gripped Dennis. The coffee bubbles; Tarquin pours out a mug, adds milk from the fridge, hands it over. Dennis sips it contemplatively, but he can't stop his hands round it from trembling.

So you used her work after all?

What?

In *Virus*. You used her work. You didn't tell me. You told me her poetry was crap.

What?

Did you meet her? Did she come round?

Tarquin: Are you still talking about Alison?

[Pause.]

You really want to forget about her, DC.

Fucking hell, Tark.

What?

For fuck's sake!

What?

I should forget about *her*?

Listen, DC. It's been a piss-off for both of us. Yes, all right, I met her, we got together. You should be so lucky: I've fucked it up with Sandra as well, *and* I'm facing serious consequences on the NMP side of things, on account of the book. It's not a good outcome on all fronts.

Well, I'm devastated for you. [Dennis, as though recovering from an unaccustomed foray into sarcasm, stares into his mug for about a minute. Then, petulantly:] I thought you were my fucking *friend*.

I am, I am!

These poems [he indicates them, on pages 46 and 47] – I suppose they were the least sentimental – I suppose it was worth it for the payoff –

Hey, man, let me remind you, you were the one who was pushing them at me in the first place –

And you were the one who said they were shit. Until she turned up on your doorstep –

She was in a bad way, it was that business with the husband. *You* know all about that. And, tell the truth, I became impressed with her integrity.

You became impressed with her fucking *body*.

They have reached a stalemate. Tarquin, who has taken off his glasses and laid them on the dresser, is furiously rubbing the bridge of his nose, which is becoming quite pink. Dennis is swivelling back and forth on the kitchen stool. Both their coffee mugs, unattended, are cooling rapidly.

After a few minutes, Dennis ventures:

You really didn't think she was going to the reading?

I told her not to go.

Why, because of me?

No, goddammit, I didn't even know you were going to show up when I last saw her. Because I thought at the time Sandra was going. Well, you know the rest of that story too. I asked her please to stay away, and she said she probably wouldn't go anyway, because she was getting ready to move out of where she was staying. Said she wanted to start a new life, something like that. It was fucking madness of her to turn up, I don't know what she was –

Move out?

She's going up north, taking her kid to live with her mother. She called it "home".

Oh, I knew *that,* says Dennis.

Alison's green eyes.

Alison's *kind* green eyes, or were they grey? Alison, bathing her son Adrian. Alison, Dennis thinks, oh my god, he's seen the tattoo, almost on the verge of *mentioning* it, the unwanted bond between them, disgusting to even contemplate. Alison, beyond them, as they meditate, each one, on her madonnaesque aspect, from which the obverse is rarely absent. Alison, with the lad with the curly hair and the bigger lad with the spiky hair. But above all, Alison/Wanda, in love with Severin. Severin, Alison remembers with a shudder, if we

222

have brief access to her thought processes, who fucked her over and fucked up generally, but had some kind of weird integrity behind all that, Severin who could have been better than he turned out to be in the end, better than the lot of them. Maybe he *was* better than the lot of them. There's a daring thought. But Alison, entrusting Adrian to the care of Justine, the city before her, the rattle of the buses, the curse of the lights, and something she still wanted to be part of, something she didn't understand, but persevered with. Alison, that idyllic week. Trying to recreate it. Alison, concluding, however, that it wouldn't do. Alison, knowing in her heart of hearts the bargain was Faustian, and therefore the archetypal bad deal. Alison, entering the pub, already knowing it to be a mistake. Alison, hoping to prove something. Alison receiving a bad shock, sitting in the window, trapped, all that language unfolding before her. So *he* was better than the lot of them, just didn't have the start in life, and then it all went spectacularly wrong. The funeral. Unbearable. The band's sympathies. Alison revolted, Alison's inner pleading, why can't they just leave me alone, Alison, loving her boy, she holds him. Mummy mummy, he says, dee-*tar,* yes my love it *is* a guitar; she holds him up, he giggles, heh heh heh. She holds him up, gazes into his beautiful laughing eyes, deep ultramarine, heh heh heh. Come with me darling, it's all right, who said so. Who says so?

Alison: she is out of the picture now anyway; the rest of her life with Adrian will shortly begin, but it is no longer of concern to us.

I'm going to bed, says Dennis, abruptly.

Certain dichotomies need to be reconciled, and it's not clear how. For a moment, he has mislaid the terms of the dialectic. The question of cognition – let's leave aside consciousness – and the illusion of simultaneity. The thesis can be salvaged, at a cost – or can it? What is a moment, anyway? What is present, what is the present? What can be shared? The light burns. It's three o'clock in the morning. Everybody else is asleep now, all the remaining and temporary residents of his household. There is what you might deem silence pervading, apart from the tiny sounds of the house itself – slight creak of the radiators, rattle of a window-frame. Do the sleepers share this? But wait, if a shared present time is not possible...? What, then, can be shared, politically, aesthetically? Can there be said to be an authentic sharing? If not, what a dismal, individualistic world! But what is this word "authentic", anyway? What about "presence"? He stares at the words and they seem to stare back at him from the glowing screen in the darkness. Suddenly, he panics – he has overused certain words, they seem to hide within themselves unwanted notions of transcendence. He needs to fix this, win back some materialist credibility. He could do some unwriting here, it *can* be fixed, a little unwriting here and there, and then a judicious rewriting, but then where does it stop? As he unwrites, more unwriting is called for, the whole thesis threatens to unravel, and the more it does the less the prospect of its ravelling back into new coherence. A horror in the darkness – that none of it makes sense any more, that the foundation-matrix of the thesis is fatally flawed. Abruptly, he closes the laptop, and the room is plunged into total darkness.

Hey, DC! Hey! Tarquin say you looking for a job.

I need some kind of job badly, Hassan.

Maybe I have something for you. I am starting new business. Art studio, with bookshop, gallery, is maybe going to be called Hassan-i-Sabbah, very exciting. Need help.

What kind of help?

Shop. Is fitting out right now. Sell books, prints, art objects. I put big money into it. I am moving into studio on top, moving out of here you understand, very exciting. But I have no time to run shop, anyway fuck-all idea how to do it, maybe you think about that?

I do have, asserts Dennis, retail experience. In fact, to be more accurate, I actually have experience of Retail Management.

No kidding! How much experience?

Oh, a year or two, lies Dennis.

Fucking supreme, exclaims Hassan. You interested? Is not much money, minimum wage. I show you premises. You come and see.

Maybe we go into music also, you very big musician, no? We have performance space? Very exciting. I show you tomorrow!

But the following day Dennis falls ill.

Dennis's sickness is a bit hard to describe; it doesn't fall easily within the parameters of a classic medical diagnosis. His succumbing begins with slight nausea, a feeling of disengagement from the actual, a mental as well as a physical disengagement, perception unlocked from its bearings so that the world is perceived as a complex weave of tattoos imprinted on the dreaming psyche. And heat begins to increase within the early course of this mystery illness. So he goes back to bed, and stays there, unable to communicate with what has arrived. It is his dis-ease, an inner, unknown planet being formed out of the wilderness of deep space. What is his body telling him? His body, a language of polysemantic devices. And the next day a baroque rash begins to appear. It erupts magnificently. Florid would form part of a standard description, were it not that aridity rather than lushness is the dominant mode. That is, at first his skin becomes friable, like sand, like a series of beaches littered by casualties. Like fucking Mars, in fact. But then more like Venus, when it erupts. Frankly, his dis-ease is all over the place by now. A flush of hot colour breaks out down one side of his body, a nuclear meltdown, a rosy stigmata. Perhaps it does start to become very like Venus. In furs? That would be a step too far, now, would it not? But deep weathers circle within his vascular system, their effects surfacing at the epidermis, where the hairs take root, of course. Yes, this is too much.

Sandra knocks, opens the door: Hey, you look pretty terrible.

I feel pretty terrible, he moans.

Shall I phone the doctor?

No, I'll be up in a moment.

Can I get you anything?

Water. That's what he needs, to irrigate the singing sands of his sickness, to flush out the invaders. Whatever little digital creatures, unseen glittery things, are trying to bunker down in his body, stirring up those awesome turbulences and lurid colours of non-human warfare.

Sandra is back with a glass of water. I just thought I'd mention, I've finally found a flat.

That's ... good, croaks Dennis.

It's a two-bed flat. Not far from here, really nice. But I need a sub-tenant to help out with the rent. Interested?

Yeah, fucking... he groans ...supreme.

Dennis's sickness takes the form of a complicated and pointless journey. He can't escape from his own mind, but must go where it takes him. The tolling of the bells. The food chain. Ultra high frequencies. Relentless fog, animals with haloes. You kicked my dog. The shadow of the garden of earthly delights. Digital solitude. Consciousness of deep breathing in a flooded kingdom. Kiss me, DC. I want to understand you, Alison. There isn't anything to understand. The prevailing winds, the howling melody of the storm. The vixen's scream. He goes scavenging garbage dumps and landfill sites. Blb, blb, blb. Endless circular diagrams. I heard there was some bad weather, no? The tiny sounds of the house, the slow footsteps on the stairs. Skin and scalp all grey with sickness, lozenge-shaped. Power and love, of which he knows not. Where is the security? I'm beginning to see the light. There isn't anything to understand.

And so on and so on, in the interminable delirium of dis-ease.

He is by no means a stupid boy, as we have already observed. But he is still not able to be thinking at capacity, let's be fair. Or his thoughts circulate aimlessly within his swollen cheeks.

Hassan says: You look better, DC. Sandra says: You're looking a lot better. Isn't he? Definitely, agrees Hassan. Dennis frowns into the mirror. The noise of the traffic outside. So you wanna see the shop, asks Hassan. Do you want to see the flat, inquires Sandra.

Yes, please, I think I can manage it now, says Dennis, squinting.

He's never going to be without a certain wariness; it's a learnt thing.

Sandra is sitting on the edge of the bed, chatting, her glasses gleaming. I feel, she says, I'm ready to move on now. I've been through bad experiences, you too, I guess, but the time comes when you think, right, closure, onward. Closure? Well, I've always been restless, I suppose. You see, DC, she smiles, I'm sick too, I have ISS.

ISS?

Inability to be Satisfied Syndrome.

Oh, right, says Dennis, relieved. So that's why you're moving out?

No.

She is in the kitchen. Hassan meanwhile can be heard elsewhere in the house, happily moaning a modal Arabic tune to himself as he goes about his business. Hey, DC! she calls. No reply. Sunshine pours in through the grimy window. Hey, DC!

He winces inwardly. What?

Do you want a cup of tea, DC?

Yes, please.

[Pause.]

Sandra.

Yes?

Please call me Dennis.

Why?

Everybody does.

Yes, the moment when the outcome isn't certain, that is the moment of revolutionary creation; surely *that* is unchallengeable, at least? but, some of his leftist critics chorus, the outcome *is* ultimately always certain, it is "the victory of working people" – how to answer this? With a poem? Perhaps he should write a 500-page poem, rather than attempt analysis or dialectic? But such critics would at best only be satisfied with a poem that mirrors the standard paradigm: personal anecdote, packed with irony and extravagant simile; epiphany;

closure. Like mainstream style, but turned on its head, so that the closure is socialist certainty. The world has truly turned upside down for Tarquin. His critics sit at their tables sniping at him, with their beer in their fists, the only difference from their bourgeois counterparts being that they sit on the ceiling, the beer remaining in their glasses as if by magic until transferred to their gullets, whence it makes its upward way into their revolutionary stomachs.

Whose side are you on? Uncertainty is dangerous, and must be banished!

Ah, fuck it.

That's a lot of words in there, a lot of words he has laboured long and hard to knit together. Check it out: 201,277 words, 1,026,512 characters, 504 pages, weighing in at a hefty 1.46 megabytes. Not to mention the voluminous notes in ancillary files. In former times, you would have had to feed the pages to the fire, one by one. Or meticulously build a bonfire in the garden. It's easier now, frighteningly easy. Drag the icon to the trash. That's it.

He takes a deep breath, and drags.

No, it's not quite done. It's now in a location that will only start to be overwritten when the computer's random access memory fills up. There's still time for second thoughts.

He must be courageous. Heart in mouth, breathing stopped.

Empty trash.

Are you sure, this cannot be undone, click.

There, it's gone.

Tarquin leans back in his chair, exhaling, eyes closed, full of horror at what he has just done, but intermingled with a little weird sense of a long-time burden being lifted.

We do not know what the future holds for Tarquin Smith, né Smythe. His world that had seemed so solid just two or three months ago has now been riven with doubt. We know that he will not admit this. If he abandons his friends, or they abandon him, he will undoubtedly gather new friends or acolytes in their place, for this, or rather the attention they provide, he craves still. We can imagine him founding his own political party – just possibly – or more likely, he will remain disaffected. He is brilliant enough to perhaps pursue an academic career, where his disaffection will continue to be nurtured in a safe environment forever. An outside chance: that he flips over, and becomes a conservative politician. Don't laugh. Or he becomes fascinated with those notions of transcendence, and embarks on a new and productively futile battle to reconcile transcendence and materialism (and of course poetry as the third apex of this trinity): the one, holy and apostolic Catholic Church, for instance, awaits with open arms.

At any rate, it is time to take our leave of him.

The future is imponderable, and we are almost done with the present. Already, it seems as though all these events happened a long time ago.

So, some time in the past, maybe a thousand years ago, who knows, as the month of May approaches perhaps, in an unknown metropolis in long-term decline, three bands of dusty sunshine, from intervening open doors, are thrown transversely across the length of a corridor, a long rug covering its worn floorboards, at the far end of which is a dining area and kitchen. The three doors in this passageway, immediately left of the entrance hall, are those of two bedrooms and a bathroom.

Two young people are wandering around in the echoing flat.

You can choose, Dennis. I don't mind which I have.

The rooms? You mean, which room?

They are much of a muchness. Each is sparsely furnished: a bed, the mattress covered in polythene, a small, badly painted or chipped chest of drawers, a couple of chairs of dark wood and uncertain construction. The skirting boards, of polished but faded and scuffed mahogany, suggest lapsed quality. The apartment badly needs airing. Sandra and Dennis together attempt to raise the heavy sash window in one of the bedrooms, but it's badly stuck. Then suddenly it lifts, taking them by surprise, whereupon they lose their grip and it crashes back down again, shivering but fortunately not breaking the glass. They both laugh at their own fright.

Sandra now notices the severed sash cords dangling uselessly.

Need to tell the landlord about that.

Right off the entrance, the living room: a rug, a basic sofa, disused fireplace with a surround of green ceramic tiles surmounted by a large mirror, bay window, uncurtained, onto the front, whence traffic hum.

Distant song of the blackbird, location unknown, fluting sweetly.

This, says Sandra, is what is meant by "semi-furnished". You look nervous, Dennis.

Me? Why should I be?

And then: This is pretty good. I like it.

He goes back and forth between the two potential bedrooms on offer, trying to make up his mind. The one on the far side of the bathroom, the one on the near. On the one hand. On the other.

What it is, I've been frustrated for a long time.

You've had a hard time, she concedes, sympathetically.

But I think I could do some good work here. I think I could start again, know what I mean?

Yeah, go for it.

OK, I'll have this one. (Voile at the window, through which the pale spring sunshine over the city, penetrating in the gap between buildings, is filtered. The bed, the chest of drawers, the chair. A Victorian wallpaper, interlacings of indigo foliage, infinitely deep, possibly fractal. No other amenities. It'll do.)

What about the rent?

Sandra names a sum. Payable in advance, monthly. The arrangement is good for six months; it will be reviewed thereafter. The landlord is domiciled several blocks hence. Sandra will be the intermediary, the official tenant.

I haven't got that money.

You can owe it to me, until you're sorted.

Elsewhere in the building, another tenant seems to be trying to move furniture, to judge from the bumpings and scrapings. A small child can be heard crying, aggressively, though the plaintiveness is muted via several sets of brick and plasterboard walls. In the back yard, another blackbird renders Debussyesque intervals with virtuosic nonchalance. Front of the building, open sky. Moving clouds obscure the sun. Vehicles – cars, buses, small trucks and builders' vans – pass back and forth. Others are parked under the line of huge, ancient plane trees on the opposite side of the road. High-pitched, even bleeps, without inflection, counterpoint the rumble as a heavy lorry backs into a side street, a man shouting the while. The world goes about its business, in a vast ocean of frequencies.

Two figures, interior. Standing at the front bay window now, gazing outward, discussing terms in a leisurely fashion, heading in parallel towards their independent objectives.

I know someone, mentions Sandra, with a van. He's coming to move my stuff tomorrow. He could move your stuff too.

Sandra, as you know, I don't have much. I don't even have a computer now. Not a viable one.

Well, whatever you need. It can be arranged.

Really, virtually all I've got is at Tarquin's now.

That's simple enough, then.

I've got the violin back. My parents sent it on. Would you mind me practising?

Doesn't bother me, Dennis. I'll keep very much to myself.

Supreme. I'll be pretty rusty at first. You know, I think after all Tarquin was right.

He was? I don't think so.

Only in so far as … he once told me I didn't need the computer. Well, maybe I don't. I could start from scratch. And it *would* sound pretty scratchy.

It isn't possible to determine exactly how happy Dennis is with this arrangement. On such matters, who can make final pronouncements? The following day, his possessions are arranged in a more or less coherent pile in the hallway at Tarquin's: a bulging rucksack, a wheelie case that once belonged to his parents, sundry pieces of salvaged electronic equipment not packed in any particularly coherent fashion, three cardboard boxes crammed with books and CDs, the violin case. Tarquin, meanwhile, will have been doing another day shift at *Lucre;* there is no need to concern ourselves further with him. Sandra's friend with the van arrives.

Is that it, then?

Dennis is delivered to his new, temporary home.

Hey, you like? Dennis looks at the white-painted walls, the white, naked shelves, the glowing boards. The smell of new. It's very, er, glamorous, Hassan.

Glamorous, that is good, yeah?

Yeah, very good, you've done a good job here.

I move in upstairs, you see my studio, very light, says Hassan proudly.

So you've moved in?

Yeah, today!

So, did you have a quarrel with Tarquin too?

Nah, nah, laughs Hassan, Tarquin and me, we are best of friends, mate, I am the last friend he has got, ha ha!

Ha ha, replies Dennis, politely.

So is bookshop here, and also can be gallery or performance space, very, you know –

Flexible?

Yeah, flexible.

I can see loads of possibilities, I'd love to work here.

You Retail Manager, no?

That's right, Retail Manager.

So what you think, I was going to call it Hassan-i-Sabbah, Old Man of the Mountains, you know, but maybe no?

Well, it's neither one thing nor the other, and also both and everything, gallery, performance space, bookshop, you could call it Duck-Rabbit.

Duck-Rabbit, why a Duck-Rabbit?

Well, you see, neither one thing nor the other, Duck-Rabbit.

Ha ha, I like it, Duck-Rabbit!

Dennis returns to the flat in the evening with some basic provisions. Sandra thoughtfully brings him a cup of coffee as he sorts his stuff, unpacking the books and CDs, stacking them on the floor against the skirting board in anticipation of some kind of shelving arrangement.

He envisaged planks balanced on salvaged bricks.

Cheers, Sandra.

Not a problem, Dennis. Do you need a hand?

The mug steams faintly on the floorboards. No, I'm fine, thanks.

How's Hassan?

I think he's done all right.

Days in the city. Immense light. Somehow a shining, from the face of things outward. There could even be some cheerfulness here. Even the tiny insects kissing each other as they meet, hard pressed against the skirting board. Flies blowing their little trumpets. Conversation with Sandra, and Sandra's friends. The problem of bed linen, and how it was solved. The kitchen arrangements, the bathroom arrangements. The economic infrastructure of the household. He imagines life in the flat, staring out of the front window at the street below, while Sandra with legs up on the sofa cradles a mug, absently flicking through TV pictures. They go about their daily business and each is careful not to infringe on the other's space. Down the booming, steel fire escape at the back and into the yard, the clatter of dustbins on a Thursday night. His music stand, assembled and stood in the corner. Charts up on the walls. The laundry arrangements. Mystery of the sounds in other apartments, in other buildings, in other lives that we shall never know, the radio playing soft, middle of the road music, a song about angels, pots and pans clanking, the baby, an argument an immense distance away, the plumbing, the traffic, a police siren, its wail rising and falling, harmonically gorgeous layers, but often very distant, almost not there, birds' soft calls from the roof echoing faintly down the disused chimney shaft. He still has the digital recorder and the mic, and could get it all down in theory, but there is no longer anywhere for the recordings to go.

Light begins to fade. Background becomes foreground. From time to time, commercial aircraft appear on the city's horizon, following each other at the specified intervals monitored by air traffic control many miles away.

They cross the dome of air above the city, one after the other, and there is no end to their coming and going.

Now they are heard above the roofs, a swelling roar in the mind's ear. Darkness quadrupled. White lights blink on one wing, red on the other. They follow market patterns: one, then the next, and the next. And as each one recedes, so the other begins to appear.

Below, under the glare of streetlamps, traffic murmurs without finish. Voices like talking drums melt into memory, strange and artificial echoes are trunked over distance. Ant-like figures move in and out of the powerful brightness of shops; each pedestrian hurries in his or her private bubble of consciousness between the shadows. A mother is just discernible pushing baby home in a buggy.

A frisson of recognition, just for an instant.

But it wasn't.

Dennis: None of them shows any awareness.

Sandra: Of what?

Of their predicament.

I don't know that you can say that. How can you say that?

I think he was right, you know. Consciousness doesn't exist.

Don't let's start that again. You know where it led to.

Look at them, they're drenched in a bath of surveillance, and they just go about their business, oblivious of it all –

So you say!

– a bath – or maybe an ocean –

You could try *talking* to them –

– an ocean of frequencies, an ocean spanning all the world, if only we knew, if only we had access to the full spectrum, but we couldn't because we would need to track them all through time, as they recede from us to the end of time – but an oceanic consciousness maybe, a consciousness of immersion, ambience, subtle variations affecting the body close to the cellular level, vocalisations picked up in swarms of aether talk, that's what could be the answer, an answer without a question I mean, an answer that you never get to the end of, or conversely a question that, well, that's given me a few ideas –

You're getting obsessed, Sandra says. Don't get like him.

OK. Sorry.

The deep, brutally repetitive bass of a passing car stereo in the street below, that, for a few brief moments, moves the whole world.

And a police helicopter comes round again. It comes in low, rotors moving to a crescendo; it drills its way across the sky. No infringement could possibly have escaped its implacable grin of surveillance, its searchlights moving over this lovely benighted part of the planet.

Tonight, she will dream of his death, many years hence, and wake up, sweating, alone in her bed, at three in the morning. Maybe an animal sound woke her. What a weird dream. She switches the bedside light on. All is quiet. What the hell was that all about? What did it mean? But this need not concern us now, so let's say goodbye to Sandra as she puts the light out again, and, incidentally, to Dennis, whose future we cannot even speculate about. The circular diagrams now pinned up on his wall give no proper clue. The music will continue to circulate in his head. It needs to break out. But it's not our business any longer.

He, too, has put his bedside light out.

Eventually the helicopter recedes, the whir of rotors dying at last, radio noise subsiding, until it's a moving point of light among many others over the complex horizon to the east. The planet Mars holds up reddish in the glory of the south-west sky. A waning moon to the south. Venus will rise at dawn. Someone's voice on a mobile phone, in the street, from an open car window perhaps: Don't give me no more grief, please.

Along the street opposite the block of flats, parked cars darkly acquire over a long period of time a thin patina of sludge – a meld of the sap descending in fine particles from overhanging boughs of the plane trees that line this side of the street, and the even finer particles of hydrocarbons from traffic emissions; the vehicles are streaked, too, with guano splashes from denizens of the same branches.

When autumn approaches, dropping leaves will add to the mix a semi-liquefied residue on bonnets and windscreens that will play havoc with paintwork and transparency.

The street is illuminated at intervals by high lamps that emit a sodium-yellow glow.

From under one of the cars a sharp muzzle emerges.

The fox retreats; then re-emerges, looks out, pricks its ears, focuses its intelligent, near-sighted eyes on the awful, sudden glare of approaching headlights. It chooses its moment; with a dart, it is across the road.

Actually, an under-sized and mangy vixen.

They are shy and uncertain creatures; they have been leaving their rural habitat via the long railway cuttings and taking up residence for many generations in the city, where, however, they rarely live longer than about eighteen months on average.

Perhaps, once, this one had progeny and a mate. Ensconced and snug beneath a great heap of tyres at the back of a scrapyard.

Anyway, she is safely across the road. Pausing only to investigate idly the fragment of a pizza carton in the gutter, she trots towards an archway cut into the middle section of the block of flats.

The night is almost spent. A bunch of young men stagger, laughing, in a southerly direction, on the opposite side of the road, on the pavement between the plane trees and the parked cars. None notice an animal so low in profile. Their faces can scarcely be seen. Only the CCTV cameras track the animal's movement. At an unknown location a drink can rattles and echoes on tarmac. Human voices emerge briefly from the low background noise, then recede. Little has been communicated.

The vixen trots under the arch and finds herself in a yard. She has a discernible limp, her left hind leg preferring to be held towards her belly; her fur is shown in the sodium lighting, which leaches the red out, to be grey and patchy, her bones angular and only lightly clad with flesh. Interesting scents waft from the dark rubbish bins, but she ignores them. There before her is the black, steel frame of a fire escape. Up that. One painful step at a time. Once, she pauses on a step, attempts with her muzzle to reach her hindquarters, to gnaw at a diseased area of skin, denuded of fur, above that left hind leg. Gives up.

Those dustbins now below, arrayed at the far end of the yard, would once have promised riches; but the glory of this world has lost its appeal for the vixen. We don't know what this animal's consciousness, if she could be said to possess such a quality, might contain or embrace: it's a black box, we might say, but who is doing the saying?

Who is doing the saying?

And why?

Only the CCTV cameras record it all, for now. We might imagine the city engulfed by a future pestilence – or perhaps the meltdown of a nuclear power station on the coast many miles from here, who knows? – and turning to shadow, its human music fallen silent, paving slabs wrenched apart by creeping vegetation, to be colonised by other beings, such as the vixen's deeply nested progeny.

All these events happened a long time ago; but the information from them continues to expand by way of three-dimensional, complexly intersecting light cones in four-dimensional space-time, without end.

One more effort, a second landing. It is sufficiently quiet here – wherever that might be. Pauses, rests, collects herself, watches – is still. For a brief while. Then the vixen revolves once, thrice; settles herself down, her muzzle resting on her paws. She will sleep now. She will dream of the death of the city. Dawn is on its way. A light comes on briefly in a nearby window, then goes out again.

Lightning Source UK Ltd.
Milton Keynes UK
UKOW02f0458221015

261147UK00002B/31/P